SOLSTICE

MIDSUMMER
BOOK THREE

JENA DOYLE

DIRTY WORDS PUBLISHING LLC

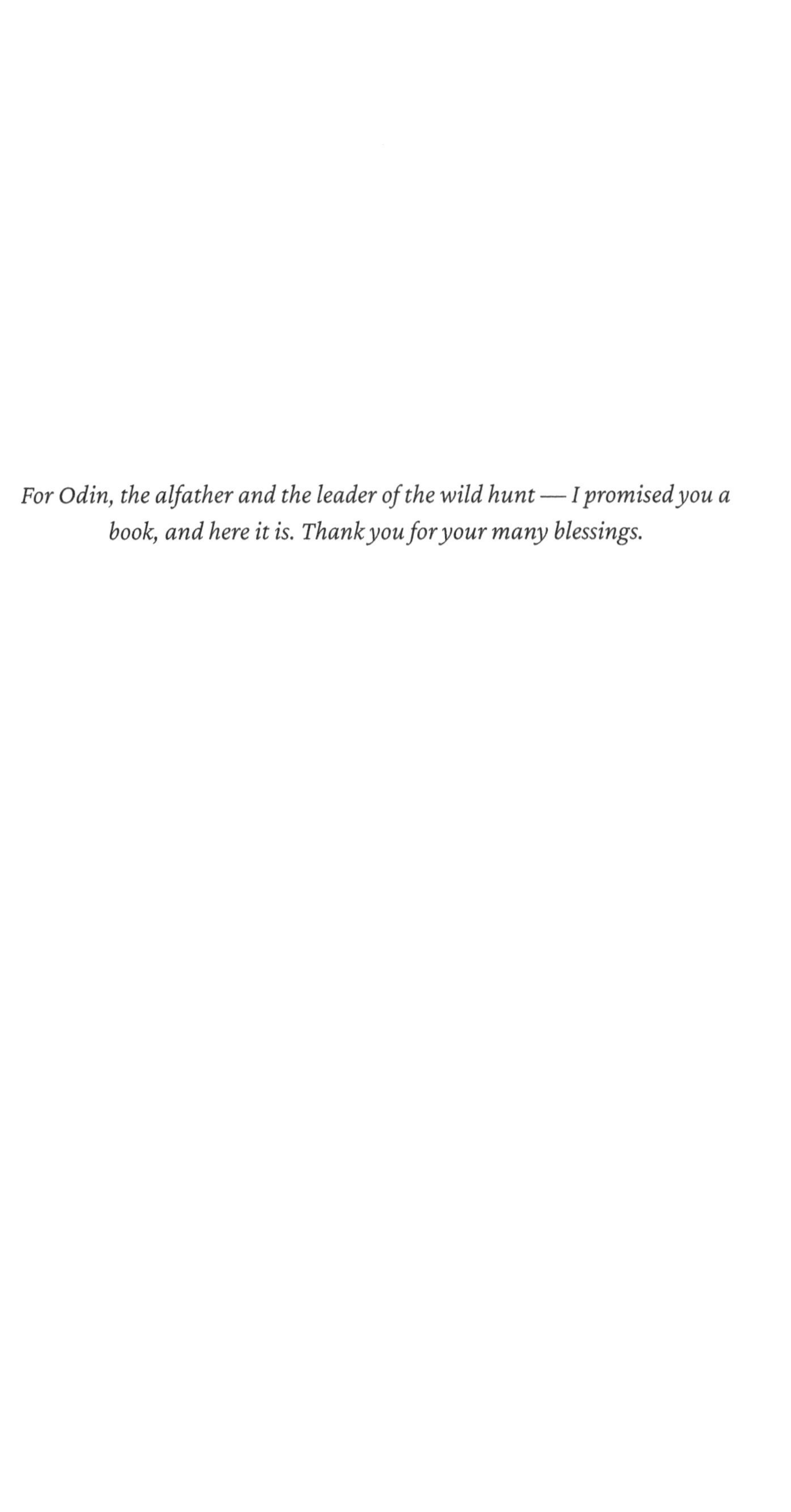

For Odin, the alfather and the leader of the wild hunt — I promised you a book, and here it is. Thank you for your many blessings.

PROLOGUE
LEX

NOW

It was a sham wedding.

Everyone knew it.

I knew it. Ivy knew it.

Four years of faking it, and here we were, staring down a night that would live in infamy for all the wrong reasons. The public wanted the glitz and the glam. They wanted the star-studded event with the free booze and the photo ops. But that wasn't us anymore. That hadn't been us for a long time. Not since Ireland. Not since Samhain and the changeling child, Poppy, and the mess in the woods with the king and the queen two years ago.

We'd be lucky to make it out of this alive.

We'd be lucky if this so-called wedding didn't end in bloodshed.

"You look pissed," Ivy's brother, Jon, said, fixing my tie. Like his sister, he had steel-gray eyes and thick ginger hair. We'd been friends since we were little, and though he reminded me of my bullheaded wife, he'd become more of an adopted brother to me over the years. "You need to fix your scowl before photo time."

Fuck.

Today, the crease between my eyebrows had more to do with the shit about to go wrong than my resting bitch face. I lit a cigarette and took a deep inhale, relishing the nicotine buzz as I looked in the mirror. The clothes were right. The hair was right. Everything about today had been planned down to the minute.

But I itched for reasons I couldn't tell anyone.

Am I really going to go through with this?

Twenty-six years, all leading up to this moment.

I looked out the window at the crowd gathering below—fifteen hundred of America's finest sycophants, here to suck the life out of what little remained of my soul. I'd grown up around them, so I could handle the pressure. But after what happened to Ivy and Miri, after how the world had reacted, these blue-blood fuckers didn't deserve to share the happiest fucking day of my life with me.

This is going to draw him out. This is a bright, shiny beacon.

Everyone I'd ever known and loved was here, well...*almost* everyone. But this was my plan, wasn't it? I cracked my neck and took another draw on my cigarette.

This is the stupidest thing I've ever done on a long list of stupid.

Ivy had been right. What the hell was I thinking?

Visions of Samhain danced in my head—thick fogs of smoke, a dark, maniacal laugh, thistle bushes twenty feet tall. Getting out of Faerie had been hell both times, and I didn't want to bring that chaos here.

Too late. All of it. All of this. Just...*too late.*

Someone knocked on the door, and my mother appeared when it opened, followed by my father.

"Malysh! Malysh!" She walked closer with her arms out, tears in her eyes, and cupped my face, leaning in to give me a kiss that didn't touch my cheek. "You look so handsome. Such a beautiful day. So long in the making."

"Yes, yes," said my father, the current president of the United

States, swirling a glass of whiskey in his hand and forcing a smile. "You're doing the right thing, Alexei."

He kept his attention on the guests outside, the sounds of the pre-wedding music echoing from the string band.

It was all so fucking pretentious, this circus and the way my mother blubbered over me, as if I chose this, as if it were my decision. She'd broken a promise to me years ago, one I hadn't forgotten about, one I could never forgive her for.

"I know you weren't thrilled about this at the beginning." Father shifted his gaze to me. "But my ratings are through the roof. Despite the scandal, people still love you both."

Despite the scandal.

There it was again, that judgmental look in his eyes, the one that reminded me the wrong son had died nearly a decade ago.

Standing here today, I'd drown you in the Boston Bay myself if it meant I'd get my son back.

He'd told me that once, but even that was my fault because I'd *made* him confess. It was the only way I'd ever gotten the truth out of him.

I sighed and shook my head. *If only Marcus were here.* If only Marcus were the one to marry Ivy instead. If only Marcus had been the one in Ireland, the one at those ruins, gifted with the ability to make anyone tell the truth.

Despite the scandal.

What would Marcus have done if he were me? What would have happened if the golden child had been cursed by fairies and doomed to live a life he didn't choose?

It doesn't fucking matter.

Marcus was dead, and I inherited this mess. Even if my father continued to be disappointed I'd lived, neither of us could change that. I stabbed out my cigarette and immediately lit another one.

"Alexei," my mother said. "I wish you would stop that filthy habit."

"We're all wishing a lot of things right now." I drew a deep, soothing inhale.

My father let out a displeased sigh and scowled. "You'll never change, will you?"

I shot my gaze to his, horrible things threatening to spill over my lips.

"Still that same petulant boy," he continued. "Angry at the world for no good reason."

No good reason.

"Is that what you think?" I blew out smoke. "That I'm angry for no reason?"

"You decided a long time ago you weren't going to be happy, and you've been living to spite me ever since."

I cleared my throat. Well, it wouldn't have been my wedding day if my father hadn't found some way to rip out my guts and eat them in front of me. He had no fucking clue what waited for us out there. He had no idea what monsters lurked in the trees, biding their time for the right opportunity to strike.

This was so trivial, so fucking unimportant. I had a thousand other things to worry about—an evil fairy king, reuniting my family, making sure this realm stayed safe. And this? This is what addles the mind of the president of the United States?

I tried not to laugh. "Thanks for the pep talk."

"We're almost ready for you," Marcia, the wedding planner, said, sticking her head into the room.

"We'll see you downstairs." My mother gave me another tearful kiss as my father turned to walk away, barely an acknowledgment for his surviving son.

After they were gone, Jon winced and then sighed. "If it helps, I'm certain things went about as well with my parents in the bridal suite."

I started to laugh, but as the sound came out of my mouth, a heaviness settled in my gut. Power shifted in the air, magic coalescing on my tongue. It reminded me of...

No. Not yet. It's not time.

I need to find Ivy.

I raced across the suite to open the door, but Ivy's sister, Kit, grabbed the handles from the other side and swung them open. She startled back a few steps when she came face-to-face with me.

"Lex, I need your help." She shifted her icy blue eyes from me to Jon and back again. "It's Ivy."

Then she took off down the hallway.

ACT I

Or, if there were a sympathy in choice,
War, death, or sickness, did lay siege to it,
Making it momentary as a sound, [...]
And ere a man hath power to say "Behold!"
The jaws of darkness do devour it up.
So quick bright things come to confusion.
-Lysander Act I, Scene I

I

LEX
NOVEMBER

The sound of Ivy's scream woke me. I'd always been a light sleeper, but my fiancée's wail could reach me even in the depths of hell. I sat up and blinked against the moonlight, grabbing my cigarettes so I could light one before standing and heading toward my door.

The stoic expression of Theo, our bodyguard on duty, met me in the hallway.

"Sir?" He raised his eyebrows, expecting a response.

I waved him away. "I got it."

"Are you sure?"

I nodded, and he turned to head back downstairs.

Am I sure?

No. I hated this. I hated that the nightmares gnawed at her. I hated that her pride wouldn't let me sleep in the same bed with her, that I had to put on this charade of going to mine so I could wake up in the middle of the night and trudge down this fucking hallway in the dark.

It was like this the first time, right after we got back from Ireland when we were in college. They'd gone away after that fairy bitch,

Siobhan, returned the ring to her. It had protected her somehow. Not anymore. Ivy had lost the damn thing on her way out of Faerie two years ago, and Siobhan hadn't put in an appearance since she saved us at the ruins.

I stalked across the soft white carpet, taking one last draw on my cigarette before putting it out in the crystal next to her bed. It already had three butts in it. I guessed Ivy had picked up my habit in the days leading up to the election.

It all ended today—now or never. She'd run out of rope to hang herself.

Perhaps it was the stress that had made the nightmares worse this week. Maybe after this was over, they might go away permanently. *Wishful thinking.*

I stood there for too long, watching her writhe and moan against her pillows.

"I won't tell you," she whimpered. "I won't tell you where she is. She's mine. Go away."

The king again this time. Or maybe the queen. Any number of those sadistic fucks could be tormenting her. I didn't know how it worked or why, but Ivy was connected to the fairies through her gift. For most people, she had to put her hands on them to see inside their head, but the fairies haunted her subconscious, showing up whenever they wanted to rifle through her dreams.

Every night, she fought it.

Something about me sent them away. All I had to do was wrap my arms around her and kiss her forehead, and she settled into peace. The same with Carter or Miri. If they came into town, they slept in her bed, and she finally got some damn rest.

"It's like you shield me from them," she'd said. *"Like being with you shields all of us."*

We were stronger together.

Truth be told, it didn't matter why it worked, only that she shut the fuck up and let me sleep. She wasn't the only one that had a big day tomorrow. Yes, I had to be the dutiful future husband and stand next to Representative Washington on her big night, but I also had a full-time job myself.

Being an appeals attorney wasn't a cakewalk, even though I knew when someone did what they were accused of. It shocked me to learn how many people were behind bars that hadn't done a damn thing wrong.

Did I cheat the system by exploiting a gift given to me by a fucked-up fairy curse? Well, I'd neither confirm nor deny those allegations, but let's say I was *really* picky about my clients, and I usually won my cases. Which was why I was so high in demand and I couldn't afford these sleepless nights.

I took a deep breath and slid in between the sheets, grabbing Ivy's wrists to stop her from flinging her hands at my head.

"X," I murmured, tugging her in close. She struggled and pushed my shoulders, clawing at my chest to get away.

"No, stop it. Get off me." She thought I was the monster in her dreams.

"X, it's me, goddamn it. Stop. Shh." I kissed her head and tucked her nose in my neck, forcing her to breathe me in deeply. Even asleep, she recognized my scent, and I knew hers. I could pick it out of a room full of people. Our lives had always been lived together, even when we didn't like it.

Then it happened, the thing we'd been practicing for years. I touched her, and our minds connected.

"It's okay," I told her through her gift. *"You're asleep. It's just a dream."*

She froze and took another deep breath, sighing and relaxing into me, her arms going around my waist, her face burrowing deeper into my chest.

"Lex," she breathed.

"Ivy," I said.

"Thank you," she murmured mentally. *"Thank you."*

She fell back to sleep, but I stayed awake and ruminated—about life, about death, about this twisted relationship I had with her.

After Samhain, Carter and Miri kept their promise. We got together every year for Christmas and took summer vacations to remote parts of the world where no one would find us, and those who did had no idea who we were.

We even visited Poppy, who I still didn't trust completely. I won't say I regretted suggesting we should leave her in Faerie because it seemed like the right thing to do at the time. But something about her still raised the hairs on the back of my neck, even after all these years.

Did it make me a cold, heartless prick that I didn't trust a twelve-year-old girl?

Maybe, but I could swear I looked into her eyes and saw someone older than any of us staring back out at me. That, of course, caused conflict between Ivy and me.

My fiancée loved her and thought she was the child that had never been given to her and Carter. Poppy took advantage of that. Which brought me right back around to this fractured, duct-taped thing she and I called a betrothal.

Carter and Miri would say Ivy and I had been in love with each other since we were children. While I wouldn't go that far, I'd admit my feelings for Ivy were complex and difficult to understand.

I loved her unconditionally. A part of me couldn't live without her and knew our square would be incomplete if she disappeared. We were a team. Partners. Together, we had to live a life we didn't choose and make the most of it.

But lately, that wasn't enough for me.

I'd come home to Ivy and Carter fucking in the shower, the sounds of her delighted giggle igniting a jealous fire in my gut. This time, it wasn't about him. I'd catch her between Miri's legs, kissing and biting and licking, and a heat rolled through me that had nothing to do with my princess. I could kiss and bite Miri anytime I wanted.

It rankled that Ivy would never do that to me, never willingly peer up from between my legs and giggle and lick me until I came on her face.

Why do I want her to?

After everything, after Midsummer and the breakup and Samhain, we should have come to some kind of understanding. Maybe that we could admit the fact we were two sides of the same coin or we could only be complete together, that half of a puzzle was no puzzle at all.

But whenever Carter left, Ivy returned to her isolation. Whenever Miri went home, Ivy retreated inside her political shell, the fake one that answered questions diplomatically and pretended like the only desire she had for me was the one that made her want to punch my teeth out.

We were political allies, faces to put on a household name.

Nothing more.

Nothing less.

I hated that, most of all. I wanted to make Ivy squeal. I wanted to be in her bed when she fell asleep and roll over when she woke up. I wanted it to be real.

I didn't know why, and it didn't matter anymore because I realized, there in the dark, listening to the sounds of her peaceful sleep, that I'd do anything to make it happen. We'd been playing this game of wills since we were children, and I so rarely denied myself the things I wanted.

I didn't know why I craved Ivy all of a sudden. Was it the jealousy of the others? Was it an entire lifetime of this insufferable urge finally catching up to me? Or maybe it was always there, trapped behind a door neither of us had the guts to open.

"You know what you both need," the deviant monster inside of me said. This was the fucker that once loved to shake Ivy's cage, the one I chained up in college when she started dating Carter and I fell in love with Miri. Now, it blinked awake and stretched, preparing to take out the years I'd spent ignoring it on her delectable ivory ass.

I groaned and adjusted my cock while I stared at Ivy's ceiling.

Yeah, I knew what turned this ginger inside out when it came to me, and it wasn't the sweet gentleman whore that Carter liked to play or Miri's demure princess slut.

With me, Ivy needed a fight. And God fucking help me, I loved to give her one.

IVY WON THE ELECTION. We'd watched the results from the residence of the White House, and after her mother gave her the fakest hug I'd ever seen Evelyn Washington lower herself to give, the recognition hit Ivy's features.

"*I won,*" she thought, seemingly in disbelief, as if she'd never considered she'd actually get here. "*I actually won.*"

After the celebrations died down, we sat in the back of the Range Rover while Theo drove us through downtown Washington, DC to take us home. At midnight, the streets were almost empty, save for the countless other political monsters out on the prowl, likewise celebrating their victories or drowning their sorrows. Perhaps both.

Warm fingers wrapped around mine where they rested on my thigh, causing me to lift my gaze to my fiancée on the other side of the SUV. She flashed me a rare grin and leaned her head back against the seat, but I focused on the curve of her lower lip, recalling how far I could sink my teeth into that tender skin before she squirmed.

"*Thank you,*" Ivy said, barging inside my head without knocking.

I cleared my throat and pushed that mental image away before she noticed it.

"*I'm proud of you, X.*" I returned her smile, forcing my attention on the connection between us. "*You were awesome.*" As much as I tried to hide the warm, fuzzy ache that had gotten desperate for her touch, it shot out of me in a moment of unfiltered adoration and vulnerability.

Ahh, fuck.

I yanked my hand away and locked my features down, glancing back toward my window and hoping she didn't feel it. To my utter horror, she stared at me until I couldn't stand it and eventually said, "What?"

"What's gotten into you?"

I shrugged. "What do you mean?"

A lock of hair fell into her face, and I almost reached out to brush it back, stopping myself at the last second because after what had happened, touching any part of her was too goddamned intimate.

"What was that"—Ivy cleared her throat and shifted in her seat, clearly uncomfortable with voicing whatever she wanted to say. Her rich vanilla smell assaulted my nose, and I resisted the urge to lean in to get more of it—"that feeling?"

I shook my head and sighed, giving her a sheepish chuckle as a response.

"Miss Washington," Theo interrupted, bringing our attention up front as he put the SUV into park. "Mister Fairfax. We're home."

Ivy looked at me one last time and pushed the button on her seat belt to climb out, clearly ignoring the predatory way I stalked behind her. It reminded me of that night in Ireland when I'd followed her through the halls of Killwater College in the dark before the lust took over our sensibilities. We'd darted into an alcove, and I dry-fucked her against the wall, savage and hard.

And she liked it.

She didn't want to, but she did.

The thought buried itself inside my brain, setting off a chain reaction of indecent fantasies I suddenly yearned to make a reality.

Would she cry out like that if I fucked her rough for real? Would she fight back? Would she—

I shook my head to clear them away. If this were the fifties, I might have said my slip was showing. I'd allowed her free rein inside my mind, and in doing so, I'd given away too much. In the four years since Midsummer, the boundaries between Ivy and me had blurred to the point where I couldn't tell where I ended and she began. Our names were synonymous with one another; they had been our entire lives.

Was I finally accepting my fate? Or did the universe know what I'd wanted all along, even if I'd been a stubborn prick about it?

I didn't know, and somewhere along the line, I stopped fighting it. What was it about *this* night in particular? Perhaps it was the glint coming off Ivy's shiny iridescent hair that had me transfixed. Maybe it was the way she smiled in that SUV, her lips so incredibly soft and bitable.

Goddamn it.

Once Theo cleared our townhouse and left us alone, I took off my jacket and helped Ivy out of hers, hanging them in the closet by the door. She bent over to take off her stiletto pumps while she rambled on about our schedule tomorrow.

"We need to meet our parents at seven a.m.," she said, but I'd long since tuned her out. Instead, I focused on the way her mouth moved and the fading remains of what had once been cherry-colored lipstick blurring into her natural skin tone.

"Well, good night," she said, picking up her heels before walking barefoot toward the stairs.

"Wait," I cut in, my chest tightening at the thought of her leaving me.

She turned and furrowed her brows. "What?"

"What are you doing with the rest of the night?"

She sighed and rubbed at her neck. "I just won an election I've been running for since I was born. Tonight looks like a bath, a bottle of wine, and a fistful of sleeping pills. Why?"

I cleared my throat and put my hands in my pockets, stepping toward her. "Do you want company?"

"To which part?"

I shrugged. "All of it."

"Is this your desperate attempt to get me naked?" She rolled her eyes and flashed a playful smile.

I grinned. "If I wanted to do that, X, I could have a long time ago."

"That's what you think," she replied with a scoff.

"There's a drop cloth somewhere in Georgetown that says otherwise." Memories of the day I fucked her in our former loft floated through my mind. We'd been heartbroken and drunk, and we swore we'd never mention it again. Even if I had photographic evidence that it happened. Even if I'd memorialized the entire thing on camera.

Ivy lifted her chin, a clear sign of a challenge, and ran her eyes over the length of me, assessing me, casting her judgment.

"Fine," she said, pointing at me. "But no sex, and I get to pick the wine."

There'd be no negotiating because she headed up the stairs to our rooms with little hesitation. I, the greedy prick with the worst intentions, happily followed her.

We stripped with no self-consciousness. We'd lived together for four years and practically another four before that. Besides, nothing said no boundaries like an orgy in the woods, so Ivy and I were beyond such trivial things as naked skin.

She turned on the faucet in the tub, grabbing a bottle of wine and two glasses from her room while I sank into the water. She climbed into the other side and handed me my drink.

"Now that the election's over, we'll announce the wedding by the end of the year." She leaned her head back to wet her hair, the heat making her skin splotchy and pink, revealing the mark on her throat. I focused on it like a target, my fingers itching to caress that delectable skin. "Our parents are aiming for the first weekend of June."

"June?" I blew out a breath. "That's quick."

"Mother wants a grandchild by the fall." Ivy took a long pull on her wine, and I let out a small groan.

"Mother will be disappointed." I relaxed in the water, resting my head against the cool tile.

"Now, now." Ivy raised an eyebrow. "You'll never spread the Fairfax family tree with that attitude."

I returned her skeptical playfulness, grinning in spite of my reluctance to encourage her. "You'd have to let me between those Washington legs before I could do that."

She laughed and splashed me before lying back against the tub, pressing her feet against a jet. "Ahh, that feels nice. Those shoes were beautiful, but hell on my toes."

Working on autopilot, I grabbed her feet and put them in my lap, rubbing my thumb and my fingers over each ridge, massaging the muscles until I found the area that pained her. I thought she might try to pull away, but when she relaxed into the touch, I continued.

"All right, spill it," she said. "What's going on with you?"

I looked up. "What do you mean?"

"Something came out of you earlier. It felt like..." Ivy shrugged and sipped her wine. "Well, it confused me. And now you're being all sweet and weird."

"Sweet and weird." I repeated her words, trying to decipher their meaning while I rubbed up her ankles and down again. Her skin felt like satin under my palm, soft and warm and decadent. "I thought that's what you liked about Chicago."

She chuckled. "It's not your style."

"And what's my style?"

"Honest and cruel."

"Ouch." I pretended to be offended, but who the fuck was I trying to fool? It was true, especially with her. Like I said, Ivy and I had no boundaries. Whatever I thought came out of my mouth or entered her head through touch. *That hurts.*

"Don't be ridiculous. Nothing I say hurts you."

"That's not true." I paused, an amused competitiveness flickering behind her eyes. "You once said comparing me to Lucifer did a disservice to Lucifer. That hurt a lot."

She laughed again, which made me smile, and I switched to the other foot, caressing that one with as much attention as the first.

"I'm serious," she murmured in my mind. *"Tell me what's up with you."*

I paused, pursing my lips while I did my best to conceal my true intentions. I couldn't tell her what I really wanted. I couldn't even think it, or she'd know. *"Just proud of you, X. That's all."*

"Proud?" She gasped in feigned shock. "Wow. Talk about things I thought I'd never hear you say."

"Can't a man be proud of his wife after she wins a seat in Congress?"

"You have two, so it only counts as half."

I didn't know why, but it bothered me that Ivy continued to think she wasn't as important to me as Carter or Miri. To be fair, what had I done to convince her otherwise? And why did I even care? Somewhere in the haze of the warm tub and the delicious wine, I forgot.

"Why didn't it ever work between you and me?" *There.* I said it. It was out in the open now.

She narrowed her gray eyes, distrust in every tense, calculating muscle. "What do you mean?"

"Why can't we be like we are when they're here?" No sense in elaborating who I meant by *they.* Between us, there could only be one *they.* "Why can't we be like that all the time?"

"Because I don't like you." She said it on a laugh, but it was a trained response, one she'd been saying for years. "And you don't like me."

The lies hit me in the gut like a slug, a palpable throbbing that squeezed my heart. "You know...you keep saying that." I shook my head and massaged up her calf, hitting a spot that made her moan and arch into the touch. Her perfect pink nipples poked out of the water and I homed in on them, my fingers yearning to coast higher. Despite my twitching cock, I behaved myself, sliding my palms back down her legs to her feet, relishing her luminous, velvety skin. "And yet, here you sit. Naked. In a tub. With me."

"So?"

"Methinks the lady doth protest too much."

She stared at me from under hooded lids, the wine now having removed the rest of the inhibitions between us. *"What do you want, Lex?"*

I took a deep breath, let it out on a slow sigh. *"A trip."*

"What trip?"

"Let me take you away. You deserve it."

"Take me away?" She raised an eyebrow. *"Like a date?"*

"Sure."

Ivy scoffed and rolled her eyes. *"We've been on thousands of dates."*

"No, no." I leaned back and smirked. *"A real date. One where you like it. One where you let me convince you."*

"Convince me of what?"

I paused, swallowing before I added, *"That what we have is real."*

"It's not." She pulled her feet away and sat up, wrapping her arms around herself. That political mask slid firmly into place, locking her emotions down like the wine didn't matter. Like the connection between us didn't matter. Like I hadn't spent hours inside that brilliant brain.

I licked my lips and sighed, realizing I'd pushed too far too soon. "X—"

"What I have with Carter? That's real. I felt it before we went into those woods. Miri, too. You and me?"

Clearing my throat, I braced myself for the worst of her venom.

"We were forced into this," she continued. "We didn't have a choice."

Lie, lie, lie. It hurt to hear and stung even worse because of my gift.

"Does that make it less powerful?" I tilted my head and assessed her, wondering why she railed so hard against the idea of us. Didn't she feel what I did? Couldn't she swallow her ego for one goddamn minute and admit I meant something, *anything*, to her?

"No, it just means that whatever this is will end once we break the curse."

If we break the curse. It had been two years with nothing but fucking nightmares to show for it. Siobhan hadn't shown up. Her sister, Ashley, had gone radio silent. Poppy hadn't heard from anyone, either. We had nothing but rumors and conjecture from ancient books with lost connotations.

"I don't think that's true," I said, using the word *true* specifically. It had implications, as it usually led to me using my fairy curse. But I hadn't yet. That, perhaps, was the only limit between us. I didn't force her to tell me anything she hadn't already agreed to share.

"Which part?" She gulped down the last of her wine and poured herself another glass.

"Any of it."

Ivy glared, clenching her jaw, gearing up for the fight. If she wanted to go, I'd fucking take her. At least then I'd get a reaction out of her. Of all the people on this great earth, I *lived* to make Ivy Washington turn red.

"I was the first person you touched after Siobhan kissed you," I said. "You drank from my chalice and shared your gift with me."

"So?"

"So." I grabbed her hand, intertwining her fingers with mine. "Take me up on my offer. Forty-eight hours, that's all I'm asking. One weekend."

She still seemed suspicious, her eyes barely slits as all the years we'd spent at each other's throats danced behind them. "That's all you want? A weekend of my time?"

"No, Ivy," I said. "I want you to like it."

She stared at me like she was trying to find out what trick I planned to play on her. "Why?"

"Do I have to have a reason?"

"You usually have an ulterior motive."

I licked my lips and answered through our bond. *"I want my wife to want me."*

"All you've ever done is try to make me hate you."

"You ever wonder why?"

"If you're about to say because you liked me, I'm about to drown you in this tub."

"It's because you never backed down from me." I tilted my head and grinned like a cat with a mouse. "And that used to piss me off."

"Oh, yeah?" Her tone dripped with sarcasm. "And what about now?"

"Now it turns me on."

She froze and tried to pull away from me, but I wouldn't let her. Perhaps the alcohol had taken what little restraint I had left because I opened our mental connection more. I made her feel how fast my blood raced around her, how I hung on every word she said, especially if we were arguing. I let the wave of my adoration for her sift through her curse, and when it hit her between the legs, she clamped her thighs shut and let out a small moan.

"Every time you fight with me," I continued, "it's a struggle not to bend you over the first piece of furniture I find. If you want it like that, it can be like that." I didn't know why I kept talking, why I let it pour out of me. This was probably going to blow up in my face like all the times before it. "But if you want it sweet, I can be sweet."

She met my gaze, and the night with the photographs echoed behind its ironclad defenses. I watched it play out in her eyes, reflecting in mine—when I'd held her hands while she moaned under me, when I'd kissed her neck and her breasts, when I let her run her fingers over my tattoos. It had been gentle and annoyingly erotic, and I couldn't get it out of my head, not in all these years.

"I remember," she murmured.

"I'm just..." I sighed and stood. "I'm just tired, and I think you are, too." I climbed out of the tub and wrapped a towel around my waist, leaning down to kiss her temple before heading toward her room. "And in case you were wondering, your pride can go fuck itself. I need a full night's sleep, and so do you."

Then I opened the door, leaving it cracked behind me as I walked out.

2

IVY
DECEMBER

When Lex said he wanted me to go away with him for a weekend, I thought he meant *only* a weekend because he had specified forty-eight hours. The farther we drove into the mountains of western Virginia, the more I suspected he'd planned something else.

"Where are you taking me?" I asked for the twentieth time, gazing out the window at the snow falling on the ground. The election had been six weeks ago, and I'd finally gotten a break in my schedule to fulfill my fiancé's request. I'd canceled holiday plans with my family to come up here with him alone.

"You'll see." He winked from across the seat, returning his attention out the window. Theo drove the SUV through the thick piles of snow, eventually turning onto a driveway that wound up the side of a mountain.

An enormous log cabin appeared out of the tree line, the chimney already smoking with what must have been a rolling fire on the inside. It reminded me of the Christmases we used to spend together at Camp David when we were kids, bickering and fighting as our parents made their grand plans. The house stood at least three stories with big glass windows facing out over the valley below.

"Jesus, Lucifer." I climbed out of the van and trudged through the white powder to climb the stairs to the deck.

"You like it?" He flashed an enormous grin and held his arms out to either side, gesturing to the woods surrounding us. We were completely alone out here, no neighbors for miles in either direction.

Only the woods.

Only the trees.

"You rented this entire place for the two of us?" I took a hesitant step toward him.

"Yeah." He shrugged, heading to the giant glass door so he could unlock it and slide it open. "For now."

For now?

I didn't ask for more information because once we were inside, words escaped me. Sunlight poured into the enormous living room containing a huge sectional facing a stone fireplace that went up to the cathedral ceiling three stories overhead. Just off to the right, two steps led to the dining room and a kitchen big enough to cook for an army. Beyond that were guest rooms. All of this paled in comparison to the second story, which housed the primary bedroom with its own fireplace and an Alaskan King bed that could sleep ten people.

Enough for all my spouses.

But they weren't here.

Like Lex said, it was only the two of us after Theo unpacked the SUV and returned to town. The refrigerator had been stocked. The pantry was full. We'd be fine on our own for the rest of our stay.

Despite this, I'd just been elected to Congress, and even on vacation, I couldn't disconnect completely. I found the office on the third floor and set up my laptop, responding to emails and confirming appointments for my return. If it were up to me, I wouldn't have left DC, but my archnemesis insisted, and after what happened the night of the election, I couldn't deny my own curiosity. When I'd touched him, an indescribable warmth had run through our connection, surging up my arm and into my bloodstream. The way fire had engulfed my arm, the way it tingled in the aftermath, the skip in my heart and the heaviness between my legs, it repeated in my imagination over and over again. It scared the shit out of me.

Of course, archnemesis didn't really describe our relationship anymore. In these last few years, Lex had become my best friend. My teammate. My ride-or-die partner in crime.

Plot twist of the century.

If ten-year-old Ivy could see me now…

The first time I discovered my fairy gift, we'd been standing in our kitchen at our old condo. I'd entered his mind by mistake and seen our life together through his eyes. In doing so, I'd taken on the emotions he had for me. There had been love there, sure, but also hate and jealousy, and that ran deeper.

Then there'd been the day he'd photographed me at our old apartment, that snowy afternoon when it had just been him and me and the vibrant, brilliant pull between us. How tenderly he'd held me, like I might break. How he'd kissed me, sweet and sinful, like years of affection existed in that one moment. Then the sun had come up and the snow melted and we'd shoved that whole experience in a box we never opened.

The only time I let myself *want* Lex was when our spouses were here. Any other time, he was my public life partner and strategic sounding board. I couldn't let it be any more than that.

The pull I felt to him, the one I sensed he was developing toward me, it was powerful. Magical. It reminded me none of it was real. Whatever was originally between us had been mutated by our time in Ireland, and if I let myself go down the path of Lex actually feeling something for me only to learn I was right, it would hurt me more than anything else we'd ever been through.

It was better to keep him at arm's length, knowing once we found Siobhan and broke this curse, he'd go back to hating me and I'd go back to hating him and the world would be set right on its axis.

I'm just tired. And I think you are, too.

Was that what I was?

Tired? Tired of pretending? Tired of sneaking around with Carter and Miri? Faking a loving relationship with Lex? Yearning to be with a child that needed a mother, knowing damn well no one in my life could ever know about her?

Lex wanted to break me down. He wanted me to admit that what we had was real, outside of the fairy curse, outside of Carter and Miri. I didn't know where this newfound desire for my returned affection came from, but as I watched him wink and smile and stand by my side through the entire election, I found myself wanting to give in to the fantasy.

What if I let him?

What if I sank into this complicated thing between us, knowing it would devastate me when it was over? I could let myself have Lex for these brief fantastical moments, completely aware that once we broke the curse, we would go back to the way things were at the beginning. Perhaps I could steel myself against it from the start.

Lex let me work for a few hours, but he soon grew impatient. I looked up when his big body blocked the door. He leaned against the jamb, one arm crossed over the other, that petulant, annoyed look on his face.

"Yes?" I raised an eyebrow, resisting the urge to smile.

"I brought you up here to seduce you, not lose you to America." He pushed upright and stalked closer, dropping his hands to his sides. He wore gray sweatpants and a white T-shirt, the uniform of a man snuggling into a log cabin for an extended stay in the snow. I traced over the dark lines on his arms, the tattoos snaking up under his sleeves, peeking out again near his collar. I'd always loved his ink, and he must have known that because he practically preened for me as he walked.

His hazel eyes shimmered in the firelight, the flames casting shadows over the angles of his cheekbones as they faded into his pouty lips and perfect blue-blood nose, making him seem like a villain from a fairy tale.

God, he could have been a model. Even when I hated him, I couldn't deny he was painstakingly beautiful.

"You know," he said, coming around the desk, making me turn my chair to face him. "The last person who eye-fucked me like that" —he leaned down, his hands going to the armrests, his face coming inches from mine—"ended their night with my cock in their ass. You sure you don't like me, X?"

I inhaled his clean scent and clenched my thighs together, an automatic response to being near someone with whom I shared the curse. It had nothing to do with him. *Not at all.* And once we broke the fairy gift, this fantasy bubble would pop and we'd realize why it was such a bad idea for the two of us to do this in the first place.

I cleared my throat and sat up straighter. "I don't."

He smiled and nodded. "Uh-huh."

Excitement mixed with trepidation in my gut, seizing my lungs and forcing my heart to pound against my rib cage. My shoulders trembled, and my cheeks burned, the X on my neck blaring to life. I dug my fingers into the leather seat to keep from reaching up to cover it. He'd see. He'd know.

He already did.

He narrowed his eyes as they ran the length of my face and settled on my lips. "I made you dinner." Then he stood, stepped back, and nodded toward the door.

I took a slow, deep breath, letting it out through my nose as I tried to slow my racing pulse, and I pushed to my feet to follow him downstairs. I stopped at the entrance to the dining room, gasping as I swept the scene. Tall candles sat at either end of the table, plates with salmon and vegetables in the middle. I glanced in the kitchen to confirm the dirty dishes in the sink.

Yes, he had, in fact, made this himself.

"Where did you learn to cook?"

He winked and stood behind one of the chairs, pulling it out before saying, "Carter, of course. And Miri."

I walked toward him and sat while he pushed the seat under for me, taking the spot immediately to my right at the head of the table.

"Lex, this is..." I didn't have words. What could I say? The last person who'd cooked for me had been Carter, and he did it because he liked to. "Thank you."

"You deserve it," he said. "You've worked so hard."

"We both have," I said, giving credit where it was due. It wasn't just me smiling and waving to the crowds. Lex had shown up for every event, fundraiser, and speech, all while working a caseload on his own. He'd been the dutiful man behind the great woman, and he'd played his part well.

A comfortable silence descended on us while we ate, and he poured wine that immediately made me feel warm and fuzzy as soon as I took a sip. Lex continued to surprise me. I hadn't expected the cabin in the woods or the home-cooked dinner or whatever that was in the office upstairs. I rubbed my left thumb over the scars on my right hand, scars he also shared. *Until the end.* I'd made that vow to him as well. Not just Carter and Miri.

Halfway through the meal, Lex took a sip of wine and leaned back in his seat, looking over at me with a dark set to his gaze. "I want to amend our deal."

I sat down my fork and wiped my mouth with my napkin before saying, "Typical."

"Forty-eight hours with me...but I meant what I said about seducing you."

Perhaps the alcohol had already gone to my head or maybe the moment in the office had unlocked a previously closed door in my heart because I only bit my bottom lip and blushed. "Oh?"

He leaned forward, his elbows going to the table, and I caught sight of the square with the X on his forearm. I'd seen it a thousand times before; I'd always assumed it was a symbol for the four of us. But he only called me X, and I was tattooed right there for the world to see. I shifted my gaze back to his.

"That time our apartment, I was gentle with you." He frowned, shaking his head, like the memories were too much for him to process or bear alone. "The way Carter would have wanted me to be." He narrowed his eyes and pulled his lips into a playful smile, and a shiver raced down my spine. "But I understand now. That's not what you need." He cleared his throat. "That's not what you want...*from me.*"

Unaware of where this was going, I smiled and rolled my eyes. "And what do I want from you?"

He straightened, leaning back in his seat with an arrogant grin that reminded me of the teenage version of himself. "You want me to fight you for it."

My thoughts stopped. My entire body throbbed. The visuals that went through my mind stunned me, and I didn't know what to say or do. I froze, staring at him with my mouth hanging open. The sharp slice of Lex holding me down with his teeth at Midsummer burned through the memory in my skin, when he'd taken what we both needed without asking. Three days later, he'd pinned me against the wall in an alcove and dry humped me until I couldn't stand, gripping his shirt to stay upright. Every time after that had either been with our spouses, under the lust, or because we were desperately heartbroken and needed a release we could only find in each other.

Lex and I had never gotten together because it was what we wanted. Our relationship had never been about romantic gestures and whispered sweet nothings. I thrived when Lex riled me up, and he lived to get under my skin.

"Ohh." He chuckled low in his chest and took another sip, lips twisting as amusement emanated in his glowing stare, hitting me right between the legs. "I'm right, aren't I?"

"No." I cleared my throat and swallowed, lying through my teeth even though there was no point. He knew me better than that, and even if he didn't, he was a walking lie detector.

He raised an eyebrow, piercing eyes daring me to keep going. Lex would pull his fairy curse trigger if he needed to. He'd make me tell him just to prove his point.

"What if that's what I wanted, too?" He raised his chin, peering down his nose at me. "What if I wanted to chase you through this house until I caught you and held you down and made you do whatever I wanted? What if I wanted to make you cry for mercy?"

Good. Fucking. God.

A hot, fiery ache clenched my cunt, almost painful in its intensity, and I adjusted my hips in my seat, aware Lex scrutinized every movement I made.

"What if I let you hit me, scratch me, claw me to try to get away? But, oh you can't, because you don't *really* want to. Do you? No, you want me to make you. You want me to overpower you, and you want to try to overpower me."

My leggings and hoodie suddenly felt too tight and the heat from the fire seemed too hot and all I could do was sit there and stare at his mouth while he said these filthy, terrible things to me.

"But you can't overpower me, not anymore, not since we were little." He took another long drink of wine before shifting his body to face me, bringing his forehead to mine and his lips inches away. "It doesn't matter that you can't; that's not what you want." His breath coasted over my cheeks, smelling like Malbec and temptation and *him.* "You want me to win. You always did." Soft, pouty lips brushed against mine, and I struggled to keep still as he continued. "Because that's the game. I'm the only one you *can* lose to. I'm the only one *worthy* of losing to."

"Lex—" I tried to tell him to stop, that a mere two sips of red had ruined my self-control, but the words wouldn't come. *They wouldn't come.* He was right about all of it, about what I wanted from him and why I wanted it. How had he known this when I didn't even know it myself?

"Ivy." The way he said my name made me shiver, and when he bit my bottom lip between his teeth hard enough to hurt, I moaned and sagged into the agony. Desire scalded my veins like undiluted ecstasy, cascading down my spine and into my legs and back up again.

Copper coated my tongue when he let it go, ruby red on his lips. He licked it away and brushed his thumb over my wound to do the same. The touch ached in the best way, making me feel alive. Shivers skated down my body when his finger came away crimson, and he stuffed it in his mouth to suck it clean. Unable to move or say anything, I sat transfixed by the connection that had suddenly snapped between us. He dragged his velvet tongue across my mouth, so soft and warm and decadent, the heat of it sparking deep in my belly.

I dug my nails into the armrests.

A mewling sound poured out of me.

I wanted him to lick me again.

He pulled back only far enough to meet my gaze. "If you get up from this table and run, I will chase you. When I catch you, I will fight you. When I win, I will fuck you." I watched him glance between my eyes. "Our safeword is 'mercy.' Seeing as you can be inside my head anytime you want, it shouldn't be too hard for you to call, even if your mouth is otherwise occupied." He brushed hair out of my face and pushed it behind my ear like I was a porcelain doll that might break if he held me too hard.

Was it more screwed-up that he suggested it or that I wanted it with a fury that almost crippled me?

"How does that sound?" He raised an eyebrow as he waited for me to say something.

My pulse pounded in my head as I stared at him to make sure he was serious. Was this a trick? Would he tease me about this until I turned into a humiliated mess?

"Is this a secret?" I asked.

His lips lifted into a devil's grin. "Do you want it to be?"

"I don't want you fighting me in front of the others. They don't like it. They don't"—I cleared my throat—"they don't understand what it is between us."

"I know." He nodded. "If that's what you want."

Shocked I was agreeing to this, I reached for my glass of wine and chugged the last giant swallow before pushing to my feet.

"Nothing on the face and if you rip my clothes, you replace them."

"Agreed."

I turned on the balls of my feet and took off.

HEART POUNDING, blood pumping, I raced up the stairs.

Thump. Thump. Thump. Thump.

The echoes of Lex's footfalls behind me thundered off the walls, fueling an intense urge inside of me. I knew he'd catch me; he gained on me with each of his strides, but the thrill was in the anticipation.

Lex had absconded with me from the Capitol, taken me to some secluded cabin in the woods with no one around for miles in any direction, only so he could primal kink his way through our bet. God, he read me so well. I didn't *want* to give in to him. I didn't *want* to admit the way he made me feel. It said things about our marriage to each other and to Carter and Miri I couldn't admit to myself, not yet. But once he started talking, I couldn't stop it. Once he put the plan out there, I wanted it with every bone in my body.

Exhilaration flared in my chest as I darted into the primary bedroom, Lex nipping on my heels. His footsteps echoed behind me as I sprinted across the room, and he slammed the door shut, the snick of the lock reverberating off the high ceilings.

I turned to face him, backing away, skirting around the bed.

"Lex," I said, playing into the game. He wanted to fight me for it? Fine. I'd give him something to fight. "Stop. This isn't right."

Yes, it is, a twisted part of me whispered, the part that knew it would always be like this between us. We could never do this with Miri or Carter because he wasn't Carter, and I wasn't Miri, and what

Lex and I had was too fucked-up for anyone else. This part of me could *only* be sated by this part of him.

What does that say about us?

"Lex, I mean it." I moved toward the second-story balcony overlooking the woods. It had a foot of snow on it, so he knew I couldn't really go anywhere. "Stop."

He smiled, clearly pleased by my mock refusal. "No."

White-hot lust puddled between my legs, and I cut right, launching myself across the bed. I scrambled on my hands and knees, but he circled my waist with his arm, slamming me back against his body. I squealed and wriggled free, rolling off the other side of the mattress while he struggled to get upright. I ran again, toes digging into the carpet to propel me to the door.

My sweaty fingers slipped on the lock, costing valuable time as I struggled to turn it. Just when I'd gotten the damn thing open, his hard body slammed into me from the side, taking me down.

Lex wrapped his arm around my hips, breaking my fall with his knees so he lay me on the floor only when I could safely land on my stomach. I tried to push up again, but he outweighed me enough to keep me firmly rooted. He circled his hands around my wrists and pinned them above my head, his hot breath pouring over my head as he panted. Then he nipped at the side of my ear and I went still, chills plunging down that entire side of my body.

"That was pathetic," he snarled.

Ugh, leave it to Lucifer to turn me on and piss me off at the same time.

I growled and squirmed, managing to yank my arms out of his hold and use my weight to roll him to the side. But he was bigger than me and quickly regained his dominance, trapping my arms next to my ribs.

"For someone who spent their childhood wrestling with me, you've gotten rusty, X."

That made me even more feral, and I bucked again, almost hitting him in the face with my head. He gave just enough for me to rip my arms away and roll under him, bringing us face-to-face.

Lex was fast and got ahold of my wrists, gathering them above my head with one hand. I kicked and flailed, nearly kneeing him right in the groin. That earned me a pissed-off glare.

"Careful," he said inside my head.

I raised an eyebrow in challenge. He wanted a fight, didn't he? And now he couldn't keep up?

"Aw, poor Lucifer."

He curled his free hand around my inner thigh to hold my knee out to the side so he could settle his pelvis against mine. My entire body tensed as his hard cock rubbed against my clit, and the weight of him on top of me combined with his thick heady scent nearly overwhelmed my senses. A surge of euphoria blasted through my chest that had nothing to do with the curse or the role-play or a pretend marriage in the woods. It wasn't driven by lust or sex with our spouses or by the way my heart yearned for another.

It was real.

This was about me and him, and God, I wanted exactly what he'd offered me downstairs. I wanted him to hold me down and take what he'd won, wring me out until I couldn't stand.

"Get off me." I shoved at his hold, jerking under him, bringing my cunt up against his cock again. The friction made me moan, and I turned my head to the side, biting at my bicep to keep from making more noise.

"Say mercy." He brought his lips to my ear, his fiery breath ghosting over my neck and sending shocks down that side of my body.

I pressed my lips together because *no fucking way* would I stop this. That wasn't what he meant, anyway. He was checking in with me, giving me an out if I wanted to take it. I could use the safeword, and Lex would leave me alone. But I'd never backed down from him, not once in my life, and I didn't intend to start now.

"No?" He let out a twisted laugh, and the cruelty in it aroused me further, forcing me to spread my legs wider. "Then tell me I won."

I shook my head and bared my teeth in a growl, refusing to admit it.

"Go on." His body encased mine, so big compared to my five-foot-seven frame. It made me feel small and protected, like the only one more powerful than me was him, and he'd earned the honor. "Tell me." He nudged his nose at my chin in a delicate, intimate gesture that reminded me this was a game.

I swallowed, the bitterness tasting like relief and anticipation. Finally, I murmured a quiet, "You won."

"There, that wasn't so hard, was it?" He kissed my jaw and chuckled before saying, "Now, shut the fuck up and let me enjoy my spoils."

Spoils.

Like he beat me for me. And hell, I didn't know that would be something that made me tremble so hard, but it did. Even more when he leaned down and whispered, "Don't fucking move. If you do, I'll tie you down." My heart kicked at the image that created, but he must have read that on my face because he groaned and shook his head. "If you make me tie you down, I won't let you up for the rest of the trip."

Well, we don't want that, do we?

When he took his hand away from my wrists, I flexed my fingers for circulation, but I didn't try to fight him again. I'd already conceded defeat, and now I was his to do with what he would.

The thought should have repulsed me. This was *Lex,* but I needed to reconcile the fact we had a complicated, twisted, thorny thing between us, and we'd been born with our roots so intertwined that we were permanently and irrevocably inseparable.

3

LEX

There were times when Miri let me smack her around or when Carter wanted it with nails and teeth and burned skin. But when I figured out what Ivy needed from me, it sent me into a whole new level of desperation.

Ivy got feminine adoration from Miri and gentle praise from Carter. But from me? No one else could match her intensity or drive for combat, maybe because we had instilled it in each other.

And now that I had a defeated, pliable, *willing* Ivy Washington under me, what was a boy to do?

I yanked off her leggings, dragging her panties with them, and chucked them somewhere behind me. Next came her hoodie... *Carter's* hoodie...up over her head and down the hall.

Then she lay naked and splayed out in front of me the way she had that night in our old condo.

My fingers itched for my camera. I'd document this whole night if I could.

But no.

It was just us; I'd promised her and myself. The only proof of its existence would be the scratches and bites we left on each other's bodies. She let me roam my fingers down either side of her torso to where it dipped at her waist and flared again at her hips, and I memorized how tantalizingly warm her skin was.

"Oh, come on, Lucifer," she said, bucking her bare pussy against my yearning cock, growing harder behind my sweatpants. "You've waited your whole life for this. Don't you dare go soft on me now."

I snarled and slapped one of her breasts, pleased with the way the fleshy sound boomed off the walls. She gasped, more shocked than hurt, and slapped me back in the same spot, sending a surge of venom-laced pleasure right down to my balls. She squared her jaw, my cock jolted, and I wrapped my hand around her throat to hold her down.

"I told you to stay still."

"You slapped me." She tilted her chin up in defiance.

I leaned in close, my throbbing dick rubbing against her cunt again. I dragged it painfully over that wet skin, relishing the ache, drawing it out. "You liked it."

She grumbled and snapped her teeth millimeters from my mouth, only missing because I reared my head back in the nick of time.

Oh, I liked this side of Ivy, and judging by the way she wrapped her ankles around my waist, she liked this side of me, too. I reached over my head to rip off my shirt, tossing it in the direction of her hoodie, and hovered over her again.

Last chance. One last out before I drive this home.

"Say mercy," I whispered against her mouth as I tugged the waist of my pants down to my mid thighs, positioning my dick at her warm, inviting entrance.

"Never."

I surged home. No preparation. No foreplay.

Correction: This whole night had been foreplay—the dinner and the chase and the torment. We had an entire lifetime of foreplay before this, and the moment I was fully seated inside her, I let out a noise that sounded like a hiss and a moan, completely humiliating me for how unprepared I was to hear it. She fit like fucking heaven, so wet and tight and perfect. It made my arms shake.

"Fucking hell," she said, arching into the touch, and I laughed, falling forward to cage her head in between my elbows, holding myself up while I rocked inside her. Hard. Deep. Halfway out. All the way in.

She turned her head to the other side and sank her teeth into my arm, the agony only urging me on, making me go faster, driving me in deeper.

"I shouldn't want you like this, Lex," she mentally said, entering my mind with no consent needed. We were already so close, so intimately connected.

"Want me however you want, X," I replied. *"I love you. I love you."*

I chanted it over and over again in her head, terrified that speaking it out loud would be too much. It would ruin the moment. It would ruin the game, the one where I *made* her do this, the one where I *took* this from her, releasing her from having to admit how much she wanted it herself.

I buried my teeth in her neck, right over that pulsing pink X, and her pussy tightened around me as she gasped and arched into the touch. I took her roughly, pushing her against the carpet with each desperate thrust, digging my fingers into her shoulders, her throat, anywhere I could touch her. The pressure was amazing, building in every part of us, growing in the small, tense space between us.

She moaned and tilted her head back, clenching her eyes shut as her emotions poured out of in her thick, heavy waves, and I kept going. Harder. Rougher. Deeper. Meaner. Until her orgasm overwhelmed her and rattled through me, through our connection, through whatever link made it so easy for us to slip inside each other's minds. Fuck, it set off mine, and my balls tightened with awareness I was on the brink of the most spectacular climax I'd ever had. I didn't know where we stood on fluid bonding, so I'd just been about to pull out, but Ivy locked her legs around me.

"Come inside me," she said.

A small part of me said I should stop and think about this, but who the fuck cared, right? We were getting married in a few months. She was on birth control, but even if I got her pregnant, so be it. In the heat of the moment, something about impregnating Ivy Washington slammed a kink button I didn't even know I had. I wanted to see her belly big with *my* baby, knowing this night, the night she finally let me win, was the night we created an even more special bond.

I never imagined having children with her, but as my climax hit me everywhere all at once, making my head swim and my knees tremble, I emptied myself inside her and whispered, "Mine."

I didn't mean to say it. She wasn't meant to hear it. But she ran the tips of her fingers down the center of my spine and moaned an appreciative noise before saying, "Mine," in return.

After I peeled myself off my fiancée, we lay in the center of the hallway, naked, panting, and sweating down our hormones, the weight of what we did between us. For the first time in our lives, our connection burned bright and vibrant. Ivy smiled at me, and I grinned back, the sting from the various scratches and bites adding a necessary torment to our unconventional bliss.

"Are you okay, X?"

She nodded and sighed, digging her palms into her eyes. "I can't believe we did that."

"Why not?"

"It's not supposed to be like that."

"Yeah, it is." I couldn't help my giddiness. Nothing had ever felt more perfect.

She shook her head and stared up at the ceiling. "What if the only reason we feel this way is the fairy curse? What happens when we break it?"

That had been her argument for months, and we were no closer to finding Siobhan today than we were when we stumbled our dumbasses into the woods on Samhain two years ago.

"Ivy." I took a deep breath and shook my head, sitting up to push back against the wall. "We would have ended up right here no matter what." She curled upright and scooted next to me, my fingers itching to touch the carpet rash on her back, but I settled for staring down into her eyes. "Our parents have been conspiring since we were children. If there's no way out of it, we might as well revel in it."

I meant that. I truly did.

Four years ago, I would have agreed with her. I knew better now. I had a man's viewpoint of my childhood memories. In all that time I'd spent hating her, I hadn't really despised her. If I were honest with myself, I'd been desperate for her attention. Even when she appeared to like Marcus more than me, even when she'd befriended Miri before I met her, even when she stole my boyfriend and flaunted him in my face for years.

Part of me feared I could never be separated from Ivy Washington, and if I were, I'd shrivel into a husk of the person I used to be. I didn't know who I was without her, and though it had been buried deep in my subconscious, I'd known that since I was born. It was one thing to understand that myself, and another to make her see it.

I led Ivy to the shower, and we washed each other, taking time to kiss and caress any remaining marks from our escapade.

"Is that what you think this is?" Ivy finally asked. *"Reveling?"*

"I enjoy you." I wrapped my arms around her waist and pulled her closer so our soapy skin touched everywhere from our chests to our pelvises. "You're worried about what happens when this is over, but it's never over, X. Not between you and me."

She tried to move away and pull up her mask, but I wouldn't let her. I twisted her back around and forced her chin up, so she had to look me in the eye. She couldn't run from me anymore; I caught her fair and square.

"We were in this together when we were kids," I continued. "We're in this together now. We'll be in this together when we find that fairy bitch and make her take back her gift."

Ivy stared at me with her incinerating gaze, perhaps trying to figure out if I was sincere, so I opened my mind to her, letting her in through our touch.

I'd never been so sure of anything in my life. I couldn't explain how I knew; I just did. Call it a punch to the gut. A throb in my heart. The damn near certainty that, if not for her, I'd be an insufferable, lonely prick. Ivy squeezed her eyes closed and tears streamed over her cheeks, but I cupped her jaw and wiped them away with my thumbs.

I kissed her, brushing my mouth against hers, tracing the bite mark from earlier with my tongue. She sighed and wrapped her hands around my wrists but didn't agree, at least not verbally. I felt it buried in the deepest parts of her mind, even if she didn't want me to see it. Ivy felt the same; she just couldn't admit it yet.

That's fine, the monster inside my head whispered. *We've got a long time to convince her.*

4

IVY

For forty-eight hours, Lex and I dissolved into wicked debauchery. He wanted to hold me down and remind me who I belonged to, who I had *always* belonged to, and Lord help me, I couldn't find it in me to stop him.

Lex had a way of being infuriatingly right about everything.

I'd wanted the fight. He understood this side of me like no one else could. With Carter, there was no competition. He liked to submit to me as much as I liked to submit to him. I was the more dominant one with Miri, which suited both of us. But Lex was the only person in the world I could lose to, I *liked* to lose to—only in private. To the outside world, we had agreed it was business as usual. I had a reputation to uphold, after all. Our two days alone passed far too quickly, and Lex had a lot of time to make up for.

"I caught you," Lex hissed, circling the table.

He did.

My heart raced, and my skin tingled where the rope dug into my wrists and ankles.

"I told you if I caught you, I'd make you pay."

He did that, too.

"And now you're blindfolded and tied to my dining room table with a gag in your mouth and a plug in your ass."

Yep. Sure am.

I let out a pretend groan of frustration, my muscles clenching around the metal in my butt.

He tsked. "You should have run faster."

Huffing out a sigh, I ground my teeth deeper into the gag. If I could see him, I'd shoot daggers out of my eyes. But no, the first thing he'd done after catching me in the woods was blindfold me. After he'd secured my hands and feet, he made me admit he'd won and slung me over his shoulders like a deer, carrying me back inside.

Now I was strung up wearing only a thong and restrained on a table in the kitchen. Deprived of most of my other senses, my hearing had elevated to painful levels, and I had become aware of every inch of exposed skin.

"Say mercy?" He clenched his hand around my thigh, slowly dragging it higher to my throbbing, wet cunt. I loved this part of our play the most: how often he checked in on me, how often he leaped into my mind to make sure I was still into whatever mayhem he'd unleashed.

"Fuck off, Lucifer."

He laughed a sick, demented noise that had driven me to fury my whole life, but tires crunching on the snow in the driveway made both of us snap to attention.

"Who's that?"

He stepped away from me, and our connection broke.

"Stay here," he said. Then his footsteps disappeared toward the front of the house.

Stay here? STAY HERE? Like I could go anywhere else. Like I could say no. I yanked at the rope on my wrists.

"LLEEXXX," I mumbled around the gag, but a distant, "Shut up," made me groan in frustration and thud my head back against the table.

Who the hell could that be?

Carter wasn't due for another twelve hours, Miri wasn't supposed to come in until tomorrow morning, and Theo had promised not to return unless it was an emergency.

Had something happened?

I tried to slow my breathing so I could hear over the sound of my racing pulse. The front door opened and closed. Boots pounded on the floor as the intruder stomped off snow and salt. Lex murmured something low and inaudible, and then two sets of footsteps came closer, echoing off the hardwood. My heart rate picked up, and I froze in anticipation, my breaths coming in slow, deep inhales through my nose. Lex would only let one person with a heavy footfall see me like this.

"Wow," Carter's deep voice said, and I relaxed against the table, my head dropping between my outstretched arms. "Is this for me? DC, you big sap, you shouldn't have."

Lex hummed. "No, I caught her for me, but I suppose I could be talked into sharing." He came to my left, and Carter stood to my right. I imagined them staring at each other over my naked body, debating which pieces they would tear off first. "If you drive the right bargain."

Carter snickered. "My lucky day, huh? Production shut down. Caught an earlier flight. And now?" He whistled. "A member of Congress tied up and spread out in front of me. Oh, the things I could do for the good of America."

It shouldn't have turned me on as much as it did. I didn't like how the public objectified me, and the thought of the two most important men in my life doing the same thing should have raised my hackles. Instead, the depraved nature of it plucked at a secret guitar string inside my freaky little soul. I vibrated with it.

My clit pulsed when there was a smack over my head, and Lex said, "No touching. You have to pay your dues."

"What do you want, DC?"

Lex made a deep sound, and a tremble went through my body when chair legs scraped against the hardwood. It creaked as he sat in it, and Carter's warmth radiated along the right side of my body, meaning he still stood next to me.

I ached to have this blindfold off. I wanted to see what they were doing. But the thrill of not knowing made me more excited, and I nearly jumped off the table when Lex put his hand on my ankle.

"Mercy?" he asked inside my head.

I shook my head and replied, *"Never."*

Carter hadn't been here when we negotiated terms. Not only that, but I'd made Lex promise we wouldn't fight in front of the others. I was well within my rights to end this scene and devise a new one with our additional partner. But I'd already surrendered, and Carter had tied me up like this before. So be it.

"I want what I always want, Chicago. Give me a good show."

Lex ran his hand up my thigh, gripping the spot right next to my pussy. So close yet so far away. I pushed into the touch, making both of them laugh.

"How long has she been like this?"

Lex hummed. "I've been edging her off and on for the better part of an hour."

"An hour?" Carter blew out a breath. "That's so mean."

"She loves it." Someone brushed hair out of my face with a gentle swipe of fingers, and I moaned an achy and desperate noise. "Don't you, X?"

Carter cleared his throat, fabric rubbing against fabric, making me envision him taking off his jacket. The sound of the zipper next meant his hoodie, and then metal clinked.

His belt.

The whoosh of the leather through denim loops had me trying to push my thighs together, but it was impossible being spread out like this. I ached for sensation, throbbing in places I didn't even know I had.

"A show, then?" Carter said, the floor creaking somewhere near my head. "What do you want to see?"

"Hmm..." The chair moved, Lex's entire arm resting against my leg now. I pictured him with his legs spread wide, his head tilted to the side, hazel gaze narrowing on Carter. "Ivy's worked so hard to win this election."

"I know."

"But she still won't admit how much she loves me."

Carter laughed. *Fucking. Laughed. The jerk!* I huffed a belligerent sigh through my nose.

I didn't love Lex, or maybe I didn't think I did. Maybe it was all so confusing and complicated, I didn't know what to do about it. Maybe I'd been saying I didn't for so long that the response came as a habit.

"It's ridiculous, isn't it?" Lex blew out a breath, annoyed with my reluctance. "Twenty-six years together, and I have to chase her through the fucking woods to get her to pay any attention to me."

"You poor thing." Carter's tone dripped with sarcasm. "You must be so neglected."

"You know what I think, Chicago?"

"What's that, DC?"

"I think X is so in love with me, she can't even stand it."

Carter chuckled again. "You might be right about that."

"I do know this." I heard Lex stand and walk around my legs, footsteps ending next to Carter near my head. "She's been in love with you since the moment she met you."

Carter hummed in agreement.

"I'd like to see how X responds to a man she loves when she's tied down. You know, for purely educational purposes."

"Right," Carter said.

"So next time, I'll see the signs for myself."

Next time?

I shivered at the notion.

I knew how this looked. Me, a strong, powerful woman, giving in to the baser desires of two men, giving them complete control over my body, letting them treat me like an object rather than a person.

But there existed peace in submission, a certain calm in giving up control, in not having to plan or coerce or strategize for however long your playmate could keep up. Which, in Lex's case, was as long as me. We'd been playing this game in some shape or form all our lives.

My beloved Mister Scott being here had upped the ante. The thought of both of them together sent anticipation through every nerve ending. Carter's gentleness contrasted with Lex's roughness, and all of that focused on me usually rocked my world. I never wanted to get up from this table.

"The thing about our Representative Washington is that"—Carter moved to stand between my bent legs, his hands landing on top of my thighs—"you gotta make her trust you first."

I sighed at the contact, relishing the familiar palms and the ridges of his scars. *His vow.*

"Hmm." Lex sounded like someone learning about calculus or astrophysics, like the thought of me trusting him was too complex or time-consuming. "How do you do that?"

Carter huffed a breath, tucking his fingers under the waistband of my thong, dragging it down over my knees so it hung around my ankles. "Patience."

"Show me."

Carter slid his hands over my waist, up my ribs to my breasts, cupping each one before cascading back down again and stopping at my hips. The denim of his jeans rubbed up against the insides of my thighs, the heat from his body radiating into me as he leaned over my body, connecting us skin to skin.

"Hello, Weeds," he said, finally addressing me. He dug his teeth into my ear and pulled, sending shivers down my neck and shoulders. I trembled, and he laughed. "He's been torturing you for a long time, huh?"

I whined and nodded, playing the poor, pathetic prisoner.

"Does it hurt?"

I nodded again.

"Want me to kiss it better?"

Good God, the hot spike that went through my lower belly should have been criminal. I nodded again.

"That's what I thought." He found my aching cunt with his fingers, massaging in just the right spots. I arched into the touch as his warm, wet mouth trailed down the center of my body, leaving cool air in its wake. When his lips rounded my clit, I bucked into him, the sensation at once too powerful and not strong enough.

Lex had worked me into a frenzy more times than I could count, only to smack my cunt or scratch me across the boobs to break my concentration. He loved to see me frustrated, and what had once been a childhood obsession with needling me had turned into a full-blown fixation. Lex was now the master of every ounce of my pain. He owned it, he controlled it, and I gave it to him because I could no longer hold it in by myself.

Now he let Carter have a piece of it. Carter, who'd only ever cared for the tender parts of me, who'd corrupted every part of my inno-cence with his wicked words and wild imagination. He surged his fingers inside, hitting all the right parts to make me sag into it. I moaned, and he sucked harder, faster, working me like he'd worked me for years.

Euphoria erupted in my brain, skating down my spine like deca-dent venom, burning and furious and amazing in its intensity. Just when I was about to climax, Lex shouted, "Stop," and Carter tore his mouth away from me with a loud *smack.*

Agony engulfed my molecules. I sobbed and yanked at the restraints, my knees desperate to close so my thighs could rub at my most needy parts.

I hate him more than I ever did.

"That's not yours to claim, Chicago." Lex's footsteps moved to the other side, next to his buddy, our husband. Carter huffed and stepped away. "I am sorry I worked you up for nothing." Lex clamped his fingers around the tops of my thighs as he took Carter's place. "This is between me and her, you see." Carter moved closer to my head. "Why don't you take that gag out of her mouth and use something else to keep her quiet?"

A sick delight went through me at the thought of where this was headed. Carter's cock in my mouth and Lex's in my cunt.

Fuck.

There had been times in our long four years together when I'd been alone with the two of them. If Lex and I happened to fuck while we were with our spouses, it was only because of *them.* Never because of *us.* But this?

This was very much about *me* and *him* and the naughty, exhausting thing between us. For years, we'd been trying to stifle it. What we should have done was let it burn. I understood that now.

Carter tugged at the buckle on the gag, unlocking it so he could pull it off my face. I stretched my jaw and swallowed a few times, my tongue raw and dry.

"Blindfold, too?" Carter said, hope in his tone.

"Hmm." Lex sounded unsure.

"C'mon." Carter chuckled. "You know I love those watery gray eyes looking up at me while she's choking me down."

Lex let out a defeated sigh. "Be my guest. How could I deny you anything?"

The fabric tore away, and I squinted into the low, flickering light. It was dark, but Lex had lit a ton of candles, the blue of Carter's kind eyes shimmering against the flames. I let out a pleased sigh, turning my hand into his touch when he cupped my cheek and leaned down to give me a tender kiss.

"Hello, Mister Scott," I said.

"Hello, Miss Washington." Another soft kiss sent a jolt right down my center, but Lex quickly silenced that with a firm *thwack* against my pussy. I gasped and arched into the sharp zap ricocheting up my body.

"I told you to keep her quiet, Chicago." Lex dragged his nails down the insides of my legs in a painful scratch, and I squealed, trying to get away from him. "If you can't do as you're told, you can get the fuck out of my scene."

Carter tucked his bottom lip between his teeth and eyed our husband with a wicked glare, like Lex making commands simultaneously turned him on and pissed him off. This was hardly the first time he had bossed us around in bed, but it was usually accompanied by some sweet and hilarious antidote from Carter, making Lex blush or break character. Now, he wilted in his submission as much as I did.

"You got it, DC," Carter said.

My excitement amplified at the sound of Carter's zipper and the sight of him reaching into his pants to pull out his big, beautiful dick.

Shaking harder, I licked my lips and opened wide.

Carter shut me up.

5

LEX

Watching Ivy suck Carter's cock always did something to me that I couldn't explain. She rolled her tongue just right and stared up at him in a way that made his head fall back on his shoulders, showing the bitable veins in his neck. She didn't know how to do that to me. To be fair, I didn't know how to do that to her, either. Did she like it when I rubbed her clit *there?* She moaned with his dick in her throat, making him hiss in a gasp.

Fuck yeah.

I leaned down to drag my tongue against the same space, pulling her into my mouth, sucking her the same way she was doing to Carter. She responded by arching against me, urging me on, turning me desperate for her and greedy for more than watching her blow the Hollywood heartthrob. I wanted to be inside her. I wanted both of us inside her at the same time. I wiggled the green-colored gem sticking out of her ass, and she squealed around Carter's cock. He gasped and stepped away from her.

"Jesus." He stroked his dick while he grinned at me. "What the fuck are you doing down there?"

"I've got an idea for our little slut."

"Yeah?" He raised an eyebrow and pursed his lips. "What's on your mind?"

I grabbed Ivy's ankle and sent a visual of me in her cunt with Carter in her ass, and the way she moaned and muttered, "Yes," almost had me doubling over.

"Let's take this party upstairs." I unhooked Ivy's ankle restraints and massaged her feet, worried she might not be able to walk given how long I'd had her spread eagle on the table. Carter unhooked her hands and solved that problem by lifting her into his arms, one under her shoulders, the other under her knees.

Such a meathead.

I stared at the sway of his narrow hips as he walked, my gaze traveling the spread of his back up to where it widened into his shoulders. Carter had always been beautifully built, and neither time nor age had dampened my attraction to him.

I remembered the first night between us, the first time he'd been touched that intimately by another man, and I smirked at the pure innocence in his eyes. How long ago that seemed compared to the filthy fucker in front of me. Today, Carter would move entire mountains if it meant my cock in his ass.

Like the dutiful king, I followed my knight and my queen down the hallway to her room. A true ruler served his loved ones first, and even if I'd never wanted the burden of this blistering crown, I'd wear it for them. I'd bear the weight of all this for them.

Carter dropped Ivy in the center of the bed and fell into the spot next to her, leaning in to steal a kiss before I could say anything about it. She pushed up on her elbows and licked her lips, biting her bottom one. I focused on the tiny cut there, where I'd bitten her hard enough to draw blood two days ago.

She liked it, and she was going to love what I wanted to do next.

"Carter came all this way to see you," I told Ivy. "Don't you think he deserves a special treat?"

Ivy nodded and turned her attention to our husband, rolling on top of him so she could shuck his pants down to his ankles and off his feet. Once he was as naked as her, she looked up at me for the next direction.

I'd told them at the start that this was my scene. I'd caught her. She'd submitted. Those were the rules.

"What should we give him?" I linked my hands behind my back, pretending to think, drawing this out so Carter could enjoy the buildup. He must have suspected where this was heading, of course. "I know. When was the last time he had your ass, X?"

She curled her lips into a smile and shrugged. "No clue."

"Hmm." I nodded. "Why don't you take out your plug and put Carter inside instead?"

Ivy made a grand show of rolling over on her hands and knees, bending and arching her back to wiggle the metal out. Blood surged to my cock, making it ache and throb. I wouldn't be able to ignore it much longer.

For as long as I'd been edging Ivy, I'd been edging myself. I enjoyed knowing the grand finale would rock my world, but I might have taken it too far this time. My dick would probably explode two seconds in, and then where the fuck would I be?

Once the plug was out, she tossed it on the bed and straddled Carter's waist, reaching for the lube on the side table. Never looking away from him, she opened the bottle and squeezed the liquid over his tip. He put some on his fingers and traced them over her ass to get her ready.

She stared down at him like he ruled the heavens and the hells and the entire universe. A fiery twinge twisted in my stomach because Ivy had never looked at me like that. I clenched my jaw before I forced myself to lock that shit away. She'd spent the last forty-some hours doing whatever I wanted. She had earned a moment with Carter.

Then she slowly, so fucking slowly, impaled herself on him. He clamped his fingers around her hips and she dug hers into his abs to hold herself upright. Once they were fully connected, she stayed like that to let herself adjust.

"Sweet fucking hell," Carter said, tucking his head into the space between her neck and shoulder. "I'll never get used to this."

Ivy laughed, and ecstasy washed over her expression. They had a connection I would never have with either of them. He had taught her everything she knew, and she, in turn, matched his drive and ambition with her own. I loved *their* love, and maybe it made me a narcissistic pervert, but I wanted to be a part of it.

Both sets of eyes shifted to me—Carter's eager and excited, Ivy's sultry and inviting. She reached out, fingers waving me closer, and for the first time in a long fucking time, I had to swallow down my insecurity.

This was my scene, and I was the master here, but I wasn't sure if I should intrude. Carter had just gotten off a six-hour plane ride. Ivy hadn't seen him in weeks. They probably didn't even want me—

"Get your ass over here, DC," Carter said. "Put your dick in her cunt and fuck us both."

Sweet sinful damnation.

I pulled the role back up around me and climbed into the bed, walking on my knees closer to them and settling in between Carter's legs. Ivy stood and turned around to face me, situating herself so she leaned on Carter's chest. He slid his cock back inside her and rubbed her clit while I sat there with my hands on my thighs, filling myself with the arrogance I'd need to continue being the dominant in this scene.

"Look at him," Carter whispered in Ivy's ear. "Have you ever seen anyone more powerful?"

"Careful," she whispered, grinding against him. "Don't give him any ideas. He'll fuck us hard."

"So fucking hard." Carter bit her shoulder, and witnessing the square of his teeth sinking into her skin shot right down to my throbbing dick. I gripped it and rubbed the tip up against Ivy's clit, groaning as the sensation snaked up my spine, urging me on. She moaned, spreading her legs wider. "Come on, DC. We're waiting."

Jesus Christ.

I'd done this with Miri before. I was pretty sure we'd done this to Ivy at Midsummer, but I wanted to make sure she was ready. I wanted to draw this out, just for us. I pushed a finger inside her, stroking the spot that made her wilt. She writhed against my hand, clearly ready for more, so I put two fingers in, pushing back against the skin separating me from Carter. The link between the three of us fascinated me, and I could have sat there for the rest of eternity, playing with Ivy's beautiful cunt and Carter's magnificent dick.

"Stop screwing around, Lucifer." Ivy tilted her head toward me, staring out with molten metal eyes gone to lust. "Just fuck me already."

I should have punished her for the outburst. I'd told her to keep her mouth shut, but I sensed this was about her urgency, and I'd been rough on her all day. Finally, giving my X what she wanted, I positioned myself at her entrance and surged inside that tight warmth, nearly collapsing at the scalding, slippery sensation that shot down my spine.

"Fucking shit fuck," I said, thrusting harder, causing her to sink into Carter. He sat against the headboard, her head thrown over his shoulder, his hand loose around her throat.

She tensed, letting out a moan of protest, and clawed her nails into my stomach to stop me. "It's tight."

"Yeah," Carter said, his voice breathless. "So fucking tight."

"Slow," she whimpered. "Go slow."

I eased in, and Carter's cock jerked against us both, and *holy shit*, it felt so good. I knew she needed me to slow down, to let her get used to it, but the way she enveloped me, enveloped *us*, made me so hard. I couldn't stop myself. Her hot breath coasted down the front of my chest, the scent of her shampoo and sweat mixing with Carter's assaulted every one of my senses. Her soft skin molded under mine, and my arms shook as I tried to hold myself up.

"Fuck, this feels so good." Once I was sheathed to the hilt, I didn't think I'd be able to hold out very long. She wiggled under me, writhing and constricting her muscles taut with how much we stretched her. *"How you doing?"*

"It's a lot." She gasped, sending a surge of pain along our connection. I winced and started to pull out, but she dug her fingers into my ass to hold me inside. "Not yet."

I nuzzled my face into her neck, kissing her windpipe, *her X,* and worked my way over to Carter, kissing him before biting Ivy's ear. "Mercy?"

She made a small moan again, but rolled her hips, rocking us together, clenching and relaxing around both of us. I hissed, Carter growled, and she did it again.

I didn't need any further motivation. I gripped the headboard above Carter with one hand and thrust myself deeper inside her. Once. Twice. Until I couldn't resist the urge to go faster. Harder.

Carter had been right. I meant to fuck both of them until we collapsed. I wanted to let them know they belonged to me. We belonged to each other. Only one piece of our square was missing, and once she got here, we'd get her caught up on the lost time.

For now, I took Chicago and X like the world would never end, like we could live between each other's legs until the heavens crashed around us. I bit Ivy's throat and clawed at Carter's hair, and by the time I came in deep, punishing thrusts, Ivy had wilted into a state of total bliss, having climaxed too many times to count. She tightened around both of us, spurning Carter's orgasm. The groans he made burned themselves into my brain. Damn me, but I loved being right here, on top of both of them.

I'd snorted everything under the sun. I'd gone on benders that had led to memory loss. But this? I'd never known true ecstasy like being in bed with my spouses. Talk about some repulsive, hopeless romantic bullshit. But I'd swear it was true.

Once we were satisfied, I rolled to the side, and we relaxed in a heap of pheromones and cum in the enormous bed, laughing down the intensity between us.

"And you thought you wouldn't have any fun," I said, kissing Ivy.

She sighed and laughed in response, her cheeks turning that adorable shade of blush as I leaned in to take Carter's mouth just as passionately.

6

CARTER

I couldn't sleep, and I was sandwiched between the reasons why. Something was going on with Lex and Ivy, something more than what they'd confessed. The sex had been amazing, another night in a long line of fan-fucking-tastic between us.

If it had been like all the other times, I wouldn't be awake at two in the morning, staring at the ceiling like a lost puppy. I loved Lex, and I loved Ivy, and for as long as I'd known them, I'd suspected they loved each other as much as they proclaimed their immense hatred.

Once upon a time, I'd even asked him to take care of her, to put her back together when he tore her apart. He'd tried his best, but without Miri and me to soften the space between them, they'd never been more than frenemies. For the last four years, both had insisted that was it. Nothing more. Nothing less.

A stinging jealousy simmered just below the surface, the one that screamed at me for moving away. Ivy and Lex lived together. They got to have all of each other all the time, and in that existed a unique intimacy I yearned to have with both of them. But a new ache had added gasoline to what ignited long ago.

The implications of tonight rattled around in my imagination.

He'd brought her up to this romantic, secluded cabin in the woods two days before I'd gotten here. When I finally did, I walked in on her tied to the table, having been edged for an hour beforehand. There had been moments where I'd swear they were communicating with more than their words.

Ivy could get inside anyone's head whenever she wanted, but her eyes typically turned white when she did. So what the fuck was going on? It smelled like Ivy and Lex were keeping secrets again, like they had uncovered a hidden side of themselves they didn't share.

Fuck, that hurt.

I should be happy they'd finally learned to love each other, but it itched like a backward pet, and I couldn't stand it. I rubbed my hands over my eyes and extracted myself from Ivy's embrace, floating over Lex's body to get out of bed. I grabbed a fuzzy throw blanket from a chair in the corner and wrapped it around my shoulders before slipping out of their bedroom to tread silently across the white carpeted hallway.

Tiptoeing downstairs for something to quench my thirst, my attention caught on the embers from the dying flames glowing in the fireplace, illuminating the room in a soft, hazy light. It reminded me of winters in Chicago, the cold wind blaring outside, the warm fire crackling all winter long. I opened the fridge and poured water into a cup, taking a long drink as I considered this new complication.

I knew what I had to do, of course. I couldn't play a knight on TV forever. If I wanted to be as close to Lex and Ivy as they were with each other, I needed to come home. Just like Lex had made me promise.

If they were keeping their secrets, perhaps that was mine. I had done all of this for the fame and glory. I'd left them both after college for my name in bright lights and a star on an already crowded sidewalk. Now that I had it, I wasn't sure I wanted it.

What would have happened if I had stayed? What would our lives have been had I fought for Ivy and Lex from the beginning? Would I get those long hours in bed with them, making love every night and taking care of them the way they wouldn't take care of themselves? Somewhere in a parallel universe, another version of me had made that choice. What a lucky prick he was.

The snow glistened outside in the moonlight, playing across the forest undergrowth like a million tiny diamonds, dancing and shimmering just for me. Maybe the early morning chill would temper down the envious stab in my stomach, so I crossed the living room to the deck and slid the door open to step outside. Inhaling a deep breath, I shivered against the sudden burst of freezing air. The shock revitalized me, cooling the boil in my veins, and I stood there with my face toward the sky, breathing in the night.

The glass door behind me slid open, and I startled, narrowing my gaze on a rumpled Lex as he stepped out half naked, boxers barely clinging to his hips. God, I could fuck him senseless like this: hair messed from sleep, pouty lips so freaking bitable, long body lithe and strong.

"It's too early for you to eye-fuck me, Chicago." He closed the door behind him, cupping his hands to light the cigarette between his lips.

I shrugged. "Never stopped you before."

He chuckled and handed the pack to me so I could take one if I wanted. I did, and he lit it while I inhaled. I didn't usually smoke, and most of the time, I gave him shit for the amount he did. But on nights like tonight, with the thoughts rolling around in my stupid skull, I needed the extra buzz.

Lex stayed silent for a moment, but eventually, he raised an eyebrow and pursed his lips in my direction. "Has anyone ever told you you're a loud thinker?"

I barked out a laugh, taking another drag on my cigarette. "Once or twice."

"What are you worried about?"

I debated whether I should say anything. Being poly wasn't all sunshine and orgies; it took a lot of communication to keep everyone from getting hurt and that was before we factored in things like a fairy curse and an adopted child from another realm. Even if I didn't say anything, Lex would have been able to pry it out of me if he wanted.

"Last night was…" I rubbed at the back of his head and took another long inhale on the cigarette. "What's going on between you and Ivy?"

Lex sighed. "I know I promised you to I'd be gentle with her, but she doesn't want that. Not from me."

I looked down to the ground between us, letting the shame of not being enough for her simmer through my veins, settling in my gut like sludge. Of course, that was the point, wasn't it? I wasn't enough for her, and she wasn't enough for me. That was why there were four of us. It still chafed.

"So you're fucking now?"

Lex narrowed his eyes. "Don't tell me that bothers you."

I swallowed, my throat burning like I'd inhaled an entire sun. "What if it does?"

Lex laughed, probably thinking I was kidding. When I snapped my gaze to his, he stopped. "Oh. Shit. Really?"

"Was she in your head?" My mouth thinned. "Were you in hers?"

The boulder on my chest grew heavier as I waited for Lex to confirm my suspicions. He didn't understand. Ivy was mine. She'd always been mine. He didn't want her until I had her and even then, he continued this farce of pretending to despise her. They'd both sworn no more secrets to me. I couldn't go through that again. Perhaps the same realization dawned on him because his features softened, and he wrapped a hand around the back of my neck, bringing our foreheads together.

"Chicago, it's not like that."

"No?" I tried to pull away from him. "Are you two telepathic or something?"

"We've been practicing on each other."

"Practicing? What does that mean?"

"Don't give me this shit, okay?" Lex's eyes radiated with adoration even as he cursed at me. "You've been on my ass for years to make nice with her, and now that I have, you're jealous?"

I didn't say anything, just hugged my blanket tighter around me. Okay, that was fair, but it still hurt to be left out.

"Where's this coming from?" He took a step closer, cupping my chin so he could force me to look at him. "What aren't you getting from me? You want me to tie you to the kitchen table?" I choked back a laugh and tried to whip my head away, but he wouldn't let me. He gripped my jaw tighter. "You want me to force you to tell the truth over and over again?"

"You did that to her?" I hated that I'd missed it, that he might know things about her I didn't. Christ, what she must have seen in his head that I never would. Yeah, I was lucky, but so what? To have that kind of connection with someone was unique and powerful, and I'd been chasing a stupid pipe dream while they'd been developing it.

He laughed that dark Lex laugh and leaned in closer. "She's seen the memory of us in London so many times, I bet she could recite the whole night for you, word for word."

"Fuck." I stabbed out my cigarette and stepped away, struggling to remember the last time it had been just him and me. "Are you happy? Is she?"

"No. We miss you every fucking second of every fucking day." Lex shook his head, narrowing his scrutinizing eyes on me. "You made me a promise."

"I know," I said. "I haven't forgotten."

Lex stabbed his smoke out in the ashtray and wrapped his hands around my blanket, tugging me closer to him. "She loved you first, Carter. We both did. We love you more."

"Stop that," I said. "It's not true." Lex furrowed his brows as I sighed and explained. "You and me, we're two sides of the same coin. Foils in a messed-up tragedy. You and Miri, she's the air you breathe, and you're her prince of darkness. But you and Ivy?" I shook my head, exhaling into the cold, quiet night. "You two are the same soul."

Lex let out another sad chuckle. "I know you've been out in LA long enough to fry your brain but spare me the new-agey bullshit."

"I'm serious."

He raised an eyebrow, still unconvinced. "If Ivy and I are the same soul, what does that make you and Ivy?"

I shrugged. "She's my foil, too."

"And you and Miri?"

"Ahh." I laughed. "She's my partner in crime. My star-crossed lover."

Lex slung an arm over my shoulder and pulled me closer, leaning his forehead to the side of my head so he could whisper, "Just tell me you want me to tie you to the table, Chicago, and I'll do it."

I shoved Lex away before reeling him back in for a kiss, memorizing how his lips melted against mine, so soft and warm and distinctly *him*. "I'm jealous you two can read each other's minds. I'm jealous you're together all the time and I get you one week every few months."

"It's not as great as you think." Lex kissed me again, lingering, licking my mouth slowly as he tried to make it up to me. "She can do it with anyone. Just ask and I'm sure she'll be happy to let you into that hellscape she calls an imagination."

I smiled again, making his teeth scrape against my lips, and when I responded by tucking my hand down the front of his boxers, Lex hissed and yanked me back into the house to make good on his promises of orgasms before coffee.

I had my cock in Lex's mouth and my fingers in his hair when Miri arrived. She, too, had caught an earlier flight and now stood in the entryway, her hands on her hips, an eyebrow halfway up her forehead.

"Figures I'd find you two like this." She shut the door behind her and dropped her luggage by our shoes. "Ivy's upstairs then? Very well. Carry on." She trudged up the steps to leave me and our husband to our own devices.

Lex throat fucked me until his eyes watered, holding me down when I squirmed under him. I loved his mouth, and when he let me go with a loud suck, I whined and tried to push his head back down.

"No, no, no," he said, nodding toward the couch. "On your knees, Chicago. You wanted me to prove I love you? I'm going to fuck you so hard, you feel my cock in your heart. You ready for that?"

I swallowed a laugh as I moved, turning over on my knees so my elbows were on the back of the couch. Lex yanked my boxers down and stepped behind me, the sound of the lube being opened making me shiver. Then he did. He gripped me by the hips and surged into me so hard, I winced and nearly sobbed. It hurt in the best way, and I sagged on the couch, arching into him as he hit the spot inside that made me tremble. He dug his nails into my skin, there'd be marks later, but I didn't care. My cock wept with his ministrations, and when I tried to touch myself, he slapped my hand away.

"That's mine," he said. "Mine. And you thought I didn't want you?" He laughed. "You silly little slut. I'll always want you." Lex pumped me, his fist like a vise, and when I came all over myself in an embarrassingly short amount of time, he laughed and took me harder. "There it is. Such a good whore for me, huh?"

"Fuck." I sobbed, but that only instigated him. His thrusts were punishing, and when I couldn't hold myself up anymore, I relented to his fury. I loved him like this—so in control, so dominating. It almost made me hard again. When Lex reached his own climax, he stayed inside me and leaned over my back to bring his lips near my ear.

"You better keep your promise, Chicago," he said. "Or I'll hunt you down and drag you home by your filthy cock. You understand me? We're nothing without you. We need you." He cleared his throat and bit my throat hard enough to leave a mark, almost breaking the skin. "*I* need you."

Then he pulled out of me, cleaned me up with a towel from the kitchen, and kissed me deeply.

"Let's go find our wives, huh?"

When I nodded, he pulled me to my feet and we went upstairs to shower, only to find them reacquainting themselves in the huge walk-in with four (that's right, *four)* showerheads.

Ivy kneeled in front of Miri, kissing and sucking the most intimate parts of her, and Miri tangled her hands in Ivy's long ginger hair. The sight of them together always lit my blood on fire, and if I hadn't just emptied my cock in Lex's hand, I would have bent one or both of them over to appease my own appetite. Instead, Lex and I shared a devilish glance while Miri cried out in release and smiled down at Ivy.

Then we joined them, and I kissed Miri to welcome her home.

That vacation was about more than early morning orgasms and butt plugs. We both had a surprise for them. Lex had always wanted us to sneak away to Miri's cottage in Aberdeen. He had envisioned our children running through the yard, me and Miri chasing after them. The older we'd gotten, the more he realized we couldn't leave the States. So we'd done the next best thing. He'd found us a hideaway here, and I'd helped him buy it.

We had purchased it together. Our accountants had figured it all out, discreetly, of course, and we could come whenever we wanted. I wrapped my arms around Ivy's neck, hugging her tighter against me, pleased when she moaned. She was the air I breathed, the oxygen I needed to survive. Now that we were together again, a sense of completeness settled in my gut that I only knew in their company.

We were whole, the four of us, and only when it was the four of us did that very specific smile grace Ivy's face. We spent the next week in domesticated bliss. We talked about a future we may never get to see, idyllic in the thought that we might actually have it. Miri and Ivy plotted to introduce a joint environmental structure into Congress this term while I decorated the Christmas tree and Lex took pictures of us all.

If I could picture my perfect heaven, it was this.

And when we told the girls we had bought the place on Christmas morning, neither could believe it.

"It's ours," Lex said with a wide smile.

Ivy squinted in confusion, brows furrowing, but Miri's grin lit up her face. "What?"

"Carter and I bought it for you...for us," he explained.

"What do you mean you bought it?" Ivy straightened.

"I used my money from *Fractured Crowns*," I said.

"And I cashed out some investments," Lex added. "Traded a few things around."

"Jesus, Lucifer." Ivy pushed to her feet.

"We have a safe space now," I said, even happier when tears bubbled in the corners of Miri's eyes.

"No one else knows about this place," Lex added. "No one except us and Theo."

"And Poppy," I cut in. "This is her safe space, too."

"Of course," Lex agreed, even if his tone made it seem like he didn't...not really.

"I can't believe you did this." Miri wrapped her arms around Lex's neck and kissed him, tender and sweet, the way she used to do when we were young.

Ivy crawled in my lap and kissed me deeply, whispering sweet nothings in my ear about what she wanted to do to me later.

And God help me...I never wanted this to end.

7

IVY

Now that Carter and Miri were here, I could ignore this newfound lust for my fiancé. What was I supposed to say? That I loved him? That despite four years of fighting this engagement, I'd come to encourage it?

I didn't know what transpired in those forty-eight hours we were alone or what it meant that I liked it so much, but once our spouses arrived, things went back to normal. I was grateful to wake up next to Miri each morning, her bright smile and brown eyes a peaceful balm to my soul. She brought out a tender side of Lex that he didn't let very many people see. Being around Carter livened both of us in a way we sorely needed. We four were made to be together; I never believed that more than those precious days we spent at the cabin.

"Solstice is the longest night of the year," Miri said, poking the fire with a metal rod. I sat on the couch in front of it, huddled under a thick, fuzzy blanket. Carter and Lex had gone hunting for more firewood about half an hour ago and hadn't returned yet, leaving me and my wife alone. "Back home, we'd sit around the fireplace all night and wait out the sun's return."

She turned toward me and bounded closer, tucking under the

covers, wrapping her arms around my stomach, her head on my chest.

"I missed you," I told her, kissing the top of her hair.

"I missed you, too." She looked up with her wide smile. "When we get the funding we need, we'll have saved the whole world, and they won't even know it."

I chuckled. "Again."

"Oh, did I tell you about the prince's gardens?" Miri launched into a story about the prince of Monaco's roses and how she'd made them healthier with barely a brush of her shoulder. My attention wasn't on her tale, but on how her eyes twinkled when she talked. Did she enjoy Monaco? I thought she'd only gone once or twice. This sounded like she'd been there more often than that.

I cleared my throat. "You've spent a lot of time with him."

She sighed and shook her head. "Yes, I'll probably have to marry him soon."

I winced, trying to hide the hot, achy rage that went through my gut. Objectively, I knew this day would come. We'd had conversations about the Prince of Monaco before, but I never thought it might be a real possibility.

"You're serious?"

She nodded. "Yes. My grandmother will need great-grandbabies before she dies."

"You have two men who would gladly impregnate you."

Her expression softened, and she dropped her eyes to the space between us. "No, Ivy. *You* have two men that would gladly impregnate you. *I* have no one."

I opened my mouth, but how could I argue with that? I took a sip of wine and swallowed down my bitterness. Lex would claim any child that came out of my body, even if Carter was the father. But Miri wasn't married. She wasn't in any long-term relationship. If she showed up pregnant, her grandmother would either make her get rid of it or make her marry the prince to cover it up. Her child would need a public father, and Lex couldn't be that for her.

"Marry Carter," I said, though it physically hurt my heart to mutter the words.

She cleared her throat and raised an eyebrow at me. "I wouldn't do that to you, darling."

"Why not?" I shrugged, pretending like it meant nothing even though it twisted my chest into knots. "I'm marrying Lex."

"Against your will."

I wasn't so sure about that anymore, but I took another drink again to hide that, too.

"If you could be with Carter, would you? Legally?" She grabbed my hand, giving it a good squeeze, but I didn't answer her.

Of course, I would. Hell, I probably would have already done it if it weren't for my family and the politics at play. That didn't help either of us, so instead, I said, "If I could be with you, I would."

She sighed and leaned in to kiss me, giving me a sad little laugh. "Now, there's an even more preposterous idea."

"Why is that so preposterous?" I mimicked her snotty British tone.

"I can see the headlines now." Miri laughed and leaned her head back against the sofa. "What would George Washington think? Daughter of American Revolution marries descendant of England's worst king."

I rolled my eyes. "We'd be lucky if that was all they printed."

"We'd be the sluts that corrupted Lex and Carter."

I laughed at that absurdity, remembering how Lex had tied me down and made me suck Carter's cock while he played with my clit. "We'd be the lesbian witches that besmirched their good reputations."

Which was even more hilarious because Lex and Carter had blurred the lines in their friendship before either of them had done it to us. She cackled harder, as if the thought of it was too upsetting to face with any real seriousness even if we knew the truth. If this were to get out, Miri and I would face the brunt of it. The guys would skate by, their respective brands too great to be blemished by an affair.

Hell, the public might even praise them for their sexual exploits. Miri and I would be the whores of Babylon, the Jezebels, the Salomes dancing half naked with severed heads on silver platters.

"You don't get to disappear on me," I said, remembering a promise she made me years ago after the lust had taken us, after we'd been reunited and sworn never to be torn apart again. "I made an oath to never let you leave me again."

"I remember." Miri smiled up at me.

"Even if you end up with some decrepit old geezer, I'll still come for you."

"You better, darling." She grinned and leaned in to kiss me, but this time, when she pulled away, she had a forlorn look behind her eyes that concerned me. It reminded me of the morning she'd shown me her gift, like she had a deep, dark secret she needed to get off her chest before it drowned her.

She opened her mouth and I reached for her, determined to see what she couldn't voice. Just before I touched her, a zap cracked out through the cabin, echoing off the walls.

Miri sat back on her feet and I pushed upright, glancing over my shoulder because that sound could only mean one thing.

Poppy.

"Come here, my darling," Miri called.

"Where are you?" I stood, glancing into the kitchen.

Big brown eyes peered around the corner, her blond hair messy with sleep.

"There you are." My heart melted at the sight, and I squatted to get on her level, holding out my arms so she could rush into them. She did, giving me a tight hug. "What's wrong?"

"It's nothing, just a nightmare." She shook her head and wiped her wet face on my shirt. "I couldn't go back to sleep there. I needed to see you."

"It's okay." I kissed her on the forehead, and we walked back to the couch where she sat between Miri and me, tucking the blanket around her body. It had been two years since we'd brought her here from Faerie, and in that time, she'd grown about a foot and a half. She didn't know how old she was, but we'd guessed about ten. Now in the body of a twelve-year-old, she struggled to fit in. Sometimes I looked into those eyes and saw a soul as old as time. Sometimes, I'd swear Poppy knew more than she admitted.

"It's Solstice," she said.

"I know." Miri brushed hair behind Poppy's ear and cuddled closer to her. "You're safe here. No one will find you."

Poppy rubbed her hands over her face. "That's not what I'm afraid of."

I narrowed my eyes, about to ask what she meant, but the front door swung open and Carter came through holding a bundle of logs. He stomped his snowy feet on the rug and hung his mouth open when he saw the girl between us. Poppy launched off the sofa and ran toward him, causing him to drop the wood to the side so he could pick her up when she jumped into his arms.

Of the four of us, Poppy had attached herself to Carter the most. Little wonder why, after the way he'd protected her in Faerie, the way he'd fought to bring her with us.

"There she is." Carter gave her a big hug and a kiss. "It's good to see you, kiddo."

"You too, Carter," she said. "I missed you lots."

Watching them together always set my maternal instincts on high alert. He loved her so damned much, and his tenderness with her made me want to yank him into the closest dark corner so we could get to work on another one just like her. That, of course, was a pipe dream because Miri had been right. Any child of mine would be Lex's, even if it had been biologically sired by Carter, and that broke my heart.

I cleared my throat and gulped down the rest of my wine to hide it, blinking back the tears in the corners of my eyes. It would tear my heart apart to see Miri and Carter together publicly, just as it had while they were in California years ago. But if it meant saving my princess from a dark and terrible prince, I'd sacrifice my true love and much more.

WE WAITED out the long night the way we would have hundreds of years ago, huddled together on the couch around the fire. Poppy sat in between Carter and me, Lex on my other side, Miri on the other side of Carter. We played cards and read stories, and once Poppy fell asleep, the four of us drank whiskey and dreamed about an imaginary future that would never exist—one where Poppy could stay with us full-time, where we'd have our own children and no one would judge us for not knowing or caring whose was whose.

"Maybe we should have stayed in Faerie," Miri said, dancing her fingers through Poppy's wild curls. "Maybe once the king is gone, we can go back."

"The king will never be gone. He's immortal," I added. "The king and the queen can't be killed."

"How do you know that?" Carter asked.

"It's what the lore says."

"Yeah, the lore also says fairies eat human flesh and demand sacrifices and sprout wings when they get pissed off." Lex rolled his eyes. "I didn't see any wings. Everything can be killed."

"So that's what you'd do?" I tilted my head at him. "You'd try to end him once and for all?"

"I told you two years ago what I'd do." Lex licked his lips and raised his eyebrows at us. "I'd lure him out onto our playing field to trap him and send him right back where he came from."

"How do you propose we do that?" I didn't bother to hide the indignation in my tone. Lex would pick it up anyway.

He looked at Poppy for a moment, only a split second, but I saw it and it pissed me off. "No."

"What?" Carter looked between us; he hadn't caught what I had.

"I obviously wouldn't let anything happen to her." Lex shrugged as if the idea weren't as diabolical as it really was.

"Then you won't use her as bait," I whispered-hissed, not wanting to wake Poppy.

"We're all bait, X." Lex pinched the bridge of his nose. "He'll come after Miri because of what she can do. He'll come after the rest of us for what we took from him, and I don't just mean Poppy."

I scowled and looked down at her, praying she didn't hear this. She already had complicated feelings about Lex because of his wanting to leave her behind.

Maybe Carter recognized this because he said, "Let me," and gathered Poppy in his arms to take her upstairs to her room. The more often she'd been coming to visit us, the better she'd gotten about teleporting herself back home before Vera woke. I'd always admired that about her, how she could control her gift even in her sleep. I supposed she'd need to be able to do that. If she didn't, she could end up in different places all the time. When Carter returned, he sat next to me and gestured Lex to continue.

"We didn't *just* take Poppy on Samhain. We're the filthy humans that showed him up." Lex blew out a breath before shaking his head. "We took the child, we built a wall of thistles, and we're keeping him out. We're making him look like a fool in front of his own people."

I knew what I'd do if I were the king, and I knew what Lex would do. I'd go for the people who embarrassed me—quick, lethal, effective. Lex would bide his time, wait for the perfect moment, and make some stupid show of strength. Until then, he'd do whatever he could to ruin their lives bit by bit.

I prayed the king never got free. I prayed the thistles held up. I prayed Siobhan knew how to play whatever game she started four years ago. Ashley said Siobhan had the instinct, some knowledge of the future, and if she'd gone to the king willingly, she must have known what she was doing.

"He'll crush us," Carter said. "If he gets out, we're fucked."

"More than fucked." I shook my head. "We'll be lucky if he

doesn't kill us. Our magic doesn't work on them, remember?" Lex had epically tried and failed to make the queen tell us the truth.

"Do you think his magic works on this side of the realm?" Miri seemed contemplative, like a secret plan brewed behind those mesmerizing eyes. That piqued my interest. What the hell could prompt her to ask that?

"Ours does. Poppy's does." Lex shrugged.

"Ashley and Siobhan could use their magic." I remembered that day after Midsummer when I went to the pub for answers. Ashley had grabbed my hand and asked me to keep quiet about what I'd seen. Then everyone in the pub turned and looked at me, creeping me right the fuck out. She must be able to manipulate the way others viewed their reality. She'd done the same thing when she helped us get away from the king on Samhain, shielding us as we snuck out with Poppy.

"What about the fairies that are still on this side?" Carter took a sip of wine and ran a hand through the back of his hair. "The halflings like Smythe, the ones that were cast out. Do you think they'd be willing to go up against him?"

Smythe had been an art professor at Killwater College when we'd been there at Midsummer. Last Samhain, Lex had used his gift to make Smythe tell us how to get back into Faerie. We'd learned he'd been kicked out of his home and now searched for his own way to get back.

"Some might," Ivy said. "But how would we find them?"

Lex looked at Miri, making my focus go to her, too.

"What?" She looked between us.

"You can tell who's fairy and who's not." Lex pursed his lips.

She snorted. "Yeah, but what precisely do you expect me to do? It's not like I have Cerebro available. I can't put on a magic hat and find all the fairies all over the world."

"I'm shocked you know that reference," Carter said.

"What? Can't a princess like comic books?"

He held up his hands in defeat. "I stand corrected."

"We can start with Smythe," I said. "I'll track him down. He has to know where more of them are staying. We can ask them for help. If not, we can try to get information out of them."

"When are you going to have time to do all of this, Representative Washington?" Lex raised an eyebrow. "Don't you think writing bills and implementing environmental reform will be taxing enough?"

I sighed and rubbed my neck. He had a point, but this was too important. "I'll have help." That was true. I had interns, research assistants, and an entire cabinet designed to make me succeed. Plus, my little sister, Abigail, had signed on to spend at least twenty hours a week with me once I returned, and she trusted me blindly. I could put her to work.

Lex pursed his lips and narrowed his eyes, reading me like a book. "Don't drag your siblings into this."

I balked, unsure if I was more frustrated he knew my intentions so clearly or he presumed to think he could tell me what to do with my family. "How dare you."

"I agree with Lex," Carter said. "If any of my sisters got hurt, I'd never be able to live with myself."

"They won't," Miri said. "We'll keep them safe."

I smiled, but deep down inside, I wasn't sure we could do that.

8

LEX

The next morning, I found Poppy sitting at the dining room table with a book outstretched in front of her and a cup of orange juice on the table at her side.

"Morning." I lit a cigarette and went to the coffee maker, pouring myself a cup of the sweet automated bliss.

"Good morning," she said in Russian.

I chuckled and corrected her pronunciation. "You were close."

She tried again, getting it perfect this time.

"Was Vera upset you were gone?" I blew on my mug and brought it to my lips, turning to face her and leaning back against the counter.

"No." She shook her head. "No one ever knows when I'm gone."

"What do you mean?"

She shrugged. "I spend most of my time in my room anyway."

I narrowed my eyes, remembering her running around with my younger cousin when I'd dropped her off two years ago. "I thought you liked Ursula."

Poppy took a deep breath, her haunted eyes shifting up at me. "Ursula's a child."

"She's the same age as you."

"Physically," she muttered like I wasn't meant to hear it.

I pursed my lips, considering what we'd long thought about her. Time worked differently in Faerie. She looked like a twelve-year-old girl, but behind those eyes, had she seen decades? Millennia?

It didn't matter. On this side, she was practically an infant. She didn't know our culture or ways of life, and from the time the queen thrust her into Carter's arms, I knew we wouldn't be able to teach her because we couldn't keep her. Perhaps we could have said we'd adopted her, that she'd been the remaining child of a long-lost, dying relative, but once that fairy fucker got through, he'd head straight for us if he knew we had her.

This distance was the only way to protect her. My spouses loved Poppy, and even if my gut still worried that taking her would come back to bite us in the ass, I had developed a hesitant affection for the young girl.

"You're bored." I tilted my head, assessing her.

"I'd rather talk with Dmitri and Vera, but they have no time for children." She said the word like it tasted foul, and I laughed, admitting she had a point.

"How can I help?"

"Tell them I'm spending Christmas here with you." Her eyes met mine, and she shrugged. "Tell them you sent someone for me, and I'm halfway to California by now."

I pinched the bridge of my nose as I considered this.

"I know it's asking a lot," she continued, "considering you didn't even want me."

My gaze snapped up, echoes of my father's voice in the back of my head.

"You were right when you said it should have been you," he'd once told me, hatred and vile in his eyes. *"And standing here today, I'd drown you in the Boston Bay myself if it meant I'd get my son back."*

"Listen to me." I walked closer to her, put my hands on either side of her book, and leaned over the table to get eye to eye with her.

"I never said I didn't *want* you, and if that were the case, you wouldn't be at my dining room table right now. You're welcome in my home anytime, and believe me when I say people want you here."

She didn't say anything, just squared her jaw and shifted her gaze between my eyes.

"But none of that matters now. I have you, and you have me." I took a deep breath and straightened. "I'll protect you, understand?"

"Not because *you* want to. Because *they* want to."

"Because you're a part of this fucked-up little family."

Poppy broke eye contact and went back to her book, pretending to ignore me while I returned to making breakfast. Eventually, Carter came down and grilled her for the same thing.

"Vera know you're okay?" He ran a hand over her hair, mussing it before sitting down next to her.

"Vera doesn't care where I am."

"What's that supposed to mean?" Carter looked at me before shifting his focus back to her.

"Vera is worried about Ursula's premiere in high society." Poppy shook her head. "The pomp is ridiculous."

Carter grimaced and looked at me. "Call it in."

"What?"

"Tell Vera I came and got her." Carter leaned back in his seat. "That way, you won't have to make up an excuse about why you didn't say hi."

"Really?" Poppy's eyes lit up as she looked from Carter to me and back again.

I paused. As much as I wanted her to be where she belonged, this was dangerous. If anyone saw us with her, if word got back to our parents or the media or any ill-intentioned fairy, we'd be compromised.

But Carter gave me a look that screamed, *C'mon, it's Christmas,* and what was I supposed to do? Be a fucking Scrooge? I sighed and pulled out my phone, pressing the contact for Dmitri's secured line before turning my back on these two idiots who had me wrapped around their fingers.

TWO DAYS.

We got her for two days before we had to figure out a way to return her that seemed reasonable. Dmitri had been furious I'd sent someone for her without clearing it with him first. But I pledged not to do it again, and he agreed to put it behind us.

For those two days, I knew what my dream could be like. We didn't think about the drama waiting for us at home. We celebrated Christmas like we might if society's rules didn't exist, as if I wasn't a Fairfax, and Ivy wasn't a Washington, and Miri wasn't a Stuart. We huddled around the fire and played in the snow, and I took pictures of the whole fucking thing. I tried to capture my vision, the one where we grew old together, the one that came to me on a Midsummer's morning under the clear blue sky.

We would need these memories anytime things got difficult, anytime Ivy acted like this inferno between us wasn't real, anytime Carter couldn't make it home for months on end or Miri threatened to marry some pretentious prick twenty years older than her.

I'd look at these photos, these happy moments, and I'd come back here. *This* was our family. *This* was our home. No matter what came for us, nothing would fucking change it. The world would have to pry it from my cold, dead fingers.

The last night we were there, I spent time on my computer, flipping through my shots long after everyone had fallen asleep. The fireplace cast the room in eerie shadows, fitting for the somber glow of the darkest time of the year. I zoomed in on a picture of Ivy, blurring something in the background before stopping to admire her eyes.

Those Washington eyes. So piercing. So hypnotizing. *How had I ever thought I hated her?*

Something shivered down my spine, a chill settling in my gut. I looked up to meet the haunted gaze of a pale blond woman in flowing white robes standing outside the balcony windows.

I jumped out of my seat, knocking my chair over. "Holy shit!"

Heart pounding, I took a few steps back, blinking and shaking my head to make sure I'd seen what I thought I saw. Between one breath and the next, she was gone.

Poof!

Like I'd imagined the whole thing.

What the fuck was that?

I took a tentative step closer, looking into the living room before crossing in front of the dying fireplace to the French doors. I turned the lock and opened them wide, bracing myself against the snowy winter air that burst into the vacuum of space.

"Darling?" came Miri's voice behind me. "Are you okay?"

"Yeah," I said.

Just seeing things. Just delusional. Nothing to be worried about.

"Did you..." She cleared her throat and ran a hand over the back of her neck. "Did you feel something strange? Just a moment ago?"

"I thought I saw..." But it couldn't have been—could it?

"Saw what?"

I shook my head as she came to stand next to me, wrapping her arms around my waist. If I didn't know any better, I'd say it was the queen. But Miri's thistles still held, and neither the queen nor the king could enter this side of the realm. Not without breaking their curse first or finding a key.

"Nothing," I said, squeezing my eyes shut. "I'm just tired."

Miri laughed and tugged me back inside, shutting the doors behind us. "Me too, darling. I could have sworn I felt the queen's presence."

I froze. "Are you serious?"

She shivered and tucked her head into my chest. "I wouldn't forget magic like that. It's...overwhelming."

"You don't sense it anymore?"

She shook her head and looked up at me. "I imagined it."

I leaned down to whisper in her ear. "I saw her."

Miri pulled back to look at me, furrowing her brows when she realized I was serious. "Do you think she's here?"

I shrugged. "If she was...she's gone now."

"Lex...I...I don't feel them anymore." She looked down at her hands, opening and closing them.

I narrowed my gaze on her. "Feel what?"

"The thistles." Tears welled in her eyes as she stared up at me, a sob catching in her throat. "Oh, bloody hell. I think they're gone."

"Gone?" My heart pounded as I leaned down to look at her. "What do you mean gone?"

"I don't know." Miri shook her head, wrapping her arms around me, holding on to me for strength.

I didn't know what else to do or say, so I tugged her close and let her lean on me, the ramifications of her confession soaking in. Even if the thistles were down, there was nothing we could do about it. If she couldn't feel them and she couldn't rebuild them, we had to pray the king never found a way through the Veil.

We huddled together, looking out those doors, holding each other like the sun might never rise, but the vision never returned. Eventually, we went back to the couch and rekindled the fire, deciding to stay the night down there just in case.

"We'll tell Ivy and Carter in the morning," I said. Even then, I didn't know what we could do about it. The thistles being gone only meant we had to be more defensive and strategic about what we did next.

Miri nodded and smiled, poking at the logs with the metal rod while I sat with my arms outstretched to the side and memorized the way the light flickered over her soft features.

Ivy told me about her conversation with Miri, how our princess might end up marrying that ancient prick sometime soon. It enraged me and disappointed me at the same time. I couldn't stop her, none of us could, but maybe I could talk some sense into her. "The Prince of Monaco."

She made a sad laugh and stood. "Ivy told you, did she?"

"She did." Ivy and I didn't keep much from each other these days.

"And?" Miri's eyes sparkled as she sauntered closer, put her knees on either side of my hips, and sank onto my lap. She linked her fingers behind my neck and pressed her forehead to mine, and her flowery scent permeated the tense space between us.

God, how I adore her.

"And I look forward to hearing how you plan to hide your three lovers from him."

She pressed her lips to mine in a chaste embrace. "With pretty lies and sugar-sweet kisses."

"Miri." I put my hands on her wrists, forcing her to look up at me. Not for the first time, I wished I had Ivy's gift. I wished I could dig around in her head until I figured out what she was hiding behind that contemplative stare. Something about her was off. I sensed it like a splinter in my mind. "You don't have to do this."

"We both know that's not true."

"Marry Carter," I suggested. "Or better yet, marry no one and move here anyway."

She rolled her eyes. "I can't do that for the same reasons as you."

We were bound by hundreds of years of tradition and public scrutiny, we political beasts. A princess of England could never marry some random actor from the US, not unless she wanted to renounce her birthright. "We miss you. Both of us. All of us."

"I know, darling." She kissed me, but my lips traveled farther south, in between her collarbones and down her sternum to her breasts. I yanked her sweater down, kissing and teasing the rosy nubs of her nipples. She tasted even better than she smelled. She arched into the touch, and soon her underwear came off, my cock was outside my pants, and I was burying it deep inside her fiery warmth.

"How much longer can we go on like this?" I said, softly showing my princess I loved her. I craved her every day. "How much longer until it drives us wild?"

She kissed my face, my forehead, my nose, my chin. She calmed me. She loved me.

"We'll be okay, my prince of darkness." Another kiss. Another coax of her fingers across my cheeks. "We'll be okay."

I held her close and fucked her slowly, praying her eternal optimism could save us both.

ACT II

And thorough this distemperature we see
The seasons alter: hoary-headed frosts
Fall in the fresh lap of the crimson rose...
-Titania, Act II, Scene I

9

IVY

NEW YEAR'S

I agreed with Lex and Miri, though it didn't make me feel better.

"Just because the thistles are gone doesn't mean he's out," Carter said, ever the hopeful ray of sunshine.

"If the queen is out, it's a good bet the king is not long behind her." Lex shook his head. "Let's just stick together, okay? If anyone sees anything strange, call it in."

Miri chewed on her bottom lip and nodded, and I gave my word that I'd report as soon as I'd heard from Kit.

Saying goodbye always broke my heart. I didn't like watching Carter leave. I didn't like wiping away Miri's tears. I didn't like sending Poppy into space and time, off to her hidey-hole with Lex's extended family. By the time Theo drove us down the mountain, the trepidation I felt on the way there had dissipated. Lex and I weren't the same two people who had gone into the cabin, and now that we'd figured out some of the mess between us, I looked forward to the upcoming term with him by my side.

We were in the limo on our way to my parents' annual New Year's Eve gala at the National Museum of Contemporary Art. Lex had been edging me all day. *All day.*

In the shower with his tongue. In the dressing room with my vibrator. And now stuck in traffic on 495.

"Don't you dare come," he said, tilting his head to the side, staring at me with those haunted eyes through narrowed slits.

I straddled him, his cock in my cunt while I rocked my pelvis slowly and annoyingly steady.

This was a game we played, one I'd grown addicted to even as I hated every part of it. Just when I was about to climax, he'd yank me off him and keep me spread and bared until I nearly bit his face off. Then he started the process all over again.

Later tonight, when I finally lost my patience, he'd let me take it out on him, and the sex we'd have would blow our minds.

"Lex, please." My whimpering sounded pathetic even to my ears.

I hated it. I hated him. I hated all of it. But I wouldn't stop it, not for anything in the world.

"Aww, look at that pout," Lex mocked, sticking his bottom lip out to tease me. "If your face wasn't off-limits right now, I'd fuck that mouth until your tongue swelled." His filthy mind was one of my favorite things about him.

"If your face wasn't off-limits right now, I'd ride it until I clawed your eyes out."

"Woo." Lex smacked my ass hard enough to make me wince and tumble forward, his dick surging deeper inside me. "You better be prepared to make good on that threat."

My cunt clenched around him, and I picked up my pace, using the leverage to hit that sweet spot inside of me.

"Fuck, X. Slow down." He dug his fingers into my hips, trying to hold me still, to keep me in place. I fought him. I always fought him. Going faster. Harder.

Right there. Yes. Yes. Yes.

He shoved me off his lap, depositing me into my seat. His absence hit like a punch to the twat, and I scissored my legs together to deal with it. He clamped his hands on my knees to hold them apart. "I said no."

"Fuck you." My heart pounded, and I clenched my hands into fists. I'd never been filled with such conflicting emotions for one person in my whole life. I needed him. I yearned for him. And yet, I wanted to punch his goddamn lights out.

"Fuck yeah, get mad," he said, a perverted glimmer in his eye. "I love taking your ass when you're pissed."

"Representative Washington," Theo said over the intercom. "Mr. Fairfax. We're five minutes out."

"Uh-oh." Lex gave me another pretend pout. "Playtime's over."

"Get off me," I snarled.

He smiled and leaned down to kiss me. When I bit his bottom lip almost hard enough to bleed, he pinched my clit until I gasped and opened my mouth.

"Nothing on the face." He pointed a finger at me like he was scolding a naughty kitten, and I snapped my teeth at him again.

I had to shake that off, though. Five minutes gave me enough time to regain my composure and tell my lady parts to settle down. Despite this intense thing between us, there was one thing neither of us would sacrifice: our public image.

Lex tucked his dick back into his pants, and I checked my hair and makeup in a compact mirror, closing my eyes to breathe down my hormones. By the time we were there, I was back in my politician's skin. My nerves had been electric for hours, but I smiled for the cameras like it wasn't there, like the sensation of Lex putting his hand on my lower back while we walked the red carpet wasn't an intoxicating caress that cascaded over my entire body.

"Ivy! Ivy! When's the wedding?" someone shouted.

"Ivy, who will you be wearing?" This one shoved a microphone in my face.

I sighed and pulled my grin tighter. I'd just been elected the youngest congresswoman in history. I had a full plate of public policy ahead of me. All these people cared about was my wedding? Sure, sure. Don't worry about the rapidly warming climate or the mass extinctions happening all over the planet. No, the overpriced mound of fabric I schlepped on my body when I relegated myself to a day of patriarchal domesticity was infinitely more important.

My mother greeted us inside the ballroom, thrusting a glass of champagne in my hand while chastising me for my haggard appearance.

"You look like you haven't slept in a decade." Her eagle eyes narrowed, missing nothing. "Are you sweating?"

Just working on your first grandchild, Mother.

Lex laughed into his champagne, and I prayed I hadn't blurted that out loud.

"Just rushing around," I said instead.

"Well, try not to look like a prized sow, yes?" She turned and walked away, catching the attention of Senator Gibson.

"How long do you think we'll have to stay?" I murmured to Lex.

"At least until midnight." He winked. "Don't worry, X. You'll wanna stay longer than that. Trust me."

I trembled at the innuendo behind his eyes, and I remembered the toy he hadn't removed in the limo.

That's right, America.

I stood in front of hundreds of elected leaders, nosy journalists, and bored housewives that loved to gossip about my family, holding an emerald gemstone plug straight up my ass.

How many congresswomen could say that?

"You don't suppose we'll hit an age where they stop inviting us to these things, do you?" Jon sipped his champagne and shoved his hand into his pocket.

I gave a sad laugh. "There's no getting off this roller coaster. Just be thankful you're not betrothed. Yet."

"Yeah, thanks for falling on that sword." Kit gave me a sympathetic smile and stabbed a piece of cheese on her plate with a toothpick, bringing it to her mouth. She trailed her steely gaze over the crowd with a sneer that always hid right between her eyebrows.

"Don't count your chickens, dear sister," I said. "Just wait until there's another election someone has to win. Some rich cousin with an agenda. Some political asshat that Mother needs to please."

"Which is why I'll take my rebellion where I can." She covertly placed a flash drive in my hand. "Your Mr. Smythe, if I do say so myself."

"Are you serious?" I'd only asked her to look into it a few days ago. She'd already found him?

"He's not that far away." Kit glanced between me and Jon. "*And he's staying with a bunch of other people with similar tattoos. The ivy and the vines.*"

Jackpot.

"Some day, you'll tell me what this is all about, right?" She narrowed her icy eyes on me.

I hoped I wouldn't have to. Of course, I didn't see how I could bring Poppy into my family without a good cover story, one that we all agreed on. I smiled at my sister and nodded.

"Yeah," I said. "Of course."

"Oh, shit." Jon turned toward me and hid his face. "Incoming."

Our father strolled our way, one hand in his pocket, the other holding a glass of whiskey. Despite his stressful marriage and his very public career, the former president had aged well. In his late fifties, he still had a full head of red hair and bright gray eyes. Washington eyes. My eyes.

"It's never good when you three are in cahoots." He straightened, his attention going from Kit on my right to Jon on my left before finally landing on me. "And you're at the head of it."

"As always." I smiled at my father and clinked my flute against his glass. "Having a good time?"

He made a sarcastic noise and turned to face the crowd. "Oh, yeah. A blast. Can't you tell?"

The wave of alcohol on his breath hit me like a slap, and I winced as he looked back at me, a little unfocused, but I'd seen him drunker at more important events. I ignored it and finished my champagne before setting it on a tray behind me.

"Well, you're in like company." Jon finished his flute and did the same. "We're taking bets on when we might be able to escape. At least you can always divorce your way out."

Our father laughed, cynical and depressed. "You're hilarious."

That hurt right at the center of my chest because we all knew there was no divorce in this family. We married once, and we married for life, and that was that, no matter what.

I'd always had a formal relationship with my father, the type expected from a man who'd sent his children to boarding school and paid someone else to raise them. I used to think he was a God, and my mother some Goddess, and together, they ruled my very soul. But the look in my father's eye when he frowned at his whiskey and took a drink shifted my perspective.

For so long, I'd seen it as me versus them, my siblings and me on one side of this war and my parents on the other. Now, I hesitated. These last few years were supposed to be their retirement. She was supposed to be done. They wanted to move to Florida and live as civilians, put away their political games and let the next generation take the reins, the way their parents had done for them. But she couldn't give it up and he'd been the man behind the curtain far too long. Would that be Lex one day? Or me?

Eventually, he turned to me and swirled his whiskey around in his glass. "Your mother wants to speak with you."

"About?"

"A spring wedding," he said.

Anxiety twisting in my gut, I nodded and glanced at Kit, whose scowl deepened at the mention of my marriage. Then I looked at Jon, who resembled our father so much, the media often mistook old pictures of my dad for my brother. He echoed my father's distant look, as if he were thinking about his own future and how it might compare to the man in front of us. Or how it might compare to mine.

We were such a traumatized family.

Lex talked to Evelyn in the crowd a few yards away, and whatever she said to him didn't sit well. The glower in his eyes intensified as they frantically searched the crowd for me, mentally shouting across the distance.

X, where the fuck are you?

I took a deep breath and headed straight for destruction.

"Oh, there you are," my mother said when I caught up to them. "Anna and I have decided."

"Decided?" I grabbed Lex's hand. *"Everything okay?"*

"April twenty-first." She said it casually, like it meant nothing in the world, but Lex's stare shifted to mine.

"Ten days before Beltane," he muttered inside my head, accompanying a hot, panicky flare of emotion. As a fire festival, Beltane marked the union between the sun and earth. In fairy lore, May first was as important, if not more so, than Samhain. It was bad enough that our wedding would be a beacon to any fairy who meant to do us harm, but to do it so close to a high holy day? We were basically giving them the finger and telling them to come get us.

"I thought we decided on June." She and I had discussed it before the election. We had agreed.

She narrowed her eyes as if my reasonable suggestion had now been deemed ridiculous. "No."

That was that. No further discussion on the topic.

"It's my wedding. I should get some say on the date, at least." I straightened and pushed my shoulders back. I'd earned a right to speak up, hadn't I? Of the two of us, I was the only one who held an office anymore.

"April twenty-first is enough time from the inauguration as to not draw attention from your new father-in-law, but far enough away from Memorial Day as to not make a national holiday about you." My mother looked at me like I was an idiot. How dare I not come to that conclusion on my own? "It will be April twenty-first." She looked from me to Lex. "Anything else?" When neither of us spoke, Evelyn scoffed and glanced at her watch. "We've got ten minutes until midnight. Ivette, don't forget you agreed to make a speech. I'll see you outside for pictures, yes?"

Then she turned and walked away.

Lex put his arm around my shoulders and pulled me into a hug.

"I hate her." I hated her so much, I could fucking sob.

Lex didn't answer, just kissed my temple and nodded toward the back of the ballroom. *"C'mon. I've got a surprise for you."*

LEX LED me down a quiet corridor and up three flights of stairs. I followed him, wondering when I'd come to trust him so completely. Four years ago, if he'd asked me to sneak away with him in the middle of a crowded museum late at night, I'd have told him to fuck off. Now, I held the fabric of my dress in one hand and Lex's fingers in the other, biting back a smirk as he lifted a velvet rope and gestured me ahead.

The sign clearly said "Employees Only Beyond This Point," but Lex had never let pesky things like rules keep him from doing what he wanted. He led me to a room with big heavy drapery hanging from the ceilings in swirling designs. I had no idea if this was an art installation or a room for cleaning canvas, but I let him guide me through it, the conversation with my mother growing more distant in my mind as we went.

The clicking of my heels on the hardwood echoed off the walls, mixing with the rhythm of his dress shoes, amping up my anticipation. He brought me to an alcove overlooking the Potomac, some of the party guests milling about in their expensive furs, their opulent jewelry glistening so bright, I could see it all the way up here. I burned with rage for it all. Biting that back, I took a deep breath and glanced over my shoulder at Lex.

"What are we doing?" I whispered. "We're supposed to be downstairs."

"Remember Ireland?" He pulled me into the curtains, twisting the fabric around us until the world fell away and it was just me and him and the dusty smell of an old room in a museum. He put his hands on my hips and yanked me closer, biting my ear and sending shivers down that side of my body. "When you dry humped me in a hallway for the whole school to see?"

I dropped my gaze to the floor. "That was because of the lust."

"Hmm." He trailed his lips down my shoulder, tugging the thin strap of my dress to the side, the soft satin drifting down my upper arm. "And when I fuck you in this alcove, in front of DC's highest society, will you blame that on the lust, too?"

I should have stopped this. It would take one nosy guest to look up this way and see us standing here. It would take one paparazzo with a telephoto lens to snap the next best-selling shot of my future husband with his hands up my skirt. But I couldn't slow down this speeding train.

"What if it is?" I wrapped my hands around his neck, fingering the back of his hair as I leaned against the wall, hitching one leg on his hip so I rubbed my cunt against the bulge in his pants.

"What if it's not?" He smiled and I melted, choosing to ignore the consequences of what he suggested as my legs drifted open farther. Since Solstice, we hadn't talked about what this newfound addiction to each other meant. He wanted to prove to me it was real, and as much as this was fun, I still believed I needed to enjoy it while it lasted. Once Lex woke up from this spell, this fantasy, he'd regret all of this and so would I. But I shoved that away, too, because I had a plug in my ass. Our filthy game hadn't stopped. Our disassociation from reality still throbbed between us.

The jingling of metal on his belt urged me on, made me wetter and more eager for him, and the sounds of the party below drifted through the window as the two-minute countdown began.

"We have to be downstairs for pictures," I mumbled through hurried kisses.

He groaned and positioned himself at my opening while I tugged my thong to the side. Lex shoved home, and I collapsed against the wooden window frame. Curtains hid us from the rest of the room, and two floors separated us from the bloodsuckers below. Here in this intimate space, nothing else mattered.

His hot breath coasted down the front of my dress, and I fisted my hands into the lapels of his jacket, holding him close while he dug his fingers into my thigh to hold me up.

"Fuck, you always feel so good," he murmured. "So fucking good."

"Remember when we used to sneak away from these stupid parties so I could kick your ass."

His hand shot around my throat like a viper strike, pushing me flush against the wood. He froze inside of me, those hazel eyes dark and piercing. "Yeah, and now I'm gonna fuck your ass instead."

I pulsed around his cock and the plug, my smile giving me away. I wanted to fight it. I wanted to shove at him and make him earn it, but the thought of doing that *here,* where I was supposed to be America's Sweetheart, yanked at a filthy, demented part of me. I gave in with little rebuttal. He twisted me around and bent me at the waist, his fingers inching the fabric of my dress up until it puddled around my hips.

"Wow." He smacked my ass again. "What a fucking beautiful sight. Green really *is* your color, X."

"You have less than a minute."

He made a dark chuckling sound and wiggled the plug out of me. I put my arms above my head, bracing against the crown molding to keep my balance, my head ducked between my elbows. The cool lube made me straighten, but when his fingers pushed inside me, all around me, I bucked against the touch.

"Right there," I told him. *"Yes, yes, yes."*

"You like that?" He crept deeper into my mind, blending our

arousal, combining our pleasure. This hadn't been like the last time; this felt like Lex was seeping into my molecules. I'd never been so intimate with anyone else in my life, not even Carter.

What was happening? And more importantly, why didn't I want to stop it?

I couldn't. I wouldn't.

"There's my X," he snarled. "You love this, don't you? Sneaking up here to do rotten things with the one person you hate most in the world."

"Do it, Lucifer. Jesus Christ." I growled the words but felt no wrath behind them anymore. I hated him, and I loved him, and I'd never be able to get enough of either.

He nudged inside me, slow and easy, taking all the fucking time in the world like we didn't have to be somewhere in thirty seconds. He put one hand on my shoulder and wrapped the other around my waist to fiddle with my clit while he fucked my ass in that tiny alcove. He filled me in every way, in my most private spot. Carter was the first person to fuck me in the ass and he'd done it so well as to make me crave it. Lex brought it to another level.

After all the edging, after hours and hours of foreplay, I should have seen this coming. Lex would be damned determined to make a mess of me, no matter what. He took me until I came in a hard, pounding climax that turned my knees to jelly. I couldn't hold myself up, and if it wasn't for his arm bracing me, I would have crumpled to the ground.

My come dripped down the insides of my thighs, and I was certain I'd left a sloppy, wet mess on the floor. Fireworks exploded outside over the river, the countdown now having reached midnight, and I moaned, loud and guttural, clinging to the curtains while my orgasm detonated behind my eyes and around my spine, curling my toes in my shoes, tensing all of my muscles, all at once.

My blood burned and my brain sparked, and the whole world stopped moving for one brilliant moment. *Finally. After all goddamned day.*

Lex kept going, chasing his pleasure until he found what he needed. He shoved his cock deep inside of me. Once. Twice. He froze on the third time, coming in deep groans and hard kicks, digging his nails into my fleshy hip.

"Happy fucking New Year." Lex chuckled against my neck, sinking his teeth in nibbles up to my ear and back down again. I tried to move away from him, conscious that we were being missed right this second, but he didn't let me go. He held me tighter. "Thank you for the wild ride, X."

I narrowed my eyes and looked over my shoulder at him. "Don't get sentimental on me, Lucifer."

A floodgate opened in his mind and images overflowed—how much he had loved our time in the cabin, how much he loved this new rivalry between us, this new intimacy, how much he realized he had loved me his whole life.

He saturated my heart with it, and I nearly drowned, my eyes burning with tears as a sob racked the back of my throat. Then he showed me how he felt during that orgasm, how his pleasure had become mine and mine was his.

"It's real," he said. *"It's always been real, X."*

My heart squeezed so hard it nearly punched out of my chest. Maybe he wanted me to repeat it back, or maybe he already had his answer by how quickly my pulse fluttered in reaction. What could I say? I couldn't deny the swell of this *thing* between us; it dominated every part of my mind and soul. Was that love? I couldn't deny that my life would be fundamentally altered if he were gone, that I would likely cease to exist. Was that love?

Maybe he was right. Perhaps this infatuation for each other had always been there. Perhaps I couldn't let myself admit it until now.

I should have thought more about that sensation of becoming one or what it meant that I'd never experienced that with anyone *except* for Lex. But the high of our connection kept me buzzed, and he gave me one last kiss before pulling out of me.

"My mother's going to be pissed," I said, wiping myself off with tissues and righting my dress before running my hands over my hair. "I was supposed to do a speech."

Lex gave me a crooked smile and leaned down to kiss me again. "Just tell her you had better things to do with your mouth."

I rolled my eyes. "Yeah, that'll go over well."

Drunk with lust and giddy with the excitement of the night, I kissed him slowly, secretly admitting for the first time in my life that I had fallen madly and stupidly in love with Alexei Fairfax.

Miracles really do come true.

Once upon a time, Lex had sworn there would never be a day we'd say we liked each other. And now? Well...

"I love you, Lex," I told him, seeing no reason to keep it to myself anymore. *"I really love you."*

"I know, X." He kissed me again. *"I fucking know."*

10

IVY
FEBRUARY

My youngest sister, Abigail, sat at the circular desk in my office with five books out in front of her, flipping through a dusty blue one before landing on the right page, her eyes flicking down the right side before going to the left. In many ways, Abigail and I were carbon copies of each other. We had the same coloring, the same steel-gray eyes, the same set to our nose. If not for the ten-year age difference, people might have been convinced we were twins.

That only made me want to protect her from however Evelyn Washington planned to dictate her life.

"Thomas Washington University, huh?" I raised an eyebrow.

She lifted her eyes from her book and smiled. "Yeah. *Exitus acta probat.*"

The Washington family motto: the outcome is the test of the act. Our parents had thrown that in our faces since we were children.

"Is that what you want?"

She furrowed her eyebrows as if the question was foreign to her. It likely was. No one had ever asked me what I wanted at eighteen. There was only what was expected, only what mother told me I had to do. I carried the great burden of history on my crown, and I wore it reluctantly. Abigail shouldn't have to do the same.

"What I want?" She shook her head. "Of course, it's what I want. It's all I ever wanted."

I didn't believe that, but I would have said the same thing eight years ago.

"What about grad school?"

She laughed, flipping the next page as she casually said, "Georgetown. Of course."

"Do you want to be a politician?"

"Sure," came her automated response, but hesitation flickered behind her gaze.

"Because if you don't"—I typed at my keyboard, absently sending an email, trying to be cool about the whole thing—"that's okay."

"Why wouldn't I?"

Again, I shrugged. "You don't have to do what Mother tells you."

She laughed. "Yeah, and spend my twenties a hermit spinster nerd like Kit? No thanks."

"Hermit spinster nerd." I didn't know what she meant. I thought Kit lived a pretty wild social life, but perhaps she hid that from our younger sister. Or maybe she lied to me about it. Abigail and Kit had lived together longer than I'd lived with either of them.

"Yeah, always sneaking around, always hiding something, always on that stupid computer." Abigail rolled her eyes and shook her head. "She hasn't gone to graduate school or followed any of Mother's plans. She hasn't had a long-term relationship in years."

Interesting. "Why do you suppose that is?"

Abigail shrugged. "She's not like us, is she? You found the love of your life when you were a child, and I'll marry Nathaniel Hancock like I always wanted."

The love of my life. Was that what she thought Lex was? And why the hell did she have her sights on a preppy douche like him? The Hancocks were ostentatious and gaudy, even on their best days.

"Lex and me…" I sighed, shaking my head. She had the wrong idea about Kit. It wasn't that she was a recluse who defied our mother just for the sake of doing so. Abigail didn't have the whole story. "It's not all sunshine and fluffy rainbows."

"Of course." She nodded. "What relationship is?"

She still didn't understand, but I decided to shift tactics. "Are you dating Nathaniel?"

She didn't answer, just stared at me.

"It's okay if you are. I won't tell Mother."

"No," she said. "I'm, uh—I'm not really his type."

"What do you mean?"

"He likes men." She laughed. "At least, privately. Despite the bimbos he has on his arm publicly. Which is why he's perfect for me." Again, I was confused, until she continued. "Because I like women."

Oh…Perhaps we had more in common than I thought. "You know I'm bisexual, right?"

She hung her jaw open, her eyebrows going halfway up her head. "I did not."

I laughed. "It's okay to be gay, Abigail."

"Mother will not approve."

And that…well…I didn't have a good answer for that because she was right. Despite Mother's liberal political agenda, she had been strictly conservative with her own children. If she ever found out about Miri and me, or the four of us, I'd be lucky if she didn't disinherit me.

"I'm not dating anyone. People are mostly disappointing." Abigail flipped another page in the book. "They either steal from me or want to steal from me, and I've gotten tired of being stabbed in the back."

Good God. It was like looking in a mirror. I thought of eighteen-year-old me, standing in a dorm room at TWU with Carter, telling him the same thing.

Abigail said it at the same time the words echoed through my mind. "What I do now will reflect on my future self." If *exitus acta probat* were the Washington motto, that might be the Evelyn Washington addendum. I smiled, recalling Carter putting his Chicago Bears hat on my head and telling me, *"People are mostly good, Weeds."*

"Who told you that?" I had asked him.

"My mother." It turned out Renee Scott had been right.

"One day, you'll be old and wish you'd done whatever made you happy." I smiled, remembering how young we'd both been.

She narrowed her eyes. "Are you happy, Ivy?"

I opened my mouth and looked down at the binder in front of me, containing the bill I'd written with Miri, the one she was flying in next week to help me finalize before I presented it to Congress.

Am I happy? Sometimes. When I was in a cabin in the woods with the people I loved most in the world. When I wasn't at the whim of a media that scrutinized my every move, a mother that had had my life planned since childbirth, and the threat of a supernatural force that this realm hadn't seen in a millennium.

Lex strolled into my office before I could answer, looking from me to my sister and back again.

"You're here late." He rubbed a hand over Abigail's head the way he'd always done, and she shoved him away. "Your mother know you're still working?"

"She's the one that told me to stay." Abigail gave him a perfect grin. Unlike Kit, Abigail adored Lex. He'd always been a brother to her, protective and teasing like Jon, annoying and affectionate like our youngest brother, Henry. Lex came to me and leaned down to plant a kiss firmly on my lips.

Abigail groaned and flipped the book closed. "Get a room."

"You're in my house, kid." Lex straightened and shifted his gaze to me. "You put up with this all day?"

"She's not so bad." I laughed. "Reminds me of someone I used to know."

"Ugh, me too." Lex looked at Abigail. "Not in a good way. That's not a compliment."

"If it's my sister you're referring to, I'll take it." Abigail shot him a teasing grin.

I laughed, and Lex shook his head, running a finger down the side of my face. *"There's been an update on Smythe. We should move soon."* Lex gave me a visual of what he'd been able to find based on Kit's initial search. He worked at Portland College in Maine, but nothing about his behavior would suggest he'd gotten nervous about the king or the queen. *"If the king is out, he doesn't know, or he's acting like it doesn't matter."*

Lex had thought he'd seen the queen at the cabin, and Miri had felt her presence. While Carter and I had slept through the whole thing, I believed them. We needed to know what Smythe knew. The reason we hadn't acted yet had to do with not knowing his motivations. Did he want back into Faerie? Did he miss his old companions? Maybe he'd be pissed Miri had built a wall of thistles around the place. If no one could get out, certainly no one could get in. Maybe he didn't know they'd fallen. Or perhaps he didn't want us to know about it.

Going to him could expose us and announce we'd brought home more than memories both times we'd gone to Ireland. Smythe knew what Lex could do, but that wasn't enough to make him come asking questions. And if he found out about the rest of us, we didn't know what danger that could bring.

"I agree. It's time for a visit."

"I'll call Miri." Lex gave me another smile and leaned down to kiss me again. "You look entirely too comfortable here, Little W." He turned to Abigail. "Don't get any ideas about moving in."

"Don't tempt me. I'll do it just to mess with you." She scrunched her nose at him as he turned to head toward his own room. "You two are disgustingly, adorably in *loovvveee.*"

Ignoring the burn in my cheeks, I thought about last night, when he'd held me down by the throat and torn my skirt off so he could fuck me on the kitchen table before dinner. Love had nothing to do with it, of course. I still hated Lex, almost as much as I loved him and knew I could never live without him. What we had ran deeper than both sentiments, and that didn't scare me as much as it used to.

"Environmental subcommittee meeting at ten thirty," my assistant, Reagan, said, running through the rest of my day. I'd been sworn in almost a month ago, and only now felt comfortable rolling up my sleeves to get started. I'd gotten involved with as much as I could, environmental policy being the start.

Two knocks on the door had everyone's head poking up.

My secretary stood in the entryway. "Ma'am, Her Royal Highness, the Princess Miriam, is here to see you."

My heart fluttered at the mention of my wife.

Miri?

Despite knowing she'd be flying in today, I hadn't expected her to show up at the Capitol. A shot of excitement jolted through me as I stole a second glance at Reagan, who shook their head.

"I'm sorry, ma'am," they said. "I don't have her on your itinerary."

"It's okay." I stood and gestured her in. "The princess is an old friend."

Miri appeared in the doorway wearing a navy blue wraparound dress that fell mid calf and matching suede pumps, clutching a handbag in the center of her body. Her bodyguards stood in the entry room beyond the door.

I drank her in, the soft waves of her brunette hair, the delicate juncture of her neck to her shoulder, where I loved to sink my teeth, and the swell of her breasts under all that fabric, perfect nipples that ached to be sucked. I'd never get over what she did to me when she looked at me like that, like I hung the sun in the sky.

"I'm sorry," she said. "I could come back later. I just assumed—"

"It's fine. Come in." I glanced around at the rest of my cabinet, ignoring Giana's narrowed gaze. "Everyone else, give us a few minutes."

"Shall I bring you some water?" my secretary asked.

"We're okay."

She closed the door as I circled around to the seat behind my desk, watching Miri look at the modest space.

"Your Royal Highness," I said. "To what do I owe this great pleasure?"

She smiled and took a step forward, making my pulse race at her possible intentions.

"I caught an earlier flight." She absently ran a finger over the chair on the other side of my desk. "And I thought to myself, who would be most pleased about my early arrival?" Another step forward. "My husband? Pfft." She rolled her eyes. "I've got two of those."

I licked my lips and pushed my chair back from my desk, making room for her as she walked around it and came to stand in the V of my legs.

"My wife?" She leaned down to bring her face centimeters from mine. "Well, boys are a dime a dozen. There's only one girl who has my heart."

I closed the distance between our mouths, a moan barreling out of my throat as her scent hit me next—flowers and springtime and whiskey, sweet and beautiful. I stood and pushed her so the back of her legs hit my desk, my hands on her waist coaxing her to sit. Desperate to touch more of her, I ran my hands up her hips to her waist.

"I missed you," I said around hungry, breathy kisses.

"I missed you, too."

It had only been a month since Solstice, but I ached for her in ways only she could understand. We needed each other, the four of us, and after she'd offered to work on a joint effort to promote infrastructure for a new sustainability plan, we'd made our visits routine. She'd never shown up unannounced before.

"Are you sure you're okay?" I pulled back to look up at her brown eyes, but she nodded and kissed me again. Something in her expression didn't ring true, and I thought about sneaking inside that brilliant brain. It would be so easy.

But...I'd promised. No telepathy without asking; only Lex and I had that free rein. If Miri wanted me to know, she would have told me. I kept my suspicions to myself and stood, but she glanced at a rough draft copy of the four-hundred-page bill I planned to present, a bill we'd planned together, sitting tidy in a binder on my desk.

She ran her fingers over it, giving me a small smile. "Tomorrow's the big day."

"It is." I'd get up in front of my colleagues and plead our case. I'd sponsor the verbiage I helped create, and hopefully, fingers crossed, it would go to the Senate. After that, it was out of my hands.

"Are you nervous?" She gave me a soft smile.

"I'm always nervous right before." The anticipation was the worst part.

"You'll do great."

"Because you're here." I ran my thumb over her knuckles, bringing them up for a kiss. "I always feel better when you're here."

I said it to make her smile, but she looked like she was on the verge of tears.

"Miri, what's—" My secretary buzzed my phone, and annoyed, I pressed the speaker. "Yes, Joanna?"

"Your committee meeting starts in five minutes."

"Thank you." I hung up and looked at Miri, but she'd recovered and pulled a mask up around her emotions, brushing whatever that was under the rug. "What's wrong?"

"Nothing, darling. Go to your meeting." She smiled and gave me another kiss before turning to head back into the front room. "See you at home?"

I nodded, my focus catching on the sway of her hips as she walked away from me. Something about that look in her eye sent a nervous twist through my gut, so I pulled out my phone and texted Lex.

Me: *Check on our wife. She just came by and looked upset.*

Lex: *Got it.*

Perhaps this was the best part of our strange relationship. If I couldn't be there for her, Lex could. And if not Lex, then Carter. We each had our own personal dynamics with the others, and though jealousy occasionally reared its head, we respected those bonds.

That was why the world would never understand, why we could never tell anyone the truth about us. Society wouldn't see the shades of gray, too focused on things like inheritance and patriarchal traditions. It wouldn't matter if Lex also loved Carter and Miri. It wouldn't matter I'd never stopped loving any of them. They'd just see something foreign and unusual, and they'd try to crush it like a house spider.

Six years ago, I'd hated my mother for trying to control my public image. I'd been raised to believe anything I did would come back to haunt me, and now that I was here, I looked back on my younger self with pity. Who would I be if I'd been honest then? Who would I be if I'd dragged Lex to California to find our long-lost loves? How would this world be different?

Existential dread aside, I gathered my things and pursed my lips, stuffing my binder in my tote before leaving for my meeting.

II

LEX

X was right. My princess seemed off.

I couldn't put my finger on what about her was different. She had the same glint to her eyes, the same springtime flowery scent, the same timeless smile. But my internal bullshit meter went sky high the second she walked into our house.

She was hiding something, and the more she lied about the fact she was fine, the more the sour taste of her dishonesty boiled in my gut.

It was in the way she quickly shifted her gaze anytime I got too close. When I wrapped my arms around her and nibbled on her ear, she curled toward herself and moved anywhere else. That made even more suspicious. Miri only shut me out when she was upset with me, and I hadn't fought with Ivy in weeks (that Miri knew about) so what the fuck?

I could demand she tell me, maybe use my magic to force it out of her, but we'd promised not to use our gifts on each other without permission. So, I sat at one end of the couch, typing on my laptop, occasionally catching her attention as she flitted around the kitchen with an apron attached to her neck. The house smelled like cookies and chocolate. She'd been craving sweets all day, so she went to work baking as soon as she arrived.

Ever since Kit had found Smythe, we'd been watching him. If he knew one of the royals had gotten out of Faerie, I'd expect more of a rush to leave town. As it was, he seemed...content. Normal. We didn't know what Smythe was planning, if anything at all. We could show up on his doorstep only to be handcuffed and gagged and sold to the king in exchange for his pardon. But nothing about the walking-talking midlife crisis in the photos screamed "preparing for war."

Hell, he wore New Balances, for Christ's sake.

After Ivy gave her congressional speech, we planned to hit the road and go after Smythe. This was the whole reason Miri had come into town. She'd been there the last time we had to interrogate him. It only made sense she'd come along again. I would have preferred the four of us go together, but Carter was in Romania filming season five. We'd only have the luck we'd been born with, and I prayed that was enough.

But none of that mattered if Miri hid her own secrets. We didn't keep things from each other anymore. We'd learned our lesson about that. So...why did she seem so guarded?

This rolled around in my mind until a plan started to form. Miri leaned over the kitchen island, licking brownie batter off one rubber spatula and peanut butter off another, her eyes rolling back in her head while she alternated between them. I paused for a moment, wondering if I'd ever licked brownie batter off her before, and then I considered what it would taste like combined with the decadence of her skin.

I zeroed in on the way her tongue curled around the end, imagining the thousands of times she'd done that to various parts of my anatomy. Fucking hell, that got my dick's attention; it jerked at the mere insinuation of being inside her.

"What?" she said when she caught me staring, wiping a bit of brownie off her lip.

"You always were my favorite show."

She smiled sheepishly and held it out. "Want some?"

"Hmm." I stood, sensing an opportunity, and walked closer, stopping next to her so I could crowd her with my height. If she wouldn't tell us what was bothering her, then maybe I could seduce her into a confession. She'd always been willing to say anything when I had my tongue between her legs.

She held up the spatula, expecting me to taste it from there. Instead, I swiped a finger across it, gathering a big dollop before smearing it across her cheek and over her mouth.

Miri gasped and balked. "Alexei. How dare you?"

The use of my full name urged me on, making me laugh as I wrapped my arms around her and hugged her close, taking a long, languid lick across her lips.

"God, you taste good." I did it again, sucking back chocolate and Miri, capturing her soft giggles on my tongue.

"Learn anything interesting?" She gave me a sexy smile and stepped back, running both spatulas under the water in the sink.

I ignored the forced distance between us, filing it away for later as I lit a cigarette and refocused on what I'd dug up today. "There's at least three or four other fairies living with Smythe. It could be a trap."

She smirked. "If they wanted to trap us, darling, they could have found us by now. We live public lives."

I narrowed my eyes on her. "Are you saying we should go?"

She sighed and shook her head, brushing hair away from her face before pressing down on a ball of bread dough. "Why not? The king's going to come for us anyway."

"We don't know that."

"Don't we?" She raised her eyebrows up her forehead, and that concerned me most of all. Miri was my springtime sunshine, the burst of a warm sun on a frigid winter's day. She saw the best in everything, in everyone, and now she lacked that same optimistic spark. Something had changed her.

"We don't know he got through."

"You saw the queen at Solstice." She cleared her throat and leaned on the dough, kneading it across the counter. "I felt it. We both know it was her. We need answers. We need to stop him."

"We need to be smart." I shook my head. "We need to be safe."

"How can we do that if we don't know what we're up against?"

I pressed my hips against the counter, pleased my plan was working. I just had to keep her talking long enough to get to the root of her issue.

"We can't just sit around—" She stopped and looked up at me, blowing a piece of curly brown hair out of her face. "Never mind. You're right. We need to play this safe."

I crossed my arms and assessed her, purposely dragging my gaze down her body and back up again. Her clothes hung off her body and her hair had been blown out but not styled. She wore two different sets of earrings, though they were close enough that I only noticed because I was looking. Everything about her seemed the smallest bit out of place, as if she'd *almost* put in the same effort this morning.

"What?" She froze and stared at me, jaw tightening, eyes wide, like she was nervous I might already know whatever it was that bothered her. She thought she'd been so good about keeping it a secret, and here I was, a man who could compel the truth out of anyone and hadn't used it against her. Yet.

"What?" I shrugged, pretending nonchalance.

"Why are you looking at me like that?"

"Looking at you like what?"

She rolled her eyes. "Don't give me that argumentative lawyer nonsense you give Ivy. I'm not your X."

"Fair enough." I took a few steps closer to her, circling around behind her, putting my hands on her hips. I bit her ear and dragged, knowing that would send a chill down her spine, and I reveled in the shiver that followed. The fact I could get to her the same way I'd always been able to turned me on, and I wanted to bend her over this counter and give Miri a reason to spill her guts. "Why don't you tell me what's going on with you rather than me fighting it out of you?"

"Nothing, darling." She shook her head and turned away from me. "I'm just tired from the flight."

The lie hit me in the gut, churning like rancid compost. I nearly wilted from my reaction to it. Instead, I took a deep breath and remained calm. I could press the issue, perhaps force it out of her. A younger version of me might have, but I didn't. I carried on with my plan.

"You're lying," I whispered, running my lips down the side of her neck in gentle kisses.

She gasped, pretending to be offended. "Are you calling the virtue of royalty into question?"

I chuckled softly, refusing to be distracted by her charm. "Even if I couldn't sense the truth, I know you better than that, Miriam Stuart."

"I'm not lying, my prince." She kissed me and turned back to her ball of dough. "Nothing's wrong."

I intended to argue, every lawyer spidey-sense I possessed picking up on the way she'd phrased it. Nothing's *wrong*, but that didn't mean nothing was bothering her. Ivy walked through the door and found us that way, her heels clacking across the hardwood as she strolled down the hallway into the kitchen.

"Hello, darling," Miri said, giving her a kiss when she came close enough.

"Hello." Ivy turned to me, pressing a greeting peck against my lips as well. *"Anything?"*

"Nope."

Ivy returned her gaze to our wife. "What are you making? It smells delicious."

"Roast chicken and peanut butter brownies." Miri smiled that fake grin and left my arms, going to the oven so she could check the state of our dinner. But I met Ivy's gaze, and we both thought the same thing.

Our princess *was* hiding something, and she really didn't want us to know what it was.

12

MIRI

I lit a cigarette and inhaled, wincing as it burned down my throat. Wrapping my robe tighter around my waist, I sat in the third-story loft with the window open, breathing in the cool winter air. February in DC usually brought snow, but this year, things had been unusually humid. I inhaled the scent of the city, vibrant with hustling politicians and reporters. Manhattan may have been the city that never slept, but DC was the city that never stopped.

I took another long drag on the cigarette and reached for my magic, calming myself in the steady hum of the surrounding plants and trees. They reminded me how small I was in the vastness of the world, that no matter how hard I beat myself against my own memory, the world continued to spin on.

Clenching my fingers and opening them, I focused on the energy of the earth flowing through my veins. I still had my gift, but the vibrant pulse that had once been my wall of thistles was long gone. I closed my eyes and took a deep breath, still sensing nothing after these six long weeks.

But that only reminded me of the secret weighing on my heart, the secret I knew about the king and hadn't told them. That Samhain, when I came face-to-face with Alberich for the first time, I remembered he'd saved me from the wreck that had killed my parents.

"Little Thistle, you'll come to owe me quite a bit before we're through."

I should have told the others by now. I'd promised no more secrets, and here I'd been holding on to a big one for nearly two years. I didn't have a good excuse for waiting. Perhaps I thought to do it in person, knowing they would want more from me than a brief FaceTime that was likely being recorded by our families. Perhaps I had hoped it was a fluke, that the king had been messing with me and it hadn't really happened that way.

The what-ifs plagued me. What if the king only put that memory there to mess with me? Or contrasting that, what if he had really saved me from that wreck? If it was all true and the only reason I was alive was because of him? Was I not strong enough? Not disciplined enough? What could I have done better?

I sound like Ivy.

Laughing, I finished my cigarette and stabbed it out, immediately lighting another.

And now, I look like Lex.

They were cuddled around each other in her bed downstairs, the space between them growing smaller both physically and emotionally the longer their engagement went on.

I liked the sight of their closeness. It pleased me to know they had that intimacy when they couldn't have Carter or me. But that pleasure had lately been laced with a bitter jealousy I struggled to contain. They lived together, spent every damnable second together, and once upon a time, it had been me in both their beds.

Marry Carter, they said. *Come home to us.*

Like it was that easy to leave my family behind. Would either of them do it for me? Doubtful. Hence the reason they were still engaged to be married in April, and I'd likely end up with some rich parasite twenty years my senior.

At least I'll make a quick widow.

I grimaced at my gallows humor, another hot jab of anxiety stabbing through my stomach as every one of my molecules revolted at the idea of being around the Prince of Monaco.

Tough. Might as well get used to it now.

I narrowed my eyes as my recollection fought through the haze. Something about the prince, about Reginald, sent up red flags. No, not the prince specifically, but the royal palace and the room I'd stayed in. The thought of going back there made my skin crawl and my lungs heave, and I didn't know why. It was more than the fact he was twenty years older than me. I'd known that my entire life. It was more than our imminent engagement and the next three decades as man and wife. I'd started to accept that years ago.

This was new and different. This made me want to claw my skin off and vomit until my insides were liquified.

Two weeks after Solstice, I'd gone to Monaco to visit the gardens as promised. Even in winter, they were blooming with glorious colors and splendor. Reginald had shown me around the grounds, and when I retired for the evening, things became hazy. I hadn't drunk that much, but this didn't seem like a blackout. There was a glimmer around this memory, almost like there used to be around the day my parents died.

When I'd woken up the next morning, I'd been sore between the legs and bleeding, but lacking any reason to think otherwise, I assumed it was my menses. But even now, I understood I was missing something, some giant piece of me had changed that night and would never be the same. It settled in my stomach like tar, poisoning me with each passing moment. It was there, just out of reach to understand it, but I couldn't grasp it. Not yet. That was even more infuriating because it barely made sense.

Deep down inside, I feared the king truly had manipulated my memories again that night in Monaco. I just didn't know what to do about it.

I pulled out my phone and texted my best friend and confidante, the only other person in the world who knew what it was to be loved by the powerful Washington-Fairfax duo.

Me: Are you awake?

Carter: Of course.

I smiled, touching my lips at the image of Carter somewhere in Eastern Europe, cold and covered in mud, filming some epic battle scene but taking time out of his day to text me back.

Carter: What's going on?

Me: Have you felt anything weird recently?

Carter: Weird how?

Me: Like fairy weird?

Of the four of us, Carter had been blessed with luck. He could best anyone in a game of cards, not to mention his sudden rise to fame on the hit TV show *Fractured Crowns*. He'd become the world's favorite knight, the one with a smoldering grin and a heart of gold. If anyone were going to get a hint that the king had broken through to our realm, my bet was on him.

Carter: I've been feeling fairy weird since Solstice.

Me: Me too.

Carter: What aren't you telling us, Juliet?

I sighed. Leave it to him to flat-out confront me about it. Lex and Ivy had been tiptoeing around it all night.

Carter: We love you. We want you to be safe.

Me: I am safe.

There in that dark room in the middle of the night, I admitted to myself that I couldn't keep this from them for much longer. I had my reasons in the beginning, but this was real now, and if the king could manipulate memories, we needed all the cards on the table. I couldn't keep pretending nothing was wrong anymore.

My phone buzzed in my hand, and I glanced down at Carter's name flashing across my screen before answering it.

"Hello, Romeo."

He sighed at the sound of my voice. "I love you, Juliet, and they know something's up."

Of course, they did.

"Though I admire your bravery, sneaking around the house with a telepath and a human lie detector." The sound of Carter's laugh warmed me, reminding me of our nights in California together. God, how long ago that seemed, ages and ages past. We were different people then. "You're goonnnna get in troooubbble." He sang it the way someone might taunt a sibling.

I laughed, shaking my head. "Who says I won't enjoy it, yeah?"

He groaned. "Aww, c'mon. Don't make me jealous."

"Hmm, come home."

"I will. Soon."

My heart pulled for him. I hated when we weren't complete, and even though Carter and I never had between us what we both had with Lex and Ivy, it was no less powerful for its uniqueness. Once upon a time, all we had was us. We loved each other, through and through.

"Are you okay, Juliet?" His tone radiated with concern.

Keeping this one secret from my spouses was killing me, and that was on top of the anxiety rolling around in my stomach about the fairy king and queen and whether they'd gotten out. If they had, it was my fault. I was responsible for it all.

Perhaps it was time we went to see Smythe. We'd delayed this long enough.

"I miss you, Romeo."

"I miss you, too." Someone in the background called his name. "I have to go. Call me back if you need me, okay?"

I sighed. "Okay. Go. Love you."

"Love you." And he hung up.

It had been good to talk to Carter, and some of his sunshine crept into my soul over the phone, but I couldn't shake the notion something was terribly out of sorts. I stared down at my hands, clenching and unclenching them before going to one of Ivy's houseplants, a beautiful pothos, and touching a tender leaf, making it grow three times its size.

It's not the gift, my subconscious told me. *Think harder.*

It had to be the impending doom. It had to be whatever happened that night, on top of the stress of trying to be HRH Princess Miriam and a loving spouse to three people and the embodiment of Mother Nature. It was all catching up to me, and I needed to rest.

"Bleeding Christ, Miriam Stuart, get your act together." I shook my head and laughed, taking another long inhale of the cigarette, mixing with the crisp winter night. Ivy's alarm went off below, and I knew she planned to get up early so she could work out before going to the Capitol. And after that, we'd head out to find Smythe and hopefully get some more information on this fairy-tale nonsense.

13

LEX

February in Maine sucked. There was four feet of snow on the ground, and the wind chill cut right through my wool coat, making me long for Virginia's humidity.

"You're sure this is the right place?" I looked out the window at the shitty run-down Victorian. Shutters hung off the siding, and one of the rooms on the second floor had a busted window with cardboard blocking the inside.

"Yes, Mr. Fairfax." Theo nodded from the rearview. "I haven't had a chance to scope out the property, but I can if you give me five minutes."

"No." I shook my head and looked at Ivy next to me.

She pursed her lips and nodded. "We should go."

"We've come all this way," Miri said from the third row, looking between the two of us.

In for a fucking penny, am I right?

I opened the door and climbed out, helping Ivy and Miri before shutting it behind us.

"Wait here," I told Theo.

"Sir, I am *strongly* against that plan." He clenched his jaw, resistance in his steely eyes.

I didn't blame him. I paid him a ton of money to keep us safe, and here we were, walking into Lemony Snickett's worst fucking nightmare without him.

"Noted," I said. "Wait here."

We turned and headed toward the entrance. Sure, the place looked creepy as hell, but I'd stood my ground against a fairy queen, so whatever waited inside could take their best shot. The rotting floorboards creaked as we walked up the stairs, holding firm while we crossed the porch to the door. I opened the flimsy screen and gave the wooden entrance two firm knocks.

No one answered.

"You think it's empty?" Ivy looked at the picture on her phone of Smythe coming in and out of this same place. This was definitely it.

"Can I help you?" came a voice from around the corner. I straightened at the familiar sight.

Smythe still had his glasses and his salt-and-pepper hair, but he looked ragged. Two years ago, he'd been healthy and attractive. Now, his cheeks had sunken, and dark circles lined the bags under his eyes. Time had not been kind.

"You." He backed away, his wide eyes shifting between us. "No, no, get off my property. I've got nothing to say to you."

"Wait, please." Ivy went down the stairs and rushed after him. "We mean you no harm."

"Your fiancé used his gift on me in broad daylight, where anyone could see. Then he left me there, a grave violation of proper etiquette."

"I'm sorry," I said, holding up my hands in solidarity. "I admit it was a shitty thing to do."

He paused and let out a heavy sigh, his shoulders relaxing. "What do you want?"

"We just want to talk." Ivy took another step toward him, but he quickly moved farther away.

"About?"

Two other people came around the side of the house, each with fairy tattoos going up their arms. I assumed these were the halflings he'd found after leaving Ireland.

"Pete?" one of them asked. "Everything okay?"

"Yes, Victor." Smythe nodded, putting his hands on his hips. "This is Lex Fairfax and Ivy Washington. Surely you know Princess Miriam."

"Aye." Victor looked between us. "What are you doing here?"

Ivy cleared her throat and glanced at me before speaking. "The last time you saw Lex, you warned us not to go into the woods."

"I did." Smythe's lips thinned. "And you didn't listen. Now there's a bloody patch of cursed thistles blocking the Veil." Smythe looked at Miri. "I assume that's your doing?"

Miri straightened and crossed her arms, but the fact he didn't know they were gone meant he hadn't heard much out of Faerie. Maybe we knew more than he did.

"I don't know what you did when you went into the woods that night, but word's spread about you four." Smythe shook his head. "If you have the king pissed off enough that he's looking for a way out, then there's no fairy on earth that will help you. Least of all me."

I didn't like the sound of that. Smythe knew more than he was telling us, but I'd been a shit to him the last time I'd come for a visit, so it made sense he was reluctant to cooperate now.

"Get off my property before I call the police." He turned and walked toward the back of the yard, Victor and the other fairy following him.

"If you change your mind," Ivy called. "We'll be at the B&B until tomorrow."

"I won't," Smythe said before the sound of a slamming door punctuated his final decision. I debated kicking down the decrepit thing and rampaging through the space until I found him. I could use my gift to *make* him spill his secrets; it had worked on him before. But I had promised myself I wouldn't do that again unless it was an emergency.

Did this qualify as one? I mean, we'd come all this fucking way.

"C'mon," Ivy said, nodding toward an anxious Theo waiting in the SUV.

I pursed my lips and hesitated, but Miri grabbed my hand and tugged me along, dragging me with my tail tucked between my legs. Granted, Smythe had a point. We'd screwed with fairy royalty, sticking our noses where it didn't belong. We were warned. We didn't listen. Now we paid the price.

"He's scared," Ivy said after we climbed into the vehicle, closing the back door behind her. Miri and I were in the third row, and Theo patiently waited for us to give the go-ahead to leave.

"We need to convince him to trust us," Miri said.

"How?" I sighed and rubbed my fingers over my eyes, exhausting seeping into my pores. "I already fucked that up two years ago."

"We could bribe him," Ivy cut in.

"Just like a Washington," I teased, shaking my head.

"You got any better ideas?" She raised her eyebrows.

Honestly, I didn't. I opened my mouth to tell Theo to drive, but the front door on the house opened and got our attention. Victor stomped down the stairs, coming closer to the SUV. I went on alert because his scowl meant he was pissed. Theo unholstered his gun just as Victor knocked on the back window next to Ivy.

"I just want to talk," he said, holding his hands up. "I swear I won't hurt you."

Ivy looked at Miri and me, and I shrugged. There were four of us and only one of him. Even if he was a fairy (or halfling), I suspected we could take him if we used our powers. Ivy bit her bottom lip and opened the door, scooting back so he could come inside.

"Theo," I said, "Do us a favor and hop out for just a moment."

Theo squared his jaw but didn't argue, just did as he was told.

"What can we do for you?" Ivy asked once the coast was clear.

Victor had dark eyes and obsidian hair. Objectively, he was beautiful, and if I didn't know he was part of a race that wanted to enthrall or annihilate mine, I'd say he was attractive. But, things being what they were, I stayed on guard. I didn't know why he was here, and until I did, I had to be prepared to fight.

He cleared his throat and looked between us. "I apologize for Peter's behavior. He forgets this is your realm. We're guests here."

"He's half-human," Ivy said. "It's his realm, too."

"Ahh." Victor smiled, softening his gaze at her. "Yes. Half-human. Half-fae. Belonging nowhere."

"Why did you come out here?" I asked. "What do you want?"

"I can help."

"With?" I didn't trust that this guy had changed his allegiances.

"You wanted answers." He straightened and shifted his shoulders. "I can give them to you."

"Why?" Ivy asked. Thank God she was just as skeptical as me.

"You're marked. Any fairy can see it. A group gift, and I recognize its signature."

I narrowed my eyes, still unsure about his intentions.

"Siobhan," he said, clarifying. "She used to do this all the time. The Midsummer festival. The lust."

"You know Siobhan?" This piqued Ivy's interest. "How?"

"She's my cousin. We were basin-mates, raised by the same nursemaid, once upon a time." He smiled, seemingly lost in a memory before continuing. "She knew what she was doing when she gave the gift to you, and I don't say that lightly. If she's wrapped up in this, I'll help her, and I think that means helping you."

"Okay." I crossed my arms, suspicious but willing to play along. "Help us. Tell us about the king. Is he on this side of the realm? Is the queen?"

Victor shook his head. "I don't know."

"Has he found a key?" I continued.

Again, Victor shrugged and frowned. "I have no idea."

"Well, gee, Victor." I pinched the bridge of my nose, frustration clawing through my midsection. "Thank you so much for your help."

"Your gifts. They're getting more powerful, yes?" Victor's eyebrows rose as he looked between us. "That's because Siobhan's vision is coming true."

Ashley said that Siobhan was a banshee, that she would get instincts about events in the future. Ashley believed we might have been a part of some grand design, especially if Siobhan continued to help us.

"The moment she saw Ivy, she had a vision. She was supposed to give the gift to her. She didn't know why, just that she had to." Victor looked at X. "After she kissed you, the queen sent her away. Siobhan spent some time in this realm, even came to visit me once or twice. She said the king was growing weary of the separation, that he planned to end the quarrel with the queen by killing the child." Victor's attention came back to me and Miri. "That didn't happen."

Ivy's lips thinned, but she didn't confirm or deny we had Poppy.

"She said something happened to the four of you when you made a vow in the ruins. She couldn't predict that. After you promised your lives to each other, the magic mutated. It took on a life of its own. She only knew she was supposed to give the gift to you, but after that..." He shrugged. "We both believe everything happens for a reason."

"If the king gets out, is there a way to put him back?" Knowing about our gifts was great, but we had bigger problems to solve here.

"I only know of one fairy that could curse him, and that was hundreds of years ago. There's no telling where to find them or if they still exist."

Great. Just fucking great.

Where the hell would we find someone like that if everyone in the fairy fucking underground hated us? Better yet, if no one even knew such a powerful fairy still existed?

"What about powers?" Ivy said. "What magic does the king have? What gifts?"

Victor snorted. "All gifts. All magic. He's the king."

"What about...time travel?" Miri held her sweater tighter around her waist. "Could the king or queen go back in time? Hurt us before we knew what was going on? Or maybe...manipulate memories?"

"I've never heard of that." Victor shook his head. "Not to say it's not possible, but all magic is elemental. We're connected to the earth, and the earth only moves in one direction. I don't know anyone who can manipulate space and time, not even royalty."

My heart plummeted to my stomach, both at Miri's question and Victor's answer. He didn't know anyone who could bend the rules of space and time...but we did. Was this why the king wanted Poppy? Could he use her to go back in time and kill us as children, ending this before it even began?

I had never even considered the possibility. Miri shared my look of apprehension and glanced at Ivy, who stayed stone-faced and stoic through the whole thing—a true politician. The only tell she had was the flush snaking up her neck.

"What will you do if he gets out?" Ivy raised an eyebrow. "Are you preparing for war? Preparing to run and hide? Will you join him or fight him?"

"Fight him?" Victor laughed, looking between us like we were ridiculous. "Ivy, there is no fighting him. If the king gets out, he'll burn this entire realm to the ground and kill everyone in it. It's all he's ever wanted to do."

"Can we stop him?" I grabbed my cigarettes and lit one, rubbing at the back of my neck with the other hand while the nicotine buzz washed over me. I'd been trying to cut back, but if ever there was a time to light up...

"I don't see how." Victor shook his head. "No one in this realm will be able to stop him."

"How many fairies are there on this side? Was Peter right? Will no one help us?" Miri's eyes pleaded with him to give us good news, to tell us we had some allies.

"Peter is right that word has spread about the four of you, but fairies are secretive. No one will say anything to a public that doesn't know we exist." Then he sighed. "But will we fight him? Will we help you?" Again, he shrugged. "Some may, if only to protect the humans they love. Most will flee. There's a reason we're terrified of him. He's done incredible things. Despicable and horrendous, but undeniably incredible."

I should have been more scared, but instead, an ice-cold, electric rage brewed just under my skin. If this motherfucker came for us, I had to find a way to defeat him. I had to protect my spouses and my family. I had to protect this whole planet.

No pressure.

"Where's Siobhan now?" I asked. "Is she still with the king?"

He nodded. "Last I heard, she and her warriors rejoined his army. I haven't seen her since, but I don't think she's with him in cause. She's trying to find a way to protect the queen."

"What about you, Victor?" I took another long drag. "Will you fight with us?"

He smiled. "I'd like to think I would."

"Why?"

Victor flashed me another grin. "Because the humans I know are loving and generous. And if they were in my shoes, they'd do it for me." He looked between the three of us before adding, "I hope you're worth it."

Yeah, I hoped we were, too.

He opened the car door and put a foot on the ground. "I have to go. I wish I could have been more help."

After he left, I turned to my wives with more questions than answers and absolutely no plan for what to do next.

14

IVY

"What are you thinking?" Carter asked, taking a sip of scotch. It was three in the morning in Romania, and weariness hung under his eyes, matching the crease between his brows. He looked exhausted, even on FaceTime. After Victor left, we'd gone back to the bed-and-breakfast to have dinner and deliberate about what to do next. This was the only time Carter could talk, so we'd taken advantage of that.

"I don't know." Lex pulled on his cigarette. "We need to think about this. Be strategic."

"I'll have Kit keep looking for Siobhan." I didn't like having my siblings involved, but there was no one as good as my sister. "If she shows up, we'll know."

"Meanwhile, we can keep researching." Lex continued. "There's got to be something out there. Some story. Some myth. Someone has to know something."

My focus went to Miri, who had remained suspiciously quiet since her question about time traveling. That made me nervous.

"When can you come home?" Lex asked.

"Soon," Carter answered. "March."

"We miss you," I said.

"Miss you, too. Love you."

We hung up, but I moved to sit on the couch next to our princess, lifting her outstretched legs so I could put them in my lap. I wanted to touch her for my next conversation, which might not be pleasant.

"Miri." I squeezed her ankle so she'd look up at me. "Why did you ask about time travel and memory manipulation?"

She shrugged. "Poppy said her gifts were from space and time. I wanted to make sure."

"You asked about the *king* being able to go back in time." I didn't buy the innocence game she tried to sell us, and it was time she fessed up to whatever she'd been keeping to herself.

Miri looked away again, but Lex moved closer and put his hand under her chin, forcing her to meet his gaze. "Do I have to do it?"

She squared her jaw and jerked her head away, glancing back at me with tears brewing in the corners of her eyes. With an exhale that sounded like it weighed a ton, she murmured, "Go on, then."

I pushed one hand under her leggings, skin to skin, and grabbed Lex's wrist with the other. Together, we watched Miri's memory of the car accident. Her fear sizzled through me like it was my own, the bite of raw terror permeating through my soul, the loud screech of metal on metal echoing between my ears. It wasn't just the visions flashing through us like a movie; it was her pain and her confusion as well. Miri's tears skated down my cheeks, and my heart broke as hers crumbled. I ached for this version of my beloved, the child who had watched her parents die right in front of her.

Then an enormous hand reached into the vehicle and pulled her out, cradling her as he carried her to the side of the road and placed her in the grass. His features seemed so kind, so at odds with the cruel snarl I associated with him.

"Yes, Little Thistle. You'll come to owe me quite a bit before we're through."

I tried to sift farther and go deeper. I sensed something else too, something that had happened to her but been put in a dark, spiraling container. Something like the car accident, but more recent. It had been encased in an impenetrable haze that even I couldn't break through. All I got was a glimpse of the prince of Monaco before the connection broke like a punch to the gut.

Miri launched off the couch, gasping as she put her hands over her face, deep, wretched sobs pouring out.

"He was there?" Lex's eyebrows shot up his forehead.

Lex hadn't felt what I had; he hadn't sensed the second part of her secret.

Miri swallowed and turned to us, crossing her arms over her waist like she was sick to her stomach. Hell, it hadn't even happened to me, and I felt like I might throw up.

"I don't know." She inhaled on a broken sigh, wiping tears off her cheeks, hiding her face from both of us.

"You don't know?" Lex's tone echoed off the walls, his eyes piercing as they glared at her. "How could you keep this from me? From us?"

"You've known since Samhain?" I stood, holding my hands up in solidarity. I didn't want to be angry with her. We all kept secrets for different reasons. Once upon a time, Lex and I had kept a hell of one from her. But the time had come for the truth. She couldn't hide this from us any longer. We needed to know all of it, if only so we could protect ourselves from whatever the fairies threw at us next.

"I was scared, okay?" Her hands balled into fists as they dropped to her side. "I didn't know what it meant. I thought he was screwing with me, putting fake memories in my head. After talking to Victor..." She cleared her throat and looked away. "I don't know what to think anymore."

My heart broke for her. *This...*This had been what she was bearing alone, and I ignored the betrayal that came with my lover feeling like she couldn't come to us, to *me,* with her darkest fears. I put my arms around her and pulled her into a hug while she cried.

"Shh," I told her. "Thank you for telling us now."

"I've been so scared," Miri said. "I'm sorry I didn't say anything.

I'm sorry." She clung to the back of my shirt, hanging on to me like I could grant her the salvation that would purify her soul.

"It's okay, Miri. My princess. My love." I kissed the side of her head. "It's okay."

"If Poppy's the only one who can go back in time, does that mean she's helping him?" Miri said into my chest. "Why does he care so much about me?"

I looked to Lex, who ran his hands through his hair and squared his jaw, his stare turning to molten rage.

"He shouldn't have been able to get out when I was a child." Miri closed her eyes and shook her head, taking a long drag. "I don't understand. He was cursed, forbidden to leave Faerie. How did it happen?"

"Miri, you should have told us." I brushed hair out of her face and kissed her forehead, her mouth, her cheeks, anywhere I could. "I love you, and I understand why you kept it to yourself. But please be honest with me in the future." I let my eyes say what my mouth couldn't.

What else are you hiding? Tell us now.

She didn't. Whatever I'd sensed earlier lingered between us until Lex sat on the couch and put his elbows on his knees. "If you remember him from your childhood, that means he gets out. That means whatever we try to do to stop it is futile. We should focus on how to defeat him when he gets here."

She shrugged and dropped her jaw, looking up to me for help. I didn't know what to say. I collapsed on the other side of her, taking a long, deep pull on the cigarette. "It doesn't matter. We know he's after Poppy, and we know he ultimately gets her. We should focus on that."

I thought about what Lex said at Solstice, that he'd use Poppy for bait. I had balked at the time, but now maybe that made the most sense. The king wanted her, and he obviously couldn't hurt her if he planned to use her to skip across time, but to what end? Had the king only gone back to mess with Miri's life? Or had he screwed with all of us without our knowledge?

"We should ask Poppy if that's something she can do," Lex said. "Or if she knows that she can do it."

"And if she can?" Miri's voice shook, like she'd been holding on to this secret so long, it physically hurt to be relieved of it.

"We'll protect you." Lex pulled her into him so he could kiss her forehead.

"I'm not just worried about me." Miri looked between us. "I don't want him forcing Poppy to do terrible things."

"We'll protect her, too." I grabbed Miri's hand and kissed her knuckles. "I promise." I'd go to my grave protecting that child if I had to. She was mine. Mine and ours, and the fucking fairy king would have to go through us to get to her.

Miri shook her head and sighed, but didn't disagree.

"C'mon." Lex stood and stabbed out his cigarette. "We're all tired. Let's take a shower and go to bed."

We squeezed into the tiny tub and cleaned each other, taking our time to make Miri come. As much as I normally loved to dominate my princess, she seemed more fragile now than she ever had before, more vulnerable for having confessed her sins.

Lex fucked her from behind and I lapped at her clit, and when she came, she dug her fingers into my hair and moaned both of our names. God, turning her to putty like this inflated my ego. I loved being able to love her, and I loved that Lex loved her, too.

If it didn't make me such a sap, I'd cry at how deep my emotions for both of them went. After we all found a release, we cuddled together in the king-size bed with Miri in the middle. Sometime later, I took them both again, needing the connection like I needed air. It was sweet and gentle and slow. We laughed and giggled, and when I climaxed for the fourth time, I swore I'd never let anything tear us apart again.

ACT III

Shall we their fond pageant see?
Lord, what fools these mortals be.
-Puck, Act III, Scene II

15

LEX
MARCH

When Miri told us about the king, I changed my perspective. He had probably fucked with our lives in other ways. Were we all victims without knowing it? We needed more information, and we had precious little time to find it. Miri flew home shortly after leaving Maine, but Ivy and I reached out to Poppy once we were back in DC.

"I've never tried it before." Poppy crossed her arms and shrugged. She'd teleported here a few minutes ago and now she sat on the couch in Ivy's office with her hair in long braids down either side of her body. She must have grown another six inches in the week since I'd last seen her. "I suppose it's possible."

"Do you think that's why the king would want you?"

Again, she shrugged. "My lady said he wanted to kill me, not use me."

"Did the queen ever use you?" Ivy asked.

"Yes." Poppy nodded. "But not without asking."

"But not to go back in time?" I narrowed my gaze on her as she shook her head. She wasn't lying, at least not that I could sense, but that didn't mean she was telling us the complete truth.

"Thank you for feeling safe enough to share that." Ivy kissed her on the temple and stood, turning to me on the other couch.

"If either of them comes looking, the king or the queen, you'll tell us, right?" Ivy asked, seemingly expecting the girl's agreement.

Poppy met my eyes with a smile and nodded. But something about the grin seemed fake, and that piqued my interest. Poppy was smarter than she seemed, and sometimes, I felt like I was waiting for the other shoe to drop, for her to turn into some kind of hell-monster, set on killing us all. It took a lot to convince myself she was just a little girl who needed a family, and even then, I kept myself guarded.

I wanted to love Poppy as much as the others, and maybe it made me an asshole to admit I didn't, that until all of this was over, I couldn't trust her completely. *Well, fuck it. Fine.* If it made me the bad guy, I'd be the fucking bad guy. We shouldn't have brought her here in the first place, and every second that ticked by was another that the king could find her and kill us for taking her.

"Thanks," Ivy said. "How are things at Vera's?"

Poppy said things were okay and talked about Ursula, but my thoughts drifted elsewhere, to what this could mean. Of course, I had the initial gut reaction any other person might have: ask her to go back and change something to see what happens. Maybe stop Siobhan from giving us this gift. Stop our parents from forcing us together. Stop Marcus from going out on that boat.

But c'mon, I'd seen *Back to the Future*. I knew fucking with time had serious consequences, most of which made my head spin. Still, it posed the question, if I could save Marcus and marry Miri and never ask anyone for the truth again, would I?

It was a compelling thought, if only because I didn't know my answer. If Marcus hadn't died, I wouldn't have gone to London. And if I hadn't gone to London, I never would have had that night with Carter. I might not have met Miri. Ivy would have happily ended up with Marcus, and Carter likely would have been a footnote in both our stories.

Sitting there in my living room with my fiancée and her kid, I wasn't sure I would change it. I missed my brother. I always would. I loved Miri, and if I had the chance, I'd marry her in a heartbeat. But I'd once told Ivy that there were worse people I could end up with, and I'd meant it. We had come a long way since those ten-year-old children wrestling backstage at her mother's inauguration. I wasn't sure I would trade that for anything else, and I definitely wouldn't trade our time at Solstice for a life where she married my brother instead.

Once upon a time, I might have, but now, I couldn't stand it if Ivy hated me again. I wouldn't be able to live with myself if I hated her. We'd grown so much. We'd done so much. I used to wish it would have been me who died instead of Marcus. Today, I thanked my lucky fucking stars it wasn't.

"Knock knock," came the voice from behind me, and I sat up, a small twist of panic seizing my gut at the sight of Ivy's little sister.

"Abigail?" Ivy pushed to her feet. "What are you doing here?"

"You said to come over for brunch." She looked at Poppy, eyebrows furrowing. "Who's this?"

"I'm Poppy," she said, her smile wide, her hand out in front of her to take Abigail's.

"She's my cousin," I said. "On my mother's side."

"Oh." Abigail seemed delighted, her gaze brightening. "I didn't know you were having family over. You should have told us. Mother would have wanted—"

"No," Ivy cut in. "It wasn't a planned thing, and you shouldn't tell Mother she was here."

Abigail's smile faltered, but she nodded. "Yeah, okay."

"How are you related?" Poppy asked, likely to be polite. She already knew everyone in Ivy's family from the pictures around our place.

"My sister," Ivy said.

Poppy nodded, her grin growing wider the longer she looked at Abigail.

"Well, I'll take Poppy and leave you two alone." I nodded toward the exit, and Poppy stood to follow, but she paused when she got closer to Abigail.

"Nice to meet you," Poppy said, eyes twinkling. "So very nice to meet you."

"Yeah, likewise." Abigail gave us a wave before turning her attention to her sister.

Poppy practically skipped down the hall to the stairs and into the family room, plopping in front of the fireplace. "She seems nice."

"Uh-huh." I didn't buy the innocent act. "Keep Ivy's siblings out of this, you understand? They don't know about you. They don't know about the king or the queen or any of that shit."

Poppy pursed her lips, seeming to mull this over before responding. "Don't you think they should?"

"Their ignorance keeps them safe."

"When the king comes, he'll go for your family first."

I paused, analyzing her words. Of course, I'd been thinking that myself, but what would prompt Poppy to say it? And what the fuck were we supposed to do about it? I couldn't see a situation in which we sat our extended family down and explained what happened to us in Ireland: how we'd been marked, how we'd stolen a child from Faerie and crossed interdimensional space to bring her here. Where does someone even begin that mindfuck of a story?

Maybe one day it would come to that, but we weren't there yet, and I prayed we never would be.

"Especially if I'm still living with Dmitri when he does," Poppy added.

"What do you suggest?" I raised my eyebrows, but she didn't say anything else, just sat in front of the fire and poked at it with the metal rod. "Yeah, I don't have any better ideas, either."

"Tell everyone I'm adopted from Russia. Let me live here with you. We can protect each other."

"Even if I could do that"—I sat down next to her and leaned back on my hands, letting the warmth from the flames wash over me—

"you don't want to live with us. Our lives are messy and complicated."

"I'm a human child born in a fairy realm. I can cut through space and time. I'm okay with messy and complicated, thanks."

I snorted. *Quick as a fucking whip, this one.* "You've been living with the Romanovs too long."

"That's my point, stupid."

Now that Ivy was elected and we planned to get married, maybe we *could* adopt her. That would certainly bring her close enough for me to keep an eye on her until I trusted her. It'd be easy to make up some cover story and pay to have her past well hidden. She could be our daughter for real.

When the king got out, he'd come for us. We already knew that, and if Miri's memory was real, he took Poppy no matter what. Perhaps there was no point in trying to hide her. Maybe this was pointless from the beginning.

If Poppy had a brain behind those eyes, then why weren't we using it? We should have been trying to teach her how to protect herself, how to use her fairy gifts to her benefit. We needed to stop denying her part in this. The king would come for her, and she needed to be ready.

"Let me work on it," I said. Maybe I could convince Ivy to talk to her mother. Maybe I could bullshit my way through the fallout now that we had our own foothold in politics. "Poppy, how often do you practice your gifts?"

She shrugged. "I teleport most nights."

"But you've never tried to mess with time?"

She shook her head.

"I want to make a deal with you," I told her, leaning in so no one else would hear us.

That intrigued her, and her tiny features screwed up into confusion as she mirrored my pose. "What deal?"

"You'd have to trust me." That would take a lot. I never wanted to bring her here, and now that she was, I had to recognize she was a liability. But, likewise, so were we to her.

"Hah." She laughed and rolled her eyes. "To quote you, why the fuck would I do that?"

I chuckled hearing her high-pitched childlike voice say curse words. Maybe in this world, she was only twelve, but Poppy was no child.

"I think the king is already in this realm," I told her. "I think he's coming for you, and I want you to be able to protect yourself when he does."

Poppy looked at me, furrowing her eyebrows. "We're stronger together."

"I know." I nodded, conceding her point. "But you may not have a choice, you understand? You may have to go with him to save yourself."

"I don't want to go with him." Poppy shook her head and glanced back to the fire. "I won't."

"I know that, too." I leaned in closer, whispering now. "You might have them fooled, but not me. I think you're smarter than that, and I think you've been hiding something from us for a while."

She swallowed but didn't comment on my accusations.

"I think when the time comes, you'll know what you have to do, and I think you're strong enough to do it." I leaned back, silent as I stared into the fire. The conversation died between us and in that silence, I felt a bargain strike, unspoken but mutually agreed. We were family because we were part of the same story, and even if neither of us liked it, we needed each other.

"What do you want me to do?"

"Meet me here tomorrow at lunchtime." A plan formed in the back of my mind, one that would help me sniff out whatever Poppy was hiding from us while preparing her for what would come next.

I DIDN'T KNOW how this was going to go, but I figured I had to give it a shot. No one else knew we were meeting. Ivy had gone out with her sisters, and I had the whole place to myself.

This plan had been forming ever since Miri showed us the memory of Alberich saving her from the car crash. I put myself in the shoes of the egomaniac that had been terrorizing Faerie for eons. I imagined living my thousand millennia as the strongest, scariest thing in the world, only to be replaced by a human child that could manipulate space and time. Poppy was powerful, quite possibly more so than the king or queen combined. Fear could be a great motivator, and if I were him, I'd want to kill it, too. Hell, I'd do worse if I thought it would protect my realm, hence the reason I wanted to leave her right the fuck where we found her.

Given that, if I were an immortal being that had broken out of Faerie into a different realm with unknown rules, I'd bide my time. I'd wait for the most opportune moment, or perhaps, in his case, the most ostentatious moment. I'd watch my prey meticulously to learn their habits and search for their weaknesses.

The fairy king wasn't one to sneak in and do the deed quietly. No. On Samhain, he had made a grand show of invading the queen's quarters after her night of rituals. He'd waited until she was weakest, until she was distracted, and then he'd shown up with his forces and easily brought her to her knees.

The wedding.

That's when I'd do it.

That would be the biggest, flashiest time to announce his presence, and that gave me *loads* of ideas.

All this time, I'd been insisting we should draw him out, make him fight him on *our* turf. I didn't know how yet, but we had fairy gifts and Miri had been keeping him out with hers. That meant he wasn't impervious to them. He could be contained. Once that spider in my mind started turning this nugget over in its web, my plot solidified while I waited for Poppy to show up.

Finally, the space around me shifted and a loud *zap* echoed through the air. She appeared in the living room, her hands crossed behind her back as she eyed me suspiciously.

"I'm here." She took a step toward me and swallowed, glancing around to ensure we were alone.

"Thank you for coming."

She nodded. "I'm still not sure what you think you're going to tell me that I don't already know."

"I want you to practice." I gave her a knowing look. "If you can control it, he can't use it against you."

She narrowed her gaze. "I already told you, I can't go back—"

I cut her off. "What if I told you I knew that you could?"

"Because the king is at Miri's car crash?" Poppy rolled her eyes. "He's the king. He can do all kinds of dark magic."

"Yesterday, I said I wanted to make a deal with you. I'm trying to get the paperwork to bring you here permanently."

Her eyes widened, her hands coming to a clasp in front of her chest as excitement flushed through her.

"That's not part of the deal. I tell you that so that you know I'm serious about what I'm going to say next." I stood and walked toward her, keeping my voice calm and level as I spoke. When I met her gaze, I didn't see the child we'd brought home two years ago. I saw an ancient soul, someone that had lived multiple lifetimes and kept her secrets closely guarded for the doom they could unlock if anyone knew them. "I'll help you survive the king. I'll work with you to figure out the breadth of your gifts, but I expect loyalty in return."

She straightened when I said the word, tilting her chin up to face me. "Loyalty."

"Yes. If I find out you're working for Alberich behind our backs?" I shook my head. "Poppy, I'll do anything to protect my family. You understand that?"

Was she too young to pick up my threat? Was I mistaken when I believed her to be older than she appeared? When she nodded and pursed her lips, she confirmed my suspicions. She understood every-thing I said *and didn't say* perfectly.

"If you turn me over to the king or betray me, I won't hesitate to use what I know against you." She steeled her tiny jaw and shot daggers at me from behind that brown gaze, saying so much with that one expression. If I betrayed her, she'd do the same. She knew where we lived; she knew where our secrets were buried. She could ruin us with barely any effort.

That should have shocked me. I hadn't expected her to reciprocate the threat, but now that she had, I respected her more than I thought I ever would.

"This is our secret, then?" I held my hand out to her, and she took it, hers so small and infantile in mine.

"Yes." She gave our clasped hands a firm shake.

"Good." I cleared my throat and took a step back. "Let's begin."

"How?" She sat down on the couch and crossed her legs up under her body.

How indeed. I had a couple of different things I wanted to try, but the one I thought might work the best was meditation. When I'd been trying to figure out how to manipulate my gift, being able to focus my thoughts and control my breathing had done wonders. Perhaps she could start there.

"Close your eyes."

She did, and I turned on a guided session I'd downloaded from an app. I didn't claim to be a great Zen master of controlling my worst impulses. I smoked like a chimney, fucked my spouses multiple times a day, and once upon a time, I'd consume anything put in front of me. These days, handling my emotions meant I didn't accidentally make people tell me the worst things they'd ever done, so I'd learned some control.

"This isn't working," Poppy said, five minutes in. "I'm not going to travel through time by breathing. If I could do that, I would have done it already."

"Try harder." I restarted the session, and this time, she managed to sit through most of it before giving up.

"This is stupid." She crossed her arms and opened her eyes,

staring incredulously at me. "My mind is already focused and centered."

"Really?" My curt tone made her glare. Agitated with her lack of cooperation, I decided to shift tactics. Seeing her stubborn cheeks get red and puffy gave me another idea. "What are you going to do if the fairy king guts Carter right in front of you?"

She squinted her eyes and twisted her lips in disgust. "He won't."

"He might." I shrugged, continuing. "He might take Ivy and break every bone in her body while you watch."

"Stop it." Poppy's eyes pooled with tears. "You won't let him."

I threw my hands up. "I might be dead."

"Lex, stop."

"I might try to kill Alberich only to have him rip me apart and force you to witness every fucking part."

Poppy surged to her feet and stomped the ground, her hands in fists at her side. "Fuck you, Lex! I didn't come here to listen to this."

"Yeah?" I stayed as calm as I could, knowing this was the right avenue to take. The more upset Poppy got, the more the air around her shifted. It charged with her fury, growing electric the longer it went on. "Why'd you come here?"

"You wanted to make a deal."

"Yeah, and you promised to be loyal to me." I kept going, knowing any second, she'd break. "How are you going to be loyal if you can't even do what you were created to do?"

The slap stopped me, and not because it hurt. Yeah, I deserved it, but the second her hand collided with my face, the world around me moved. I fell back on my ass, landing in the mud on the side of a river. All the oxygen whooshed out of my body, and it took a few seconds before I could force my lungs to inhale again.

"What the fuck?" I croaked, holding up my hands to shake off the crud, trying to push to my feet. Nausea rolled through me, arching up my throat, and if it weren't for the fresh air blowing in my face, I would have yakked all over the place.

Poppy stood next to me and groaned, wiping her palms off on her jeans. "What happened?"

"What do you mean? You took us to some random fucking shitho—" I stopped myself because I recognized this place. We were standing on the shores of the Charles River in Boston, and out in the middle of the water, rowing teams sporting Harvard sweatshirts sailed past us.

"I feel really weird, Lex." Poppy grabbed her head with one hand and twisted her fingers into mine with the other. "That wasn't normal."

I took a step closer to the water's edge, narrowing my gaze on someone at the end of the last boat, his dark hair shimmering in the light. I hadn't seen my brother in eight years, but fucking hell, I'd still recognize him anywhere, even this far away.

My heart dropped into my gut. My knees shook. My head got so foggy, I thought I'd fall over any second.

"Lex, we need to—"

Between one breath and the next, the world whooshed around me, splitting me apart and putting me back together again. My molecules soared, twisting and reforming and, God, it hurt in places I didn't even know existed. When we were back in my living room, every nerve in my body revolted. I hunched over and vomited in the middle of the vintage Persian rug Evelyn had insisted we take from Mount Vernon. I didn't know if it was the shock of seeing Marcus again or the absolute blinding agony of ripping through time. But whatever happened to me, I couldn't pick myself up from that spot. I lay face down on the floor, tears streaming over my cheeks, trying to suck air into my lungs to restart my aching, bleeding heart.

Marcus, my soul cried. *Marcus.*

"Are you okay?" Poppy's tiny, cold hands gripped my shoulder, bringing me back to reality. "Lex?"

I nodded and rolled to sit up, rubbing my trembling hands over my face. "Jesus fucking Christ, that was him."

"Who? You knew those people?"

"My brother." My voice shook as I tried to process it. "You took me to see Marcus."

Realization sank into her eyes, her childlike features dropping. "Are you saying it worked?"

"Yeah, Poppy." I nodded. "Yeah, it fucking worked."

My phone vibrated in my pocket, indicating a number from New England, and a tremble of excitement went down my spine. Ignoring the implications of what had just happened with Poppy, I climbed to my feet and lumbered into the next room so she didn't hear me.

"Hello?"

"Lex, it's Victor." He cleared his throat. "Siobhan is in DC, and she's asking for you, all four of you. The whole gift must be present."

I paused, playing out the scenarios in my head. This could be a trap. If I were the king of fairies and I wanted to lure out the people who had hidden an abominable child of space and time, I'd use Siobhan as bait.

She was the one who had our answers. She could get rid of the gift. She could make this all go away. At the very least, I could finally get the truth out of her, assuming my gifts worked on the one who gave them to me.

"Why all of us?"

"I don't fucking know, do I?" Victor let out a frustrated sigh. "You asked me to call if she showed up. I did. She wants to talk to you. So go see her, ya wee bloody bastard."

And he hung up on me.

16

IVY

Siobhan had asked all of us to come, but Miri couldn't get away from her royal duties so soon after visiting us last month.

"I wish I could, darling," she said. "But it's better if I stay here for the time being."

I clenched my eyes shut at the strange tone in her voice, telling myself it was just my own exhaustion creeping up on me.

"Are you sure you're okay?" I remembered finding something else in her mind when she'd let me see her memory of the king, something buried so deep that I wondered if she even knew about it.

"I'm okay. Truly." It sounded like another lie, and I secretly wished Lex had been the one to call her instead. "I love you. Please be safe. Call me when you get home."

"All right. I love you—" She hung up before I could get the rest of it out. Something else was going on with her, something more than her memory of the king, and if she didn't come clean soon, I'd hop on a plane to London myself. I'd once promised her I wouldn't let her get away from me again, and I meant it.

Theo picked Carter up from the airport and brought him to our townhouse. Tomorrow night, we'd go see Siobhan at the address Victor had sent to Lex and hoped three out of four would suffice. For now, we took the opportunity to reacquaint ourselves with our husband. We hadn't seen him in weeks, and for someone magically bound to us, that felt like years.

Having his smile against my cheek, his hands in my hair, his words on my lips, it soothed some of the ache of his absence. It wasn't completely right, and it wouldn't be until we could be a four again, but it sated us enough...for now.

Lex took us both the way he'd been doing for years: rough kisses and deep scratches and slow, passionate fucking. He forced us into the shower and watched while Carter fucked me within an inch of my life. Then he pinned my arms down on the mattress with his knees and fucked my mouth while Carter ate his ass until he came in a low, desperate roar. He loved us and unloaded on us and then passed out on his side of the bed with me in between him and Carter. His soft snores hinted at how deeply he'd fallen into unconsciousness, which pleased me because neither of us had been sleeping well recently. He deserved the rest.

The next evening, we left to meet Siobhan at a park and ride on the outskirts of Northern Virginia. There was nothing out this way except for vineyards and cornfields. Theo sat in the driver's seat, Lex and me in the second row with Carter in the third.

"She's late." Lex checked his phone for the fifth time, his knee bouncing, his fingers twiddling over his thigh.

"She'll be here." She had to be. We were long overdue for a conversation. Even I had to admit, fifty minutes didn't bode well. Anxiety coiled in my stomach, and I ignored my vibrating work phone. Again.

Giana had balked at my taking the time away so close to my bill going through the Senate and now needed to contact me immediately, but I couldn't focus on that. With Siobhan and Alberich and all this fucking mess, the Senate would have to wait. There might not even be a world to save after this was done.

Movement by the trees caught my attention, and I glanced up, trepidation shooting through my nerves as Siobhan ran closer, a giant male following behind her. I hopped in the third row with Carter when she opened the back door and climbed in next to Lex. A bigger male fairy with short pale hair climbed into the passenger seat, his face grim and scarred.

I opened my mouth to ask who he was, but Siobhan snapped, "Drive," at Theo, looking from Lex to me and Carter in the back seat. "Where's Miri? I told you to bring everyone."

"Well, seventy-five percent is still a passing grade, right?" Lex pulled his lips into his devil's grin. "Who the fuck is this?" He nodded at her companion.

"Finn, my commander." Siobhan grimaced at Lex's arrogance but shifted her attention to me, turning toward the center of the SUV, one arm across the back of the seat. "It's good to see you again, Ivy."

"Yeah, likewise." I raised an eyebrow. "Where the hell have you been?"

She laughed. "There's that fiery spirit. Tell me, how's the engagement going?"

"Oh, great." Lex shook his head. "Do you know what it's like to live in a family of politicians and be able to sense when someone is lying?"

Siobhan sighed, her smile faltering. "It wasn't supposed to be like that."

"Then what?" I crossed my arms. "What the fuck is going on with us?"

"Look, I know you have a lot of questions. I don't have many answers to give you." Siobhan rubbed her forehead, her brown eyes mesmerizing and timeless. She hadn't aged a day in four years, but that was the thing about fairies. A hundred years to us was a blink to them.

"Okay, let's start with the obvious." Lex lit a cigarette and cracked the window so he could blow the smoke out. "Take this fucking gift back."

Siobhan matched his demanding tone with one of her own. "No."

"Why not?" Carter asked.

"Because I'm not supposed to."

"What is that supposed to mean?" I hissed.

"I'm a banshee." She looked between us. "I know when things are supposed to happen. Sometimes, it's death. Sometimes, it's giving a gift to a ginger-haired human girl with boyfriend drama." Siobhan's stare focused on me. "It comes to me randomly, but the first time I saw you, Ivy, it was the clearest instinct I've ever had. This?" She gestured between all of us. "I didn't expect this. I didn't *do* this."

"What do you mean?"

"Something happened when you made that vow in the ruins. What I gave you was supposed to wear off after the ceremony. You'd wake up with a few fun memories, no big deal. But you vowed forever on our sacred lands." Siobhan shrugged. "You made it permanent."

My heart sank into my gut. "What?"

"I can't remove it, Ivy, even if I wanted to." She shook her head, her surprised expression squeezing my chest. "This is ancient and powerful magic. It's bigger than me."

"Bigger than you?" Carter pursed his lips and considered. "What, like destiny? Fate?"

She nodded. "You were made for each other, and whatever happens next, you four are at the heart of it."

"So you don't know how to fix it?" My hopes for clarity were quickly diminishing, and the sinking feeling at the base of my chest throbbed harder.

"There's nothing to be fixed."

I didn't like that answer, and suddenly, every ten-year plan I had went up in smoke. I'd have to live with this forever, and I didn't know what to do with that information.

"Do you know what Alberich is going to do?" Carter asked.

Siobhan sighed. "I have an idea, but he's mercurial. He changes his mind faster than I can keep up."

"What happened after we got out?" Lex flicked ash out the window, taking another long drag. "Did he kill the queen and all the other fairies?"

"No," Finn cut in. "He'd never be able to kill the queen. They're equals in every way. He couldn't exist without her."

Something about that sounded alarm bells in my brain, but I couldn't put all the pieces together at the time. I tucked the information away for later when I'd be able to dissect it with a clear head. "Where is the queen? Why isn't she handling this?"

"He took her captive at first, but she escaped," Siobhan explained. "I don't know where she is now. We've been sent on a mission to find her."

"Is that why you're on this side of the realm?" The urge to put my hand on hers and sift through her memories nearly overwhelmed me. I clamped my fingers into fists to keep from doing it. I didn't even know if my gift would work on her or just piss her off. "Is Alberich here, too?"

"I think so," she said. "The thistles slowed him down, but once they disappeared, he found a way to break his curse. I got out before he did." Siobhan rubbed her fingers over her forehead. "Listen to me. You don't have much time until he comes for you. If he's out, he's only waiting until he has all the pieces in motion. You have to be ready for him."

"Does he want Poppy?"

Siobhan nodded. "She's the key. Is she safe?"

"She is," I said. "For now."

"Where is she?"

"No fucking way," Lex said. "You're the right hand to the Dark Lord or some shit. I'm not telling you that."

"Watch your mouth," Finn snarled, focusing his glowing green eyes on Lex.

Siobhan held up a hand, and her commander grunted before staring back out the front window.

"I'm not loyal to the king," Siobhan explained, "and I hold no great love for his purpose."

"Why is Poppy so important?" I cut in before Lex ended up strangled. "What can she do? Can she go back in time?"

Lex softened his features and looked away, taking another long drag on his cigarette. That subtle move may have seemed innocent to everyone else, but I recognized it. That was his tell. The X on my neck had always given me away, but Lex's lies were in his eyes and always had been. I kept that in the back of my mind as well.

"Maybe." Siobhan sighed. "She's strong, maybe the most powerful human I've ever known." She looked between the three of us. "The king wants to destroy her. He mustn't be allowed to do that. He mustn't be allowed to win."

"Then why are you helping him?" Lex's curt tone sliced through the ominous tension in the air, like he still didn't trust her.

"Because it's the only way I can help my lady and Poppy. I was friends with her mother. I love her, and I'll do whatever I can to protect her."

That didn't make any sense to me at the time, but before I could question it, Carter cut in.

"How can we help?" He looked between Siobhan and Finn, praying one of them would answer his question. "How do we end this?"

The SUV stopped at a red light, and I looked outside, recognizing the dim streets of downtown Arlington. The normally overpopulated sidewalks were surprisingly vacant this time of night, and I wondered if that too was some kind of fairy trick. Siobhan could see the future and create rings of power. What could Finn do?

Siobhan laughed at Carter's question. "You think I have any idea? I get instincts, not visions. I was supposed to give you a gift. I did. Now it's in fate's hands. This is ordained, foretold. No one else could have given this to you. Use it." Siobhan's serious brown eyes met mine. "I've warded your house and your cabin in the mountains. No fairy may enter without a welcome, including the king and queen."

"You did?" That touched my heart, if only because I had believed Siobhan forgot about us a long time ago. "When?"

Siobhan rolled her eyes. "I've been keeping tabs on you, Ivy Washington. I never forget someone that has been given a gift."

The kindness in her expression made me blush, and I smiled to let her know I appreciated it.

"Why us?" Carter said. "It could have been anyone."

"No." She shook her head. "It couldn't. I know some things have happened that you don't particularly like, and when you find out the rest of it, you'll hate me. Everything has been leading up to this, and you're almost done."

I opened my mouth to ask what she meant by that, but the SUV slowed in the middle of the street.

"Uh...guys..." Theo called.

"Fuck," Finn growled, glancing at us with an angry glower. "He's here."

When I focused out the front window, my pulse picked up and my stomach churned. The vehicle had been completely surrounded by dark wisps of shadows. The air sizzled with power, crackling and zinging through the smog like electricity. I remembered this feeling from Faerie.

The king.

Bodies appeared out of the darkness up ahead, faeries, a lot of them. An entire army of the king's henchmen glared at us, prepared to take us down. With only six of us in the truck and half of us armed, there was no way we could win, even if we drove through the crowd with the SUV. They'd swarm us and drag us back to Faerie, and then we'd be fucked.

I focused on my breathing, resisting the urge to panic.

This is it.

This is happening.

"Gods be damned," Siobhan said, taking a deep breath.

"Drive," Finn snarled, his hand on the dashboard to direct Theo. "Fucking drive, goddamn it."

I lurched backward as Theo slammed on the gas, and Siobhan grabbed two of her daggers from the holsters at her sides, palming them in her fists. Finn ripped the sheath off his enormous sword, keeping his attention on the chaos outside.

I had only a moment to wonder how to defend myself when we crashed into a hard, invisible force, and I tumbled forward, slamming my head on the back of the seat in front of me. Pain ricocheted through my skull and down my spine as hot, sticky blood squirted over my chin.

"Shit," I shouted, grabbing at my busted nose. I couldn't see, the agony radiated through my entire face. I didn't have time to wallow in it because obsidian swirls of smoke seeped in through the cracks in the windows on either side, making my chest cave inward with panic.

"Theo, drive!" Lex shouted.

"I can't." The wheels burned against asphalt, the taste of rubber pungent on my tongue, as something none of us could see held the vehicle still. Siobhan sliced at the tendrils with her blades, cutting them as easily as snipping the heads off flowers.

Finn growled again and muttered a loud, "Fuck," before slamming his elbow into the side window, shattering it. I grabbed on to Carter, my eyes wide, my head pounding, and Siobhan kicked the glass out on the side closest to her. Both fairies stabbed at the smoke, slicing through bodies and flashes of bone. They moved so fast I had a hard time keeping up with what was happening.

I didn't know what to do. I couldn't fight. I couldn't do magic. I was just some weak, telepathic human. We'd thought we'd been prepared. We'd thought we'd done our research. How inadequate that seemed now that we were up against the real threat. I sat there stunned, and when a monstrous arm of smoke reached inside the driver's side window and yanked Theo through it, I realized nothing I could have done would have made any difference.

I gasped as the cloud consumed him.

Everyone froze for a heartbreaking second, as if trying to make sure we'd seen what we thought we had. Finn shouted a louder, "Fuck," and Siobhan grabbed Carter's shirt, tugging him forward.

"Get us out of here," she said, her brown eyes wide. I didn't know Siobhan very well, but I'd never seen her this scared.

I didn't want Carter to be the next Theo, so I started to protest. He gave her a timid nod, seeming to understand something I didn't, and lumbered over the seat, cramming Lex against the window as he tried to get up front. Siobhan moved to the back next to me, smashing me against the wall as she fought off another thick arm of smoke.

An icy-cold rope wrapped around my throat, and I tried to claw it off me, but my nails dug into my overheated skin, scratching me instead. I couldn't breathe. I couldn't think. I struggled against the tether as Carter got the car moving again, my body jostling around. The air sucked out of my lungs and my chest caved in like I'd never be able to breathe again.

Stars danced in my vision, but not because I was dying.

No, something else was happening, something that terrified me even more.

I had only a moment to process it before I collapsed under its weight, letting the darkness consume me.

17
CARTER

When Siobhan grabbed me and told me to get us out of here, I didn't immediately understand what she meant. Once I climbed into the driver's seat, I got the picture. It was too dark to see, the thick clouds of Alberich's energy blocking out all the light.

"Go!" Finn snarled from the passenger seat.

Go where?

I didn't have a goddamned clue. I wrapped my fingers around the steering wheel and slammed my foot on the gas. The SUV lurched forward, only to slam into something hard. Metal crunched and I grimaced, fear slicing through me that I might be the next person to get sucked out the window.

Poor Theo.

"Ivy!" Siobhan yelled from the back seat.

I glanced in the rearview mirror, watching as one of the dark swirls choked the life out of my Weeds.

"Don't worry about her," Finn said, snapping my attention up ahead. "Drive!"

Fuck. Fuck. Fuck.

What was I supposed to do?

Close your eyes, the magical part of me said, the one that told me which cards to pick in a poker game. Intuition could be an asshole sometimes, but I didn't have any better ideas, so I listened to it. I closed my eyes and put my foot on the gas, and when it told me I should turn left, I did. The tires hit a rough patch of asphalt, gaining traction, and we surged forward. I white-knuckled that steering wheel the whole way, and when I felt like I should head straight, I went with it. It shouldn't have been possible, but fuck it. A lot of stuff that had happened to me shouldn't have been real. I stopped questioning it years ago.

The delay cost us. A heavy weight hit the side of the Range Rover, sending it up on its side for a gravity-defying millisecond. I opened my eyes and met the gaze of a fairy dressed in black with a hood over its head perched outside the passenger side window. Finn wrestled with it, trying to get it off, but it was too quick for Siobhan's friend. As the tires slammed back down on the earth, the dark fairy sliced through Finn's chest with an enormous smoky sword before falling off the vehicle.

I gasped, and Finn let out a monstrous yell, grinding his teeth together as he grimaced. When he sputtered up blood, I reached out to touch him to make sure he was okay.

"Get off me." He glared, his eyes gone completely white, glowing with the intensity of his rage. He emanated a powerful physical fury, vibrating in the front seat.

"Drive!" came Siobhan's panicked shout.

Another fairy ran next to us on my side, just as fast as the SUV, gaining on us. Finn groaned and shook next to me, his form pulsing so fast he'd gone blurry.

"What's happening to him?" I struggled to form the words, adrenaline racing through my veins. I could barely focus. If he went nuclear in the passenger seat, he was going to take all of us out with him, especially me.

"Go, Carter. Go!" Lex slammed his hands on the back of my seat.

Close your eyes, the voice said again. *Don't worry about them.*

This time, I had to force myself to listen, maneuvering around things I couldn't see, speeding through invisible streets at almost fifty miles an hour. As long as we were driving without hitting stuff, a win was a win.

"How's Weeds?" I shouted. "Is she okay?"

"We're okay," Siobhan said. "Just keep going."

We weren't out of the woods yet, but we still had our favorite ginger and as long as we were still alive, we'd make it through this together. I snuck a glance at Finn who had one hand on the dashboard in front of him and the other to the wound on his chest, his eyes clenched shut. He took deep breaths in through his nose and out through his mouth, no longer glowing or vibrating. I figured that was good news for us.

Here, my intuition said. *Stop here. Be quiet.*

I cut the SUV to the right and slammed on the brakes, shutting off the engine.

"Carter, what the—" Lex said.

"Shut up," I hissed, ducking down in my seat. "Everyone just shut up for a second."

No one argued, and everyone except for Finn sank under the window line to wait this out with me. I didn't like the rattle in his lungs when he breathed. Not that I was a fairy expert, but it sounded wet and desperate, like he couldn't get enough air on his inhales.

The darkness started to dissolve, slowly creeping away from us like a retreating tide, revealing brick buildings on either side of the vehicle. A dumpster sat to the right, and several trash bags lined the other side. I'd hidden us snugly in an alley between a gas station and a gun store, the rest of the street dark and empty.

Time ticked by at an agonizing rate, dragging on as my pulse pounded in my ears. Any second, I expected a fairy to step out from behind the corner to tear us to pieces, and I'd have to figure out how to use the horseshoe up my ass to talk us out of this nightmare.

That never came. I didn't know if it was because they couldn't find us or my gift had gotten us out of it, but after fifteen minutes of silence, I sat up and restarted the car.

"They're gone," I said, knowing it in my gut. My fairy gift told me so, and it had never steered me wrong.

Siobhan sprang into action, jumping over the second seat and into the first, straddling Finn's lap so she could examine the wound on his chest. Likewise, I turned my attention to the back. Lex had already climbed into the third row, finding Ivy with her eyes open and rubbing her head.

"You okay, X?" he murmured.

She nodded and sat up. "What happened?"

"You scared the shit out of us, Weeds," I said.

"One of those fairy assholes got ahold of you." Lex ran his fingers over her neck, tracing the spot where she'd been strangled. It was red now, and she winced when he brushed a tender spot. "Are you okay?"

Lex brought their foreheads together, and I thanked the sweet Lord she was still alive and we hadn't lost her. She was a fighter, but seeing her go down like that sparked a panic in my veins. I couldn't lose her.

I *couldn't.*

The mere thought of it made me tremble with rage. I'd often said Lex and Ivy were the same soul in two different people, and I stood by that. He was ice cold and she was fiery hot, and in a lot of ways, I didn't think they could exist without each other. For me, Ivy was the sun in my solar system. She was the enormous burning ball of light that guided me in my orbit. If she died, I would be a husk of a person. If she were gone, truly gone from this earth, I wouldn't want to be on it anymore.

Lex kissed Ivy, and I smothered the small flame of jealousy that surged up my spine. I'd always considered Ivy mine, and I still felt that way today, even if somewhere deep down inside, I believed we were all Lex's. I knew that now in the best and worst possible ways.

Ivy snorted out a sad laugh, but a groan and a cough to my right got my attention again.

"All right, all right," Siobhan said, ripping Finn's shirt open. "Let me see it."

"It's deep," he groaned, coughing again. This time, ruby-red liquid sputtered over his lips and down his chin.

Siobhan grabbed his jaw and held it up, forcing him to look her in the eyes. "Six hundred years, Finn. This is not how you die."

He tried to laugh but ended up falling forward on her, his eyes rolling back in his head.

"Shit!" Siobhan looked at me. "Take us to Ivy's house. Now."

I yanked the gear into drive and took off, alarm blaring through me. I didn't know Siobhan or Finn well, but they'd helped us. Yeah, this shit started because of her, but she'd also said we were important, that we had a role to play. I didn't want Finn dying on us before he had his chance to do his part.

18

IVY

I said I was okay, but someone had taken a sledgehammer to my head, scooped my brain out, blended it, and dumped it back in.

Diana's laugh and her impenetrable stern gaze, a swell of adoration and unyielding envy burning in the center of my chest.

The glint of the sun shimmering off a ruby ring, my most prized possession, the one I'd spent millennia looking for, the one that would get me out of Faerie once and for all.

Seeing Poppy for the first time and knowing, deep down, she meant something important. She would be my downfall.

I had to destroy her. I had to absorb all that energy. I had to—

These weren't my memories. They weren't my emotions, and yet, as I tucked myself in Lex's arms for the drive home, worried about both Siobhan and Finn, I struggled to understand where they'd come from. My stomach churned and my chest tightened, screaming at me that I already knew. There could only be one explanation, but I didn't want to face it. Not yet.

My heart ached for Theo and his family. I didn't know if he was dead or gone or if he would find his way back to our house, disheveled and aching from his experience with the king. My conscience slapped with shame. Even though he knew the risks when he signed up to be our bodyguard, I still hated the fact he'd gotten involved in this because of me. We owed him a debt we'd never be able to repay, and my heart hung heavy for his sacrifice.

When we arrived at my townhouse, Lex and Carter hopped out to help Siobhan with Finn, but I recognized the vehicles parked along the alley. My siblings were here.

"Shit." My voice sounded hoarse, and considering I'd been choked within an inch of my life, I was surprised I could talk at all. I ran my hands over my hair, trying to brush it out of my face, and wiped at the blood under my nose. I was a mess. "It's my bachelorette party." I'd completely forgotten. With my upcoming nuptials, trying to get my bill through, going to see Siobhan, and researching any possible way to defeat the king, it had slipped my mind.

"Who's here?" Siobhan said.

"Kit, Jon, and Abigail."

She nodded, urging me forward. "It's okay."

I narrowed my eyes at her. "What?"

Finn groaned as Lex and Carter struggled with his weight, but the big fairy somehow managed to get his feet under him. The wound on his chest dripped with shimmery crimson blood, and I winced as I imagined the pain. It likely would have killed a human.

"They're a part of this, too." Siobhan gave me a reassuring glance and gestured me toward the door.

"I think the fuck not." I rebelled against getting my siblings involved, swearing to protect them no matter what. Drawing them into this fairy-tale bullshit would only put them in danger.

"You don't have a choice," Siobhan said as a sedan pulled up behind us, the headlights blinding me for a moment. She pushed me behind her, a hand on her weapons, but relaxed when the driver got out.

"Lieutenant," she said, rushing to jump in his arms.

"Hiya, Banshee," he said, giving her a kiss. He was tall with dark hair and bright blue eyes, almost glowing in the moonlight. When he lifted his gaze to Finn, his expression sank and he pushed past me to get to the wounded fairy. "Commander?"

Finn could do little more than groan and wince. "It's not as bad as it looks."

"We need to get him inside," Siobhan said.

I took a deep breath and led them through the yard and up the stairs to the back door, pausing before I opened it. My hands and clothes were covered in my own blood. My hair was a fucking mess, and running my hands through it only made it knottier. The welt around my throat burned from where the king had strangled me.

This was going to suck.

I pushed inside, walking through the kitchen and steeling myself as my siblings came into view. They stood around the dining room table, sipping champagne and laughing with each other. When three sets of eyes landed on me and our new guests, they all froze.

We reeked of defeat. The last several months had been stressful. I'd been working eighty hours a week, sunup to well past sundown, trying to protect Poppy, trying to figure out what happened to us, trying to find Smythe and Siobhan, all while dealing with a media that wanted to chew me up and spit me out. That didn't even take into account my predominantly male coworkers that didn't know me or support a damn thing I proposed. After whatever happened with the king tonight, well, I didn't know how to hide this.

"Ivy?" Abigail balked. "Are you all right?"

"What happened to you?" Jon took a step closer.

"Who the hell is this?" Kit straightened, her eyebrows going halfway up her head as she looked at the crowd of beat-up fairies forming behind me.

"Where can we take him?" Siobhan asked.

"Upstairs," Carter said, helping her and Donnelly get Finn to the steps.

Lex moved to stand behind me, perhaps sensing what was about to happen. I'd hit a breaking point, and I let out a sound that was half laugh and half sob, startling even myself. Abigail tried to reach out to me, but I'd lost it and couldn't stand the connection, so I moved away.

"What happened to me?" I laughed harder, unable to get air into my lungs fast enough. "Jesus, Abigail."

"X." Lex put a hand on my shoulder, and if I'd been in any right mindset, I would have sobered at the touch. But I was covered in my own blood, and maybe some of Finn's. The king was out, and the world had officially gone to hell. We were all at risk, even them. Lex wanted to keep this between us, but I couldn't hold my tongue. I'd officially lost the last part of me that could handle the stress.

They're a part of this, Siobhan had said. *You don't have a choice.*

No, I never had a choice, and neither did they. If I was a part of this, then they were at risk because of me. I had to tell them to protect them. They had to know so they could protect themselves.

I opened my mouth and the last four years spilled out—the affair with Miri at boarding school, Lex and Carter in London, the trip to Ireland. Midsummer. The curse.

"Until the end, we promised." I held up my hand, showing them the scars as proof. I explained that it hit us again two years later and drove us back together, back to Ireland. I told them about the king and queen on Samhain and Miri's wall of thistles.

"That's how we know Poppy."

Lex put his hands on the back of a chair and hung his head between his shoulders as I went on, unable to stop me but also unable to fault me. Perhaps he knew this would happen. Perhaps we had already waited too long.

"And tonight?" I ran my hands over my face. "Tonight, he came after us and he strangled me." I pointed to the burn on my neck. "He —" I almost told them he was inside my head, but I paused because I wanted to make sure I hadn't imagined that before I told anyone. There was no sense in scaring everyone if it turned out to be nothing. "He's coming after us all. Nowhere is safe. We need to call Miri. We have to make sure she knows."

No one said anything for a long moment, my heart thundering in my head.

"I know how it sounds," Lex added, taking a deep breath and letting it out through his nose. "I didn't want to believe it myself. But the gifts are real. I can tell when anyone's lying. Carter's lucky. Ivy can read people's minds. Miri can grow plants by willing it to happen."

Kit narrowed her piercing stare on me before she asked, "Have you read mine?"

I sighed. "No, I wouldn't do that without asking. I try not to, anyway. I can't always help it."

Abigail remained quiet, slinking into a chair with a dazed look on her face.

"This is incredible, Ivy," Jon said.

"It's horrible," I corrected. "It's a goddamned nightmare."

"You've been able to do this for four years?" Kit looked between us. "Is that what all that Siobhan and Smythe bullshit was about?"

I nodded as Carter came back into the room, his eyes sympathetic like he'd overheard what we were talking about.

"The woman who went upstairs," he said, "that's Siobhan."

Kit blinked and glanced toward the steps, a longing expression in her eyes like she wished she'd gotten a better look.

"I'm sorry to rope you into this, but the fairy king could come after you." I ran my hand over the heated X on my neck. "You could be in danger."

"I can't believe you've been keeping this secret this whole time." Jon shook his head.

"Who would believe me?" I let out a breath, relieved to finally be able to share this with the people closest to me.

"What's the plan?" Abigail crossed her arms. "If he's out, he's heading here, right? How do we protect the place?"

I admired her tenacity. She really did remind me of a younger version of myself. "My house is warded," I said, remembering what Siobhan told us earlier in the night. "We'll be safe for now."

"We know what he wants," Lex said, reaching into his pockets for his cigarettes.

"And that is?" Kit looked between us.

"Poppy." Carter shook his head. "She's more powerful than us. We've been protecting her by hiding her."

"And Poppy is the little girl you rescued from a fairy realm?" Jon narrowed his eyes, glancing at Carter and Lex as he scratched the back of his head.

"Yes," Carter said. "It sounds incredible. We didn't believe it ourselves for a long time."

"It's still unbelievable most days." Lex straightened, shoving his hands into his pockets.

Jon looked at Kit before shifting his gaze to Abigail. She nodded and returned her attention to me. "What can we do to help?"

"Wait, you believe us?" I looked between them, certain that any moment, I'd wake up and this would be a dream. They'd commit me and put me on a psychiatric hold. Once that got out, my mother would never let me leave the house again. My siblings were grounded in reality, as logical as I was, if not more so, especially Jon.

"I don't think you'd go along with this if it were a stunt," Jon said. "Neither would Carter or Lex."

"You look exhausted, Ivy," Abigail said. "It's been weighing on you."

"I've known something was up for years." Kit sighed and pulled half her mouth into a smile. "You should have told me sooner, you fucking loser."

Tears burned my eyes, and I blinked them back. "Shut up, you fucking twat."

Kit laughed and stood, coming over to give me a hug. For someone who balked at affection of any kind, she held me tighter than ever. Then, like something out of a corny Christmas movie, Jon wrapped his arms around us, followed by Abigail. We formed a Washington sibling group huddle that broke me to pieces.

I wanted them to stay with us where it was safe, but I couldn't honestly expect them to move in. I didn't know where the king was or when he would strike again. Our lives didn't just stop because some fairy king might be after us. I still planned to go to work the next day...*right?*

Fuck, my brain hurt.

"What happens now?" Kit stepped back, looking between me and my husbands.

I took a deep breath at how much my siblings supported me, how much I cared for them and wanted to protect them from all this.

"For right now, we need to rest and recoup." Lex looked at me, reaching out to take my hand so he could intertwine his fingers in mine. "We'll ask Siobhan to ward your houses tomorrow. Sleep here tonight."

"Slumber party!" Abigail threw up her fist. "Fuck yeah."

"Wait, you've known about Siobhan the whole time?" Jon turned to Kit, who rolled her eyes.

"Don't give me that 'you always leave me out' bullshit."

"But you do!" Jon whined. "You do always leave me out."

"He's right; you do always ignore him when he's around." Abigail gave Kit an affirmative shrug.

"Okay, first of all," Kit rebutted. The two of them bickered while Abigail instigated further, but I wanted to go check on Siobhan and Finn. Lex and Carter followed me up the stairs, groans and muttered curses echoing down the corridor from my office. I didn't know what to do for an injured fairy in the human realm. Did they heal the same way humans did? Should I call a doctor?

When I peeked inside the room, Finn lay stretched across the couch, his head resting on Donnelly's lap. The darker-haired fairy wiped sweat off his commander's face with a white rag, holding down his shoulders so Siobhan could stitch up his chest from her spot on the chair next to them.

"Damn it, Banshee. That hurts," Finn growled.

"Stop being a baby," Siobhan hissed, yanking at a piece of thread. Where the hell had she found stitches? I didn't have—no, it wasn't stitches. It was dental floss. I grimaced when I noticed she was using a sewing needle to yank it through his skin. "I've stitched up fledglings who were worse off than you."

Finn's once glowing complexion had now faded into a dusty pallor that would indicate near death on a human.

I cleared my throat, and three sets of eyes shifted to me.

"No need to lurk by the door," Finn weakly muttered. "This is your house."

"Do you need anything?" Lex took a step around me and glanced at the littered supplies. "I can call for a doctor."

"He'll be healed by morning," Siobhan said.

"We think," Donnelly muttered.

Siobhan's eyes lifted, shooting daggers into him when she repeated, "He'll be healed by morning."

Donnelly glared back at his counterpart, but didn't argue.

"Please forgive their poor manners," Finn struggled to say. "I trained them both better than this."

"Rest," Donnelly said, kissing the side of Finn's head. "You need to conserve your energy."

Finn groaned and leaned in to the touch as Donnelly's hand stretched down over Finn's chest to connect with Siobhan's. I wondered about their relationship, but I didn't pry. It wasn't any of my business.

"We're all set for right now, thank you." Siobhan sat up straighter, stretching her back muscles. "You look wrecked. Get some sleep, mates. We'll talk in the morning."

"Okay," I nodded and turned to leave, stopping when she called out again.

"Ivy?"

I raised an eyebrow.

"Don't sleep alone, yeah?"

I nodded, noticing she'd said that in front of both Lex and Carter. Neither would let me get away with breaking that agreement, especially not tonight.

AFTER WE SHOWERED and dressed for bed, I tried to call Miri again, but it went straight to voicemail. Lex tried after that, and she still didn't answer. It was early in London, or late depending on one's point of view, so we promised to try her again once we woke up.

"Princess," Lex said, "we're okay, but we have news. Call us. Immediately. Stop fucking around. I love you." When he hung up, he set his tired stare on me and Carter. Under any other circumstances, I imagined Lex would have wanted to fuck us both before calling it a night. But I didn't have it in me, and perhaps he could tell that because he simply crawled into bed on my other side. Carter passed out as soon as his head hit the pillow, but Lex only narrowed his eyes at me and licked his lips.

"You should have told us you were going to tell your siblings." He tapped his cigarette into the dish between us.

"It just came out." I shook my head and sighed. "I didn't plan on saying anything."

He nodded, an echo of something sinister behind his eyes. It was there for a moment and gone, almost like I'd imagined it. I knew Lex better than anyone, and it reminded me of the look he'd gotten earlier tonight when Siobhan had mentioned Poppy. But I was exhausted, so I figured I'd deal with that tomorrow.

Lex leaned down and kissed me before putting the ashtray on the end table and sinking farther down into bed. "You scared the shit out of me tonight."

I ignored the churn in my stomach. "Yeah, me too."

He intertwined his fingers with mine, the vows on our hands brushing up against each other as we slid palm to palm. "I can't do this without you, X."

"Don't tease me. I'm tired." I rolled my eyes and scoffed, figuring this was another sarcastic tease from Lucifer reincarnate, but when he grabbed my chin and forced me to look back at him, I paused.

"I mean it." He looked between my eyes, his hazel counterparts wide. "Whatever happens next, don't fucking die on me."

I grabbed his wrist and tried to slide inside his mind the way I always had, but he put up a shield, something he'd never done before. I furrowed my eyebrows and tried harder, but he broke the contact and rolled over so I couldn't see his face.

"Get some sleep," he barked.

As much as I wanted to lay my hands on his skin again and make him show me, he'd had enough for the night. Hell, I'd had enough, too. My body was tired from the fight with the king, so when I finally closed my eyes to give in to unconsciousness, I fell in like an anvil.

My dreams took me back to the woods on Midsummer. The humid air choked me, and the sun radiated as warm and heavy on my skin as it had four years ago. Voices echoed on the wind, and I glanced to my left to see four bodies dance and twirl their way into the ruins. *Us.* Versions of us from four years ago. Those were hallowed grounds, the walls full of magic we barely understood.

From this perspective, it was like I was looking through the eyes of a bystander. Off in the distance, Siobhan peered from behind a tree, smiling to herself as she watched us. But if I wasn't in my own head and I wasn't in Siobhan's, then whose dream was this? Whose memory was I in?

The answer chafed at me, but I couldn't quite grab it.

The memories flipped forward and backward, reorganizing in my brain before coming to a stop in front of the queen.

Samhain.

I recognized the platform with the enormous tent on top of it. The king had long since chased us out of the realm, and now he leered over Diana with red cheeks and furious eyes. Except...I *was* the king, and I looked down his long, narrow nose at the fairy he'd loved for centuries.

"Give her to me," the king snarled, but the queen only smiled.

"How weak you look"—she shook her head—"storming in here

the day after Samhain. All these years, and you're still so desperate for my attention."

That set him off. He whispered something in a language I didn't understand, but I vibrated with his intentions.

Suffer in silence, suffer in solitude. Then you will know the pain you have caused.

He opened his palm and blew a ruby-colored powder in her face. She coughed and rubbed her palm over her nose, sneezing as she scrambled away from him.

It shocked me, and I gasped, a red-hot fury sizzling down my chest, even in sleep. The emotion got Alberich's attention.

"Ivette? Is that you?"

He closed his eyes, relegating both of us to the darkness of his mind.

"I can hear your human heart racing, Ivette."

I didn't know what to do or how to wake up. Certainly, this was a dream. I slept soundly next to Lex and Carter; he shouldn't have been able to get inside my head. But...he wasn't. I was in his head. At least, I thought I was.

"You're smarter than this, Ivette. Give me the child, and all of this goes away." The dark tendrils of his magic circled the part of me that connected us, caging me in, trapping my arms to my sides. *"Give her to me! Give her to me!"*

The pressure squeezed. All the air pushed out of my body.

I tried to call for Lex or Carter, tried to reach out for Miri, anyone who could help me. But no one came. No one could. It was just him and me and this strange tether that had formed when he touched me. Now I was dying and there was nothing I could do and this was it, the end of the story, nothing more for Ivy Washington.

Wait, a voice said. My own voice. My own consciousness. *Stop panicking...This is a dream, an illusion, nothing more. I am smarter than this.*

I reached out for Lex's presence. Even this deep in sleep, he hummed through my veins as cool as ice. He always had, no matter how many times I'd tried to get rid of him. I latched on to that energy, that manifestation of him inside my soul, and I yanked.

The more I tugged, the more he pulled back. I had no idea if he even knew he was doing it, but it brought me back to reality. My eyes snapped open, and I inhaled a deep lungful of air, running a hand over my face to make sure I was back in my own body.

Calm down. It's okay.

Soft snores on either side of me confirmed Carter and Lex were still asleep, and that neither of them had been inside my head when that happened. My secret was still safe...for now.

Except when I sat up, Donnelly leaned against the doorjamb with his arms crossed. His bright blue eyes focused on me like a predatory cat's, glowing with their strangeness and intensity. He pushed upright and nodded toward the hallway as he turned to leave.

Not sure that I would go back to sleep anyway, I extracted myself from Carter's hold and grabbed my robe from my closet. After shrugging it over my shoulders, I tied it closed and walked down the hallway to my office.

Finn slept on the couch, his wound somehow looking worse than it had several hours ago. Siobhan sat on the other sofa, a blanket over her lap, her hair undone and hanging in soft waves down her shoulders. Big puffy bags hung under her eyes, accenting the grim set to her mouth and making her appear as exhausted as she must have felt on the inside.

Donnelly pointed to the spot next to Siobhan and took his place next to Finn, gently lifting the commander's head so he could put it on his thighs again. "Sit. Hang out for a while."

"How's he doing?" I absently followed his orders, slumping down in the empty seat. Siobhan pushed the blankets over my lap, sharing her warmth with me.

"He's alive," she said. "That's all that matters right now."

Donnelly narrowed his eyes. "How are you?"

"I'm in better shape than Finn." I gave him half a smile. "So there's that."

"Hmm." Donnelly looked at Siobhan, who grabbed my hand.

"Have you talked to Poppy?"

I shook my head. "I tried to call her, but she didn't answer. She'll come when she can."

Siobhan glanced at Donnelly before swallowing hard and taking a deep breath. "There's more to the story of her birth, more that I didn't tell you."

I raised an eyebrow, silently asking her to go on.

"The night you came to Faerie the first time, the night of the Midsummer festival, that's the night she was born. She came into the world at the same time you made your vows."

"What?" I squinted, trying to put the pieces together. "That can't be true. She's at least twelve—"

"Time passes differently on that side of the realm. That Midsummer was the last celebration where the king and queen blessed their union. After her birth, it all fell apart."

"You said her powers are of space and time." I looked between Siobhan and Donnelly, hoping one of them would explain.

"And you asked if she could go back in time." Siobhan pursed her lips. "Care to elaborate?"

It wasn't my story to tell, but I didn't see how they could help if they didn't know all the details. "When Miri met eyes with the king for the first time, it unlocked a memory from her past. He was there the day she got into the car accident that killed her parents. He pulled her from the vehicle."

Siobhan glanced at Donnelly again.

"That's not possible." He absently ran a hand through Finn's hair.

"His powers are unimaginable," Siobhan argued.

"We followed him for six hundred years, Banshee. If he could go back in time, don't you think he would have done that, I don't know, when Halifax nearly decimated our entire *Fianna?*"

Siobhan hummed a noise of reluctant agreement.

"What's the *Fianna*?" I looked back and forth between them.

"It's the king's army, his most elite soldiers. They were there the night he attacked the queen."

I remembered. They had nearly caught us when we were running for our lives out of Faerie. We'd only made it because Siobhan found us before they did.

"When we asked Poppy, she said she didn't know if she could do it." I rubbed a hand over my tired eyes.

"The next time you see her, bring her to me, please." Siobhan squeezed my hand in a show of solidarity, and I remembered the twenty-two-year-old girl I'd been when I first met her. How we both had changed since then, how we both had stayed the same.

"I have a question," Donnelly chimed in. "Where's Miri?"

I sighed, wondering what was going on with her that she wouldn't say. She'd been distant the last time she visited, almost like she was keeping secrets again. "She was here just a few weeks ago. She said she couldn't get away again so soon."

"Uh-huh." Donnelly looked at Siobhan again.

"What's with the secret looks? What am I missing?"

"You share a group gift," Siobhan said. "You need each other to survive."

"I realize that." I rubbed my tired eyes, praying I didn't have a headache leading into the day. We had a lot of ground to cover, and precious little time to do it. Not to mention my real life. I had meetings and congressional committees to attend. I had no time for fairy nonsense. "She's the royal princess of England. She can't just drop everything because you've decided to come out of the woodwork."

"She's vulnerable by herself, all the way in England," Donnelly said. "She needs to be here, at least until this is over."

"What am I supposed to do? Break into Kensington Palace and abduct her?"

"There's an idea," Siobhan said.

I rolled my eyes, defeated. "I wasn't being serious."

"Why not?" Siobhan balked. "Human women like that kind of shit."

I scoffed at the utter ridiculousness of that notion. "Yeah, there's a good headline. Congressional representative abducts British royalty for sapphic fairy war."

"Fuck the headlines, Ivy," Siobhan said. "This is about saving both realms from destruction. This is bigger than a stupid trash magazine."

"I called her," I said. "She knows we need to be together."

"That's not good enough," Siobhan countered. "If she's alone for too long, he'll get to her. He'll hurt her. He might have already done it."

I winced at the possibility, all the horrible visions in my mind churning the anxiety in my chest.

"I'll deal with Miri," I said. "What happens next?"

"I'm still formulating the plan." Siobhan pursed her lips, seemingly in concentration. "I'll have all the pieces in place tomorrow."

I shivered, remembering the dream I'd had, and looked at Donnelly. He stared at me like he had in my bedroom, like he could see straight through my guards, all the way down to my secret heart.

"The night of Samhain," Donnelly said, "the king put a spell on the queen."

Suffer in silence, suffer in solitude. Then you will know the pain you've caused.

I cleared my throat and forced the words away. The fact the king had sensed me in his memories terrified me. I didn't know what that meant. He had always been able to haunt my nightmares, but now that I was haunting his, did that mean he could see more? If I was connected to him, he might be connected to me and...God, this was all so confusing.

"If she's out," he continued, "both realms are at risk. Faerie cannot exist without them both, and this realm cannot contain their energy for long. We need to find them, and we need to put them back where they belong."

"How are we supposed to do that?" I looked between them. "We're three humans and two and a half fairies."

"I heard that," Finn growled, making both Siobhan and Donnelly chuckle.

"You're supposed to be sleeping," Donnelly said.

"Your incessant scheming is keeping me awake." He cracked his eyes open and attempted a smile.

Donnelly grinned, and Siobhan rose to walk closer to her lovers. I recognized the shift in intimacy and my lack of place in it, so I stood to leave. Siobhan stopped me with a hand on my wrist.

"We'll talk more in the morning," she said. "Try to get some sleep, okay?"

I should have told them about this strange connection to the king. I should have told them about what I'd seen and what his intentions had been when he'd cursed the queen. But I didn't yet know what it meant or what I should do about it, so I kept my silence and headed back to my room.

19

LEX

I planned to personally see to Theo's last requests. He'd been required to create a will when he started working for me, and now that I was pretty sure he was dead, I wanted to make sure his family was well taken care of. Did it make me a monster that I couldn't do more for him? Maybe. But I had the rest of the world to think about.

"It's about time." Poppy crossed her arms and squinted her eyes. We were in the woods where I normally met her for lessons, far away from the prying eyes of Washington high society. "I've only been waiting forty-five minutes."

I raised an eyebrow. "Don't take that tone with me."

"What's going on? Ivy's been calling me every five seconds, and I know Carter's around here somewhere."

There were a lot of things I should have told Ivy in the weeks after Poppy took me to see Marcus. But I didn't. I continued to practice with her, and I encouraged her to train on her own, employing basic movie time travel rules like not interacting with any prior versions of us and *definitely* not trying to change anything. So far, Poppy didn't feel comfortable doing it without me, and I didn't particularly enjoy going with her. It ripped my body apart, and I was but a lowly, fragile human.

"It's more than that." I tilted my head at her, debating whether I should tell her or let her find out on her own. "But you need to spill first."

She rolled her eyes and groaned. "I've been practicing ever since we saw Marcus."

"And?"

"I can control it." She squinted up at me. "I can choose where and when I go."

"Are you sure?" My plan relied on that. If she thought she couldn't do it, I'd have to reassess and reevaluate.

"Yes, I'm sure." She sounded indignant, and I swallowed down a laugh. Such an impudent little thing, she reminded me so much of myself when I was younger...and Ivy. "I can do it."

"If you get scared—"

"I won't."

"If you do, pull out. Come find me. Don't keep going just because that's what you promised."

"I know." She nodded. "We should tell the others."

I took a deep breath, reminding myself Ivy and I had no boundaries between us. The next time she got in my head, she'd see this, and she'd know I'd been keeping it from her. She'd hate that I'd put her precious Poppy in harm's way, even if Poppy insisted on doing it herself. She'd hate that I hadn't asked or at least consulted her before going through with what was probably the dumbest thing I'd ever done. And I didn't even want to think about what Carter would do.

Fuck it.

"Not yet." I cleared my throat and glanced away, hoping she didn't see the truth in my eyes.

"Then when?"

"I have to convince them to go along with it first, the wedding and the big showdown."

She screwed up her features, seeming confused. "You really want me to do this?"

I nodded. "Yes, Poppy. It's the only way to protect everyone. He has to believe it, understand? And no one else can know."

Poppy nodded. "Now, your turn. Spill it."

I grinned and rubbed a hand over her head. "Siobhan is at the house."

Her big eyes turned the size of saucers and she smiled, giving me a solid shove. "Why didn't you tell me?" Then she disappeared, and I knew she'd gone home to visit her long-lost friend. They were deep in conversation when I made it there myself, reminiscing about the old days. Poppy sat on Siobhan's lap, laughing and hugging the older fairy.

Finn looked better when they dragged him up here, but still not back to perfect. Siobhan had been sure he'd be cured by now, but from the looks of him, I doubted he'd be back on his feet by our wedding. Donnelly lurked in the corner, sitting in a chair with his feet out on an ottoman in front of him, an old book open on his lap. He seemed deep in thought, but I knew he was well aware of everything in the room. He gave off that "hunter in the shadows" vibe, and I didn't want to find out the hard way if he had fairy powers like Siobhan.

I went to find my own partners in crime, walking down the hallway to the spare bedroom Carter claimed when he was here. Finding it empty, I checked my room and Ivy's before heading upstairs to the third floor loft.

Ivy sat at the desk at the far end, her laptop open in front of her, her shiny red hair twisted up on top of her head with a pencil. By the time I woke up this morning, she had long since been out of bed. I hadn't had the chance to follow up with her, so I wrapped my arms around her shoulders and leaned down to kiss the side of her head.

"How'd you sleep?" I lingered on her ear, giving it an extra kiss so she'd understand my affection. I'd been too raw and emotional last night, so when I told her not to die on me, it bordered too close on baring my soul.

She whipped her attention to me and narrowed her eyes, pulling out of my hold. "What do you mean?"

The reaction made me pause because I hadn't meant anything. "Did you get any rest?"

"Yes." Ivy pushed to her feet, her features going calm and steady, the politician's mask in place. "Did you?"

Something about her seemed off, but I couldn't put my finger on what it was. Her guarded answers knocked at memories I hadn't thought of in years. Ivy and I didn't keep each other out. We were on the same side these days.

Were we?

I had an entire plan set in motion that I hadn't told any of them about. I kept a secret with Poppy that neither of us planned to share with anyone else. And if I'd been capable of keeping that from her, then what was she capable of keeping from me?

"Yes. Fine," I answered.

She nodded, gathering her laptop and books in one arm. "Good. Siobhan and Donnelly would like to talk to us at dinner once Poppy has gone home."

I thinned my lips and watched as she headed downstairs, that annoying stoic look in her eyes. Ivy could be a good actress when she wanted to. She could turn on the Washington charm with an effort-less grin. But Ivy never could beat me in a game of poker. I knew her tells like I knew my own, and now that I suspected she was hiding something from me, I wouldn't stop until I knew what it was.

Ivy had her door closed when I passed by it on my way to find Carter. He was in the gym, running on the treadmill, sweat dripping down his naked torso. God, he was beautiful, a Greek statue come to life before my very eyes. I could stand here and watch him move for the rest of my life.

Carter always had a way of sensing my presence no matter how stealthy I'd tried to be. He stopped the machine when I stepped forward, grabbing his towel so he could wipe his face. I focused on the curves in his arms as he did, his muscles bunching in all the right ways.

"Keep staring at me like that, DC, and I might do a trick." Carter's grin almost brought me to my knees.

"If you do a trick, you might get a treat." I leaned against the doorjamb, waiting as my proverbial knight hopped off the treadmill and stalked closer. His gym shorts hung low on his hips, reminding me of the time I'd fucked him right here on this rubber floor. How long ago that seemed compared to today.

"Is that a threat or a promise?" He eyed me with a smug expression that made me want to force him to shut up in the most despicable ways. If I wasn't so damn caught up in all the other bullshit, I might have done just that.

"A gentleman never divulges all his plans before the endgame."

Carter made a low laugh and leaned in to kiss me, smelling like sweat and man and deodorant, an alluring intoxicant for a hedonist like me. My cock throbbed, and I had to remind myself I'd come down here for a purpose.

All these years, and only one person could *really* break through to Ivy. If she was keeping a secret, Carter might be able to sniff it out before I could.

"Have you talked to Ivy today?"

His smile faded, replaced by concern in his eyes. "Yeah, why?"

"Did she seem strange?"

Carter narrowed his eyes, flipping his towel over his shoulder as he moved past me toward the showers. "No, I don't think so."

I followed him. "She was up before us this morning. I don't think she slept well last night."

He shrugged. "She's shaken up over the fight with the king. We all are."

Could be, but my gut told me otherwise. "No, this is different."

When we got to the bathroom, he shucked his shorts and boxer briefs down to the white tile floor, stepping out of them before he reached into the shower and turned on the water, looking back at me with confusion in his eyes. "How so?"

"She's hiding something."

He snorted and shook his head. "Well, you're the truth teller. Make her reveal all her dirty secrets." Carter eyed me up and down, a sexy smirk coming to his lips as he grabbed at the ends of my shirt. "You staying for the show?" He leaned in and kissed the side of my neck, pressing his hard body against mine.

Fuck, Carter could always make me weak. Ever since I met him, I'd never been able to resist him. When his soft lips worked their way up my neck and collided with mine, I groaned and let him lift my T-shirt over my head. My jeans hit the floor next, followed by my boxers. When we both stood naked, the steam building between us, I pulled back to look him dead in the eyes.

"Promise me you'll check in on her." I raised an eyebrow, one hand going to his hair, the other to his cock between us. I gripped the tip and squeezed in just the right place to have him buckling at the waist.

"Of course, DC." He gave me another kiss, accentuated with a bite on my lower lip. "Anything for you."

I liked the sound of that. "Yeah?"

He sensed the devil in my tone because his grin deepened, and he nodded eagerly. "Yeah. Tell me what you want."

I shoved him down to the ground and pushed my thumb in between his lips. "Open wide, Chicago."

"My PRINCE," Miri said. "I'm happy you all are safe."

"You need to come home," I said. I'd just spent the last thirty minutes making sure the fairy king of motherfuckers hadn't gotten to her and replaying everything that had happened thus far. "Siobhan and her fairy lovers are plotting the king's downfall. We need you."

"Alexei," she said, her tone sounding more shallow than it ever had...like she was depressed or tired. "I understand this is important, but I can't leave right now."

"Why not?" I'd grown impatient at her absence. Sure, it had only been a few weeks since the last time she'd been here, but this was a fucking fairy war. Now was not the time for her to go AWOL. "You're more vulnerable by yourself. You need us. We need you."

"I know that, darling," she said. "Look, I have to go. I'll be okay, and I'll visit when I can."

"Miri—"

She hung up, and I glanced at Ivy, who stood with one arm clutched around her middle, biting at her thumbnail.

"See?" she said. "There's something up with her."

"I agree with you." I shook my head and sighed. "What do you want to do? Get on a flight to England? Abduct her from her ivory tower?"

"What if the king has already gotten to her?" Ivy said, stepping toward me. "What if he's already messing with her mind? Would we even know?"

"X, let's not jump to conclusions." I ran my hands over her upper arms in a sore attempt to calm her. Admittedly, I worried about Miri, too, and I didn't know how to fix whatever was causing her to keep her distance. "If he wanted to get to her, he already would have. She sounds stressed. It's probably her wicked grandparents fucking with her."

"Hey, you all ready?" Siobhan nodded toward the dining room, where the rest of the family had gathered to figure out our next steps. "Have you talked to Miri?"

I nodded. "She's...uh...busy."

Siobhan pursed her lips and furrowed her brows, but didn't comment.

We crammed around the dinner table like one big fucked-up family. Donnelly and Siobhan teased a barely healed Finn, and Poppy giggled at whatever bad joke Carter blurted out. Ivy talked to Kit and Jon while Abigail recited the research she'd done during the day. If I squinted just right, it would almost be perfect. Except, we were down one spouse and she left a void in my heart the size of a small planet.

"I still think waiting around here is a terrible idea," Siobhan cut in, her voice echoing over the suddenly lowered conversation.

"I agree," Carter said. "We should relocate to the safe house."

"How do you expect me to get married from a remote cabin in the woods?" Ivy raised an eyebrow.

"Postpone the wedding," Carter said. "You didn't want to get married anyway."

She laughed and shook her head. "If I could do that, I would have years ago."

I ignored the sting in my heart. Ivy and I had long since moved past hating each other, so I knew she didn't mean it the way it sounded. Given all we'd been through together, we deserved more than empty insults.

"We need to draw him out," I said. "If he's here, then the other night was child's play. He's fucking with us, batting us around. Theo was just a warning. Next time, it'll be someone closer." I looked at Ivy's siblings, then at Carter. "Have you checked in on your family?"

He nodded. "Yeah, they're safe and blissfully out of town. I'm more concerned about Miri."

I knew my princess well. If she thought she could protect us by staying away, she'd do it. I feared the worst, imagining that smoky fairy bastard with his greedy hands all over her, tricking her or forcing her to stay away from us so it isolated her into complying with whatever he wanted.

Of course, all of this was conjecture because the stubborn brat wouldn't tell me the truth. She wasn't *lying,* but she wasn't being completely honest.

"I hate to say it," Donnelly cut in, "but I agree with the human."

I tried not to be offended. The way he said "human" reminded me of the way humans say "piece of shit." Siobhan pursed her lips, and Finn made a noncommittal noise.

"What? You too?" Siobhan looked at her commander.

"It's not perfect, but it's a start." Finn shrugged.

"What about the thousands of people in attendance? Or the millions more watching at home?" Kit crossed her arms.

"I can handle the people there." Siobhan ran her fingers over her eyes. "Ashley may be willing to help."

Finn shook his head. "She'll want conditions."

Siobhan nodded. "I know."

Donnelly started to talk, but Finn held up a finger to stop him, perhaps indicating they'd talk more about that later, and Donnelly shut up.

"Can you handle the broadcasts? Can you disrupt them?" Siobhan looked at Kit, who sighed and pinched the bridge of her nose. A few moments passed in silence.

"Kit?" Ivy asked.

"I...I don't know," Kit finally said. "I'm good, but even I have my limits."

"Try your best." Abigail grabbed Kit's hand.

"I know a few people who could help." Kit nodded. "I think I can do it."

"Wait," Carter cut in, his gaze darting between Ivy and me. "Are you seriously sabotaging your wedding? You're inviting him to show up?"

"No," I said. "We're preparing for him to show up. He hasn't struck until now. Why?"

"He's a maniacal narcissist with unlimited magical power." Finn's voice sounded rough, and his weakened state made him look even rougher. "The human is right. He'll wait until he thinks we're distracted. He'll want a big show, and without me around to temper his ego—"

Siobhan nodded and shook her head. "And without the queen around to stop him—"

That got my attention.

"What happened to the queen?" Carter glanced from Siobhan to Donnelly and Finn. "You said she escaped?"

Siobhan's mouth opened, but she didn't answer. Donnelly eventually said, "Before he took her captive, he blew ruby dust in her face, hypnotizing her. After that, she couldn't speak. Her mind is fried."

"It's a spell," Finn said.

"What spell do you know calls for ruby dust?" Siobhan rubbed a hand over her face, seemingly as exhausted with Finn as she was with the whole situation.

"Well, I don't know all the spells that have existed since he was born, do I?"

"Now that she's out and still bewitched, it's only a matter of time before she ends up in a hospital somewhere." Donnelly refocused the conversation. "She's wandering around, half dressed, speaking in tongues. Someone will pick her up." He took a sip of beer, his icy blue eyes narrowing on Poppy for a moment, long enough to draw my attention to her. She squirmed in her seat, avoiding all our gazes.

"You haven't seen her, have you?" Carter nudged Poppy on the shoulder and she looked up, ignoring me in favor of her favorite human.

"Nope." She forced a grin. "Haven't seen her since Samhain."

The lie hit me between the eyes hard enough that I almost winced. It soured my stomach, and the urge to make her spill her secrets nearly overtook my willpower. I could do it. I could force her to tell us all the goddamn truth for once. But I didn't. I took a drink and made a mental note to call my uncle after this was over. Poppy looked from Carter to Ivy and finally to me.

I stared right back at her.

All this time, I had my suspicions about the changeling. There were things she didn't tell me, and as long as it didn't endanger the ones I loved, I let her keep her secrets. But I couldn't forgo this. I didn't want her to suspect I knew, so I gave her a playful wink and returned my attention to Donnelly.

"I think Lex's plan is the best course of action. We'll secure Poppy to make sure he doesn't get what he wants, and when he shows up, Ashley will keep a container on the optics."

"If we go along with this," Ivy said, "what are we supposed to do when he gets there? Isn't he the biggest, strongest fairy in the world?"

"He is," Finn said. "But this time, I'm not on his side. This time, I'm defending the humans."

"And that means?" Ivy pursed her lips, waiting for an explanation.

"For six hundred years, I was the leader of the king's army." Finn's gravelly voice hinted at how much pain he must have been in. "I did whatever he wanted. I went wherever he told me to go." He reached to grab Siobhan's hand, his other going to Donnelly's. "Even at the expense of my loved ones. I swore never again. My banshee believes we must help you, so I will help you. When the rest of the *Fianna* finds out what side I'm on, they'll join us. We can contain him together."

"You sound sure of that." I narrowed my gaze.

"They are blood sworn to me."

"But oath sworn to the king first," Siobhan said.

Finn shook his head. "I know where their true loyalties lie. I wouldn't risk your life on it, Banshee."

She swallowed and nodded. "I trust your judgment, Commander."

"Can you get word to your soldiers before the wedding?" Jon said. "That way we can be sure?"

Finn looked at Donnelly, who sighed and rubbed a thumb over his brow. "It's tricky."

"How tricky?" Siobhan looked at the lieutenant, concern in her deep brown eyes.

"I'd have to reach out to old friends, people I swore I'd never talk to again."

Finn growled low in his chest like he didn't like the sound of that. My throat tightened and my heart hammered, a natural response to a literal fucking monster baring his teeth at my dining room table. They looked and sounded so much like us that I forgot they were magical beings from time and lore and shit. They didn't belong here, just like we didn't belong in Faerie.

"Do it," Siobhan said. "I'll go with you."

"No, absolutely not," Finn cut in. "Lieutenant, I forbid it."

"I'm missing something here," Abigail said. "Who does he need to talk to?"

"It doesn't matter," Donnelly said at the same time Siobhan said, "Donnelly has friends in low places."

"When I found you in that trash heap, I swore I'd never let you go back there." Finn's anger turned to Siobhan. "Either of you."

"We can do it," Siobhan said to Jon. "We'll figure out a way in. We'll give them the warning."

"It's getting out that I'm worried about." Finn started coughing and grabbed at his wound, evidently over-exerting himself.

"In the meantime," Donnelly continued, "pretend like nothing's wrong. Siobhan has warded your homes and those of your parents."

"Won't he suspect something when Mount Vernon is the only place that isn't warded?" Kit pursed her lips. "Won't that be a big fat sign saying 'It's a trap?'"

"It won't matter." Donnelly sighed. "He won't be able to deny himself the opportunity."

Ivy met my gaze from across the table, raising a brow when we connected. "Are we really doing this?"

I laughed at the irony. For four years, we'd rebelled against this inevitability. We'd fought it as long as we could, and we lost. Now that I'd finally come to accept the rest of my life with her, we were going to destroy it. Maybe I was ready to rip this apart because, in my mind, we were already married by vow and soul. Or maybe I didn't give a shit anymore because I never had a choice about any of it. "Yeah, X. Let's do it."

Ivy smiled, but it didn't reach her eyes, and I remembered what happened when I went to find her earlier today. She was still hiding something, and so was I. Weren't we a fucking pair? Weren't we past this by now?

"Great," Siobhan said, focusing her attention on Ivy. "One more thing."

Ivy sat up straighter.

"You need to get Miri to come home."

Ivy's features dropped. "I know. I tried."

"Not hard enough." Siobhan let that sink in before reiterating. "You need each other."

"Yeah, yeah, group gift." Ivy sighed and pulled up her politician mask to protect herself.

"Not just that," Siobhan said. "When this all happens, when the end comes, it is the four of you. Not three. Not two. Four."

Siobhan met my gaze with a discerning one of her own, seeming to suggest I needed to drive this point home with Ivy, that I had the most sway. What did she expect me to do? Short of standing outside Miri's bedroom with a speaker and a classic love song, we couldn't *make* her do anything.

"That's enough for one night." Finn clapped his hands on his thighs and tried to push to his feet. Still unable to support his own weight, Donnelly and Siobhan got under each arm to help him. "We'll regroup tomorrow. Fare well, friends." The three fairies lugged the commander up the stairs, and now that their homes were warded, Ivy's siblings said their goodbyes. Carter and Ivy went upstairs to her room, leaving me alone with Poppy.

I wanted to ask her why she'd lied. I wanted to dig into why she seemed so uncomfortable with talking about the queen, but I didn't. Instead, I acted like nothing had happened.

"We're still following your plan, right?"

I pursed my lips and nodded. "Remember, it stays between us, okay?"

She agreed and stood, coming around the table to throw her arms around me. I reciprocated the hug, reminding her to be good before she disappeared back to Vera's house.

And then I pulled out my phone.

20

IVY

Life didn't stop just because Alberich may or may not be after us. I still had to report to Congress and stroke the egos of my colleagues so they would consider passing my bill through the Senate. I put on the fake smile and shook all the right hands. I made videos for social media and took time out of my day to answer questions live. But at night, when the politics were over, I went home to my husbands, who plotted and schemed with Siobhan, Finn, and Donnelly.

"The timing needs to be perfect," Lex said. "If you can't get the army back in time for the wedding, we're screwed."

"If the *Fianna's* not there in time for the wedding, assume we're dead." Donnelly stabbed his cigarette out and immediately lit another one.

"Don't listen to him," Siobhan said. "Don't assume anything until you see it with your own eyes."

"Even then," Finn added, "question it. We're dealing with powerful beings that have no hang-ups about squashing tiny humans like you."

Siobhan smacked his arm. "You're scaring them."

"They should be scared, Banshee," Donnelly said. "This is the stupidest thing we've ever done."

Finn pursed his lips and shrugged. "Maybe third stupidest. Calgary was a clusterfuck."

"You said you'd never talk about that again." Donnelly pointed at him while Siobhan sighed and looked between me and Lex.

"This is a long shot, Ivy." She patted my shoulder. "But I've got a good feeling about it."

She said it to give me reassurance, and the fact a banshee didn't have a bad gut instinct about our plan gave me a spark of hope. I should have said something about invading the king's mind. I hadn't been completely honest with them, and holding on to this information didn't do anyone any good.

If he could reverse the connection, he could see us right now. He could be watching. Of course that had occurred to me, but I had to believe I could control who entered my mind and who didn't. I believed I would feel it if that sort of tether opened up, just like I had that night with the dream. So, I stayed quiet. I kept it to myself, holding it in my back pocket in case I needed to pull it out at the last minute.

That conversation had been four days ago, and the day after that, Siobhan left to go find her sister. Finn was finally healed enough to head north with Donnelly. Carter had rented a room in a hotel a few blocks away to keep up pretenses, but he spent most of his time at our house. Tonight was the last night he'd be in town before he left to go on his press tour.

"I hate this part the most," I said. Lex was sound asleep next to us, the long days at the office catching up to him. "The anticipation of the next morning."

Carter held me tighter and kissed the top of my head. "It's only for a little while."

"It's always too long."

"I'm worried about you, Weeds." Carter kissed my forehead and wrapped his arms around my torso, pulling me in close to him. "Talk to me."

What could I say? My mind had connected to the king's, and in that intimacy, I'd seen things I shouldn't. I didn't know what this meant for all of us, and between everything else, I was falling apart. My upcoming nuptials were approaching faster than I wanted, my bill was unlikely to pass through the Senate, and we had no idea what was going on with Miri. She had all but stopped taking my calls.

I knew how I looked. I saw it in the mirror every morning, the bags under my eyes, the loose clothes hanging off my bones. If I stopped to let myself think about it, I'd lose my composure and never get out of this bed again. So I couldn't stop. I didn't stop. I worked until I was exhausted, and if I had a spare moment, I focused on Poppy or Abigail or research.

"You don't have to bear this alone." Another kiss to the side of my neck. "I'm here. Let me share it with you."

Whether it was his words or the years of trust and intimacy between us, I turned in his hold and wrapped my arms around his waist, tucking my head under his chin.

"It hurts when she's gone." I let myself sink into despair for a moment, here in the dark with Carter where I was safe. "She made me swear to never let her stay away for too long, and now she's acting like none of this matters. I don't understand what went wrong."

"She misses you just as much." Carter pressed his lips to the side of my temple and held me tighter. "I'm sure of that."

"Have you talked to her?"

"No, but...I know her well. So do you. This is her grandparents, nothing more."

The affection in his tone made me look up at him, balancing my chin on his sternum. "I would burn it all down for either of you."

"I know."

"I'm teetering on the brink of doing that," I whispered, terrified saying the words any louder would cause my utter collapse.

"What do you mean?" Carter looked between my eyes, perhaps searching for the truth. "Are you gonna stalk into Kensington Palace and demand to see her?"

I searched his gaze for sincerity. "Do you think that would work?"

"No." He furrowed his brows like he couldn't believe I was serious.

"Carter, it's more than her family. There's something else going on, I can feel it." I'd been feeling it ever since I went inside her mind to find the truth about the king. Something had been kept from her, just like the car accident. Something that was slowly eating its way through her soul. Despite the distance between us, whatever it was had infected me, too.

When we made that vow in the woods, the four of us had been linked on more than a physical level. Each of their souls echoed in my bones, in my molecules. I had been inside their minds. We were soul mates in a million different ways. The fact she was hiding from me meant something, and it didn't have to do with what those cunts in the media printed about us.

I believed Miri would let hell freeze over before she'd willingly be separated from us, the ones who loved her the most. She'd made me swear never to let this happen again. So whatever was keeping her away this time, it was bigger than her family, bigger than all of this.

"They're keeping her prisoner or she's sick or"—my voice shook at the possibility—"something, Carter. It's something."

"Shh." He leaned down to kiss me, wiping away my tears with his thumbs. "She's okay, Weeds. She's okay."

I stopped to pull back and look at him. "Would she tell you if she wasn't?"

He nodded and answered without hesitation. "Yes. She would."

He hummed and put his finger under my chin, forcing me to look up at him. Indigo eyes shined with that eternal light Carter always emanated. It had been the thing that attracted Lex to him in the first place. I'd seen that memory so many times that it had sort of become my own, almost as if I was there with them that night.

"What's going on with you?" Carter whispered, leaning down to kiss my lips.

I sighed and sat up, pulling away from him. "What do you mean?"

"Lex thinks you're hiding something." He raised an eyebrow. "I told him that couldn't possibly be true. We don't keep secrets from each other anymore. Isn't that right, Weeds?"

I bit my bottom lip as heat blossomed up my body. Leave it to Carter to sneak past my defenses. All he had to do was make me limp and pliant with oxytocin.

"He's hiding something, too." I narrowed my eyes at my husband. "I see him and Poppy sneaking around, whispering to each other in dark corners."

"Aren't you happy they're getting along?"

No, something wasn't right. The king's voice echoed from the depths of my subconscious. *Suffer in silence, suffer in solitude. Then you will know the pain you have caused.*

That had been the curse he used on the queen. I'd had my chance to tell Siobhan and the others, but when the time came, I sat there like nothing was wrong. I went along with this idiotic plan because, for some reason, the thought of telling them the truth terrified me more.

Suffer in silence, suffer in solitude.

Earlier, I had opened my mouth to say something when Carter asked Poppy if she'd seen the queen. Poppy said she hadn't, and Lex gave her a look that seared itself into my memory. She was lying and he knew it; I saw it in his eyes. Yet, he hadn't said anything. Not then, and not since then.

Why?

The only reason I could think of was that he had an ulterior motive. He'd proposed we lure Alberich out at the wedding in an attempt to get him on our turf, under our control. Out of all the other scenarios, why that one? And why had he been so sure of it? The answer, of course, was obvious. Lex had been plotting and scheming *on his own* while appearing to go along with ours.

"It's more than that." I took a deep breath and rolled so I sat on top of Carter's pelvis, my knees on either side of his hips. His hands went to my thighs, rubbing his thumbs over my skin in a gentle caress. "He won't let me in."

Carter rolled his eyes and shoved at Lex's sleeping form. "You two are ridiculous."

"Wait, stop," I said, but it was too late.

"What?" Lex grunted, not bothering to lift his head.

"What are you doing with Poppy?" Carter asked.

That got Lex's attention, and he pushed upright, whipping his head around to face us. "What?"

Carter looked back at me. "Both of you. The truth." When neither of us said anything, he cleared his throat and forced the issue. "Now."

Lex sighed and sat up, scooting back against the headboard and reaching for his cigarettes.

"I'm inside the king's head," I said, deciding to bite the bullet and go first. Lex's incredulous gaze met mine and I held it, knowing he had his own skeletons to air out. "The night we found Siobhan, he wrapped a tendril around my throat and—I don't know. I saw things."

Carter ran a hand over the back of his head and let out a breath. "Fucking hell."

"Why the fuck didn't you say anything?" Lex said.

"We need to call Siobhan and tell her," Carter added.

"No," I said, every impulse I had balking at that idea. "Look, it's not that I don't trust them. I just...I think we should keep this between us for now, just until we know what it means."

Lex shook his head and stared at me with his incinerating gaze. "Is he watching us right now?"

"I—" I started to deny it, but I didn't want to lie to them, not anymore. My chest felt lighter the more I spoke, the burden not as heavy now that they knew, too. "I don't know. I can usually tell when my mind has been infiltrated. This feels different."

"How?"

I grabbed their hands and showed them everything, all the disorganized mess that had dumped into my mind's eye. I'd been able to see memories the king thought were tucked away forever. When Alberich choked me, I'd latched on to a piece of him that he didn't know still existed inside of him.

Just as I went to pull away from Lex and Carter, I got a hint of a memory from Lex I hadn't seen before. It was recent. One of him and Poppy...and Marcus? My curiosity got the better of me and I remembered that look in Lex's eyes when Siobhan brought it up earlier in the night. I wanted to dig deeper, but Lex yanked away, slamming the door between our mental connection so hard, I gasped.

"What the fuck was that?" Carter's indigo gaze cut to our husband.

"Was that Marcus?" I couldn't believe it. I just...I couldn't fucking believe it.

Lex ignored our questions, narrowed his gaze at me, and twisted his lips into a sneer. "I thought we were asking before we went skipping through each other's minds."

I climbed out of bed, needing to be on my feet for this conversation. "Was that Poppy and Marcus?" Venom rolled through my veins, my naked body flushed with the heat of our argument. "Did Poppy take you back in time?"

"Yes," he admitted, hanging his head. "I've known she can do it for a while."

"A while?" It erupted out of me in a growl. I could have clawed his eyes out.

He confessed what he'd been up to, that he'd been working with Poppy to hone her skills. "She can control it. She can manipulate him with it."

If I could kill people with my mind, Lex would have been burned to ash on the spot. The fury radiating in my body could have brought a weaker man to his knees. Truth be said, I had been hiding an H-bomb of a secret myself. When he sent his frustration right back at me, I allowed it because fuck...we were two fucking peas in a pod.

"If she can control it, she's a weapon he can use against us." I tried to keep my voice low, but arguing with Lex always brought out a different side of us both.

"Don't you think I fucking know that?" Lex found his sweatpants and slid them up his legs. "Poppy will follow my plan because she loves you both. Now that Siobhan is involved, even better." He ran a hand over his hair, brushing it back from his face with a tired sigh.

"What's your big plan, huh? Train her up and send her to him like bait?"

When Lex didn't answer, my heart sank into my gut. I had to get to Poppy. I had to stop her. "How could you put her in danger like that?"

Lex shook his head. "She's not in danger, not yet. He'll want to use her against us first. He'll need to put us in our place, and until he does that, he has to keep her around."

"That wasn't up to you to decide."

"No." He eyed me with an incredulous glare. "It was up to Poppy."

I almost accused him of manipulating her, but there was more going on inside Poppy than she let us see. She played the child card, but behind those eyes existed a knowledge I could only guess at. "And she agreed to this, knowing what he might do to her?"

Lex nodded. "She's got an out. She can teleport anywhere she wants, anytime she wants."

"What if he turns her against us?"

He made a sad noise and turned to our husband. "Nothing will turn her away from her beloved Carter."

I looked at Carter, who up until now, hadn't said a word. He seethed with rage, staring at our husband as betrayal burned behind his red-rimmed eyes.

"How could you do this?" Carter's voice broke, like he didn't know how to filter his outrage and stay calm. "How could you do this...*to me?*"

"Poppy's lying to you, Chicago," Lex said, his tone softer. "When we asked her if she'd heard from the queen, she said no. The lie hit me so hard, I almost threw up."

"So what? She knows where the queen is. She's keeping herself safe." Carter pushed to his feet, getting in Lex's face. "Does that mean she deserves to be used like a pawn in your sick fucking game?"

"This isn't a game," Lex snarled, remaining the cold, stoic monster he wanted everyone to think he was. "And in case you haven't noticed, she's more powerful than anything anyone's ever seen. Pretending she's not will put all of us in danger, including her."

I couldn't argue with him. Once again, Lex had been the bad guy for the greater good, the anti-hero in this fucked-up fairy tale, the one that had to fall on the sword so everyone else would be okay.

"You should have told us." Carter's jaw squared. "This is about trust. You knew we'd be pissed, that we'd try to stop you. That's why you didn't say anything."

Lex didn't argue, just redirected his focus to me. "What about her, huh? Your precious Weeds is a fucking sleeper agent for the fairy king. Don't you think that's something we should discuss?" His sharp hazel gaze cut right through me.

"It's not like that," I said. "Up until now, it's felt like he's been invading my mind. This time...I'm invading his."

Carter swallowed his anger and hung his head between his shoulders. "We're a family. A team. It's not supposed to be like this between us."

"Every family has fights." Lex tried to take a step toward him, but Carter only wiped away tears and stepped back.

"I guess I ought to come clean, too." He put his hands on his hips and held my gaze. "I'm going to see Miri while I'm on my tour."

My heart bottomed out, sinking into the abyss of my aching gut like a boulder. "What?"

"Part of it goes through London. I've scheduled a stop at Danae Enterprises on a day that Her Royal Highness is supposed to make a rare public appearance."

"How?" Lex's one word held so much anguish, I almost rushed to hug him before remembering I was upset with him.

"My agent is her cousin, remember?" Carter shrugged. "She's sneaking me in. Miri doesn't know."

I sighed and closed my eyes, everything in me growing heavy with his confession. Jealousy flared to life harder than it ever had before, and not for the first time in my life, I wished I could trade places with him. I wished I had what he had with her, that unconditional friendship, that trust that meant he could reach out to her when she wanted to be unreachable to everyone else.

"Tell her I love her," I whimpered. "Tell her I'm sorry. Tell her to come home."

"What a fucking match we all are, huh?" Carter shook his head and sighed. "Keeping secrets and hiding away in foreign palaces."

"I promised to rescue her from her evil grandmother." I swallowed the sob that threatened to climb up the back of my throat as I remembered that night. I still wanted to keep it; I just didn't know how to get to her. This seemed like a viable approach. If I couldn't go myself, I could send Carter.

He took a step closer, brushing a pinky down the side of my face. "You still might have to. When it comes to our princess, my knight's heart is no match for your royal one."

Now it was my turn to roll my eyes. "That's bullshit. You have your whole California bond. *All we have is us*?"

"She's my soul mate, same as you, Weeds. But she loved you first, and she always has." Carter turned to Lex and pulled him closer, grabbing our hands in his. "We promised until the end, the four of us. No more secrets. No more lies."

If my heart could have shattered any more, it would have.

"Promise me," Carter said, glancing between Lex and me. "We are never going to defeat him if we don't work together. Promise me."

"I promise." Lex nodded, glancing at me with sincerity in his eyes.

"I promise," I agreed and met it with my own.

We had made this same vow before, God knew. But this time, I meant it. This time, Lex and Carter meant it, too.

ACT IV

Come, sit thee down upon this flow'ry bed,
While I thy amiable cheeks do coy,
And stick muskroses in thy sleek smooth head,
And kiss thy fair large ears, my gentle joy.
—Titania, Act IV, Scene I

21

IVY

APRIL

I stared at myself in the mirror, twisting to the right, then to the left, admiring this catastrophe of a dress. My mother had picked the designer, the hemline, and the details. All I had to do was show up and let them put it on me. It weighed a ton and cost even more due to the overwhelming amount of diamonds embedded in the lacing. I'd admit it made me look like a princess, but it wasn't me.

I'd get married in cut-off shorts and a tank top as long as I got to have my spouses afterward, as long as the person at the end of the aisle was someone I wanted to marry.

I used to hate Lex, and the ten-year-old year girl inside of me cringed at the thought of saying "I do" to someone who'd only ever made me want to say I *definitely* don't. Putting on the dress made it real. In less than a month, it would be legal. I'd worked my whole life to get to Congress, to implement change, to prove to my legacy that I was a worthy addition. But all anyone cared about was this stupid dress and a promise to a man I'd hated for most of my life.

"Suck it in, Kit." Abigail yanked on the zipper behind our sister, her ginger hair falling over her shoulder.

"I'm trying," Kit said. "It's too tight."

"Mother is going to kill you." Abigail grimaced. "We only have a few weeks until the wedding."

"Mother will get over it," I cut in. "If you need a bigger dress, we'll get you a bigger dress."

Abigail and I took after our father's side of the family—tall and lean with a high metabolism. Kit took after our Aunt Victoria on our mother's side. She had hips and an ass and big breasts that I had envied in my adolescence. She'd never been a "sample size," much to the chagrin of our mother and most of the media. Kit loved her curves, and she'd never diet for anyone except herself. Definitely not our mother.

"Give it up, Abigail." Kit reached back and unzipped it, peeling it off her body before hanging it back up.

"Maybe with another layer of Spanx?" Abigail anxiously picked at her fingers, a tick I was sure annoyed Evelyn Washington to no end.

"If I put any more Spanx on, I'll be a stuffed sausage."

The bridal shop attendant came into the dressing room, eyeing a nearly naked Kit. "Everything okay?"

Kit shook her head. "We're going to need a size twelve."

The attendant's fake grin widened. "We don't carry a size twelve. I'll have to have it specially made."

"Great. Get to it." Kit turned toward me, reaching for her jeans. "I'm done here, right?"

"Wait, come on." Abigail sulked closer. "We never hang out, the three of us. I miss my sisters."

"We've never been the hanging out type." Kit narrowed her eyes, suddenly suspicious of our younger sister's motivations.

"Don't you want to change that?" Abigail looked from Kit to me and back again. "Shouldn't we like...look out for each other or something?"

"We do." Kit pursed her lips. "It's called living our own lives to make it more difficult for our mother to control us. If we scatter like rats, we're harder to pick off."

"C'mon, Kit," I said with a laugh. "I could use the camaraderie."

She sighed. "Okay, okay. Fine. But only because you're getting married. What do you want from me?"

I shrugged. "I don't know. Don't normal sisters do like…sleepovers and stuff?"

Abigail gasped, pushing up on her toes as she looked between us with big eyes. "A sleepover!"

"Jesus Christ, really?" Kit groaned and ran her hands over her face.

"Why? Do you have somewhere better to be?" I put my hands on my hips and gave my sister the *c'mon* look. Abigail activated the puppy dog eyes, layering on the guilt.

Kit shook her head and gave in. "No, I guess I don't."

That was how we found ourselves spread out in my living room, drinking wine and laughing our way through a game of Monopoly. It might have seemed like a boring domestic evening to anyone else, but I hadn't spent much time with my sisters in, well, ever really. Maybe not since boarding school for Kit and longer for Abigail. I had missed them more than I thought.

Abigail grinned. "Are you excited to get married?"

"Don't be ridiculous," Kit cut in. "You know they didn't choose this, right?"

"That doesn't mean they don't love each other."

My phone rang, but I ignored it. I wanted to stay in the present. Whoever it was could wait.

Kit rolled her eyes and groaned. "Lucifer and X? It might look like true love now, but they've spent decades making each other miserable."

"Better than dating no one at all." Abigail pursed her lips at Kit.

"You're the one to talk." Kit rolled her dice and picked up her top hat to move it four spaces, landing on a railroad. "Buy it." As banker, I gave her the property, and she handed me the money.

"You know why I'm not dating." Abigail took another sip of wine. "But you could have any man you wanted."

Kit chuckled and did her best Disney villain impression. "You poor naive girl."

"No?"

"No." Kit shook her head, taking another long drink of wine. "Mother has had her eye on Hugh Kennedy since I was in diapers. I'll be married shortly after Jon."

Abigail's mouth hung open. "Really? You think she'd do that to you?"

"She did it to Ivy." Kit pointed at me, and I grimaced. "You know Ivy dated Carter in college, right?"

"Kit—" I tried to cut in, but she held up a hand.

"Lex was in love with Miri. And after college, Carter broke things off out of the blue. Poof. Like it never happened."

"So?" Abigail looked confused.

"Carter says he didn't do it." I took another drink of wine, swallowing back my bitterness. "He got a similar text from me."

The pieces fell into place in Abigail's mind. "Was it Mother?"

"I don't know," I said, shooting my other sister a death glare. "And neither does Kit." My phone vibrated again, but I silenced it, sending it to voicemail.

"Of course it was Mother." Kit rolled her eyes. "Who else has the connections to hire someone that good? I tried to find them, but they covered their tracks. No one is better than me, Ivy. No one."

I squared my jaw, the fire in my belly surging at the mention of the breakup. We'd never found out how it happened or who prevented us from seeing each other. I thought about sifting through my mother's memories, but what good would that do?

If I found out she did it, I'd hate her, but I wouldn't even be that surprised. If it wasn't her, then it doesn't change the fact that it happened and I might never know who did it. All my skepticism had done was make me suspicious of my own family, and that had always been the case with Evelyn. I hated to hear that she'd done the same thing to my siblings. Someone had to take a stand. Someone had to stop this.

I balled my hands into fists on the table.

"What if it was the fairies?" Abigail raised her eyebrows and looked between us.

"We don't know it wasn't," I agreed. "But it doesn't matter anymore. The wedding is happening, no matter what."

"I'm sorry, Ivy." Abigail put her palm over my knuckles, genuine sympathy in her gray eyes. "If it's any consolation, it doesn't matter who she arranges for me to marry; it won't make me happy."

"None of us are happy, Abigail," Kit said. "That's the price we pay to live the life we do." She almost said it with a straight face, and I laughed because I'd been drinking and needed something to do besides cry.

The front door burst open, startling me, and Lex rushed through, slamming it shut behind him. I only caught a glimpse of his face as he stormed up the stairs, but with his tense jaw and piercing eyes, he was pissed.

"Lex?" I called after him, gesturing for my sisters to stay there. My phone buzzed in my hand, flashing Giana's name, and I realized she had called me six times already. I sent her to voicemail again in favor of chasing down my fiancé in his room. "Lex?"

"Shit." He stormed around his space, digging through bookcases, toppling things to the ground while he rummaged through the shelves. My gut clenched. Something was wrong. "Fuck!"

"Lex." I went closer to him, stopped his pacing, and put my hands on his face, forcing him to look at me. "What happened?"

He froze, his mouth open. Of the two of us, I was usually the one that flew into a blind panic. I usually assumed the worse until I knew the outcome, but his eyes were so wide, I could see whites around the pupils.

"You haven't checked your phone, have you?"

"No, why?"

It buzzed again, this time flashing my mother's name. I ignored it.

"Ivy…" He shook his head and sighed, pulling up something on his phone before handing it to me. "It's bad."

A headline on *The Puck* stopped me.

Breaking News: Congresswoman Ivy Washington and Princess Miriam Stuart spent Christmas together at a secret romantic hideaway. "The tryst goes back to boarding school," our source says. "They were together when they were roommates at Mount Oberon." Representatives for Miss Washington and the royal family could not be reached at this time.

Below that was a picture of the two of us, naked in bed together. It was censored, of course, but undeniably us.

I remembered the shot. Lex had taken it Christmas morning when it was just the two of us and I'd fucked her before anyone else woke up. The look in my eyes screamed love, and hers equaled mine in intensity. It was more than that. These were artistic shots that bordered on pornography. What we were doing couldn't be confused. And there it was…right on the internet, for all the world to see.

Then the realization hit. *The whole world had seen these pictures.*

My mother. My father. My siblings. Her grandparents.

My heart pounded behind my ribs. My clothes felt too tight. I couldn't get enough air into my lungs quickly enough. My phone vibrated again. *My mother.*

"It's all over the place." Lex went back to the shelves, finally finding what he was looking for, a folder of pictures from our time at our cabin. "There's only one way someone could have gotten ahold of them."

"You printed them out?" I balked.

"Yes," he said. "These are the only copies. I deleted the digitals because I thought we'd get hacked. Again."

"Fuck!" I ran my hands over my face, ignoring the eighth call from Giana, the tenth from my mother. "Fuck, Lex. This is bad."

"Yeah, no shit." He scrambled through them once. Twice. A third time. "They're not here."

"What?"

"Those prints. They're missing."

"Someone was here?"

"Someone broke into our house, came to my room, found the pictures, and took only the ones that incriminated you and Miri." There were far worse ones in there. Ones with Carter on Lex. Ones with me on Carter. Why had they only taken the ones of Miri and me? Why not expose all of us?

"Ivy?" Abigail stood at the doorway, a concerned look on her face. "Mother is calling. You should talk to her."

I took a deep breath and steadied myself, opting instead to dial the one person who had as much to lose as I did.

"We're checking the security footage," I said to my wife over a video call. This was the first time she'd talked to me in weeks, and it was about horrible news. That hurt worse than anything else, more than this stupid headline. "I don't know how this could have happened."

Miri sighed and ran a finger over her forehead. "It's okay, darling. It's not your fault."

"I should have seen this coming." I cleared my throat and choked back a sob.

"How could you?" She wiped a tear away, giving me a small smile.

I inhaled my cigarette, stabbing it out before shaking my head. "Are you going to deny it?"

Silence rang on her end as she bit her lips between her teeth, which meant she wouldn't be given a choice.

"I don't want you to be my dirty secret. I love you more than that," I said. "Let's just be honest. Fuck them, Miri. Fuck all of them."

"X," Lex cut in, giving me a knowing stare.

"You can't do that. Your wedding is in three weeks." Miri sighed and looked away. "We couldn't openly be ourselves even if you did."

I pretended like my heart hadn't shattered into a thousand pieces. I hated that she was so far away, all alone and vulnerable in a different country.

"I love you," I told her, blinking back tears. Letting them fall meant the asshole who violated my privacy won. I wouldn't give in to this bullying and harassment.

"I love you, too," she said. "Tell our prince of darkness I love him and I'm sorry."

My focus drifted across the room to Lex, who sat on the bed with his fingers digging into the mattress. "I love you," he called.

"Darlings," she said. "It would be best if we don't talk for a while."

"We won't be able to do that," I said. "You know why we can't do that. It's already been too long."

"We'll have to appear like everything is normal, like this is the media grasping." Lex pinched the bridge of his nose. "We'll say it's a fake."

"You need to come home," I continued. "Things with the king are escalating."

Miri steeled her jaw and swallowed. "*I* won't be able to see you for a while."

The tone in her voice set off alarm bells in my heart and my gut. "What? Why?"

"They're threatening to take everything away from me," she whispered. "The titles, the money, the houses. My life. My entire life. This phone call is probably tapped."

"Let them, Miri. You don't need them." My pulse raced and my knees wobbled, panic rising in my chest as reality closed in around me. I looked at Lex, who only shook his head and inhaled his cigarette. "We have to stick together."

"I can't." Her voice cracked and tears streamed down her face. I hated this. Everything in me wanted to jump on a plane to England and rescue my princess. They couldn't do this to her just because she loved me. "I can't."

"Yes, you can," I said. "Miri, you must. He'll come for you if he hasn't already. How can I protect you if you're—"

"Ivy, stop," she cut in. "You're making this harder."

No.

The sharp ache of panic tightened my chest. I couldn't get air down my throat. My stomach rolled. I didn't care if the whole goddamned world found out. I couldn't lose her. I couldn't.

Why wasn't Lex saying anything? Why wasn't he fighting for this?

"You know what will happen if you stay away," I said. "*Until the end.* You promised."

"I don't have another choice," she said. "Please don't call me again. I plan to deny it. You should do the same."

The line went dead.

Four years ago, I believed Miri had broken my heart over text message, and I spiraled into a sadness like I'd never known. When I sank into the mattress next to Lex this time, the overwhelming *loss* of her made me furious.

It was real. She'd meant it, and I was so damn angry at her, at the world, at myself, that I could burn it all down. I could go in front of the cameras tomorrow and admit the whole thing. I'd tell them I loved Miri from the first moment I saw her, and fuck anyone who dared judge me for it. I'd tell them Carter Scott was my other half and so was Lex, and they loved each other, too.

But—that would only satisfy me temporarily. Miri still had a public image to maintain and an entire royal legacy to uphold. If that meant more to her than our love, *our marriage,* then how could I stop her? Once I had that running around in my head, the real terror set in.

She isn't coming back. This is real.

"She'll get over this." Lex grabbed my hand, intertwined his fingers between mine, and pulled them to his mouth so he could kiss my knuckles in an attempt to soothe the ache in my soul. "Trust me."

In college, he and Miri were on-again, off-again for several years, but they always got back together.

"She's not like this with me," I said. "We don't treat each other like this."

The sincerity in Miri's eyes would haunt me forever. With nowhere else to direct my fury, a sob barreled out of my chest. Lex wrapped an arm over my shoulders, pulling me in to kiss the top of my head and hold me while I fell apart. Everything in my body burned with a brilliant hot rage, and whenever I found the person who did this, I would direct every ounce of it in their direction.

Banging at the front door brought my head up, and Abigail's voice echoed up the staircase followed by Giana's and my mother's.

"I don't care if she's not taking visitors," my mother said.

"Is she upstairs?" Giana marched into Lex's room, pausing at the threshold to find us in an intimate embrace. "I've been calling for two hours."

I took a deep breath and stood. "I know."

She looked pissed, but on my account, not at me. "I need to speak with both of you. Immediately." Giana's dark gaze drifted between the two of us before she turned to walk toward my office at the other end of the house.

I wasn't ready to talk about it. I didn't want to see Giana or my mother or anyone related to covering it up. Miri had just reached inside my chest and ripped my heart out, and even if she claimed she didn't have another choice.

We did.

Of course, I didn't actually know if I could do what I proposed. Bring her into my marriage? Tell the world that the three of us...*four* of us…had made a secret vow in a magical forest, that we were poly and fuck anyone with an opinion about it? If I were any other person in the world, I might have been able to get away with it.

But not me.

Not Ivy Washington.

So I got up and squeezed Lex's hand. Together, we followed Giana into the office. My mother sat on the couch in front of my desk and Lex's father stood over by the window, the room lined with secret service agents. I stopped when I entered, the president turning with his arms crossed and his eyebrows furrowed.

"Ivette, what have you done?" My mother's voice made my skin crawl, and I looked at Lex, gripping his hand tighter.

"It's a fake," Lex said.

"Obviously," I said. "I've been adamant about pushing through this green plan. We should look to my political enemies."

"No," Evelyn cut in, pushing to her feet. "No, you'll do nothing. You'll sit here and keep your mouth shut. Wait for me to clean up your mess." She shook her head, rubbing at her forehead with her deep maroon nails. "How long has it been going on?"

"What?"

"The affair, Ivette. The scandal with your boarding school room-mate. Were the papers correct?"

I balked at her question. Of all the scandals *The Puck* had ever reported about me, why had she taken this one so seriously? We were three weeks out from the wedding. Lex and I had never been more emotionally attached to each other. I'd put on her stupid dress and attended every social function, and now? Now she believes the papers?

But this time was different, wasn't it? Because this time, it *was* true, and everyone knew it.

"I told you they were photoshopped." I squared my jaw and held my chin higher. Lex tightened his fist around mine, giving me his strength. "Why don't you believe me?"

"It doesn't matter whether they were or not," Giana cut in,

holding her hands up between us. "The only thing that matters is what the *public* believes. We don't have much time to respond."

"Respond?" I raised my eyebrows. "No, there'll be no response."

"Reporters are going to ask questions," Giana said.

Mother scoffed and shook her head, and my eyes caught on the way the light reflected off the silver in her dark hair. The presidency had aged her, as it had started to age Kellan. It reminded me that the crown lay heavy on the head that wore it, and I didn't know if I wanted that responsibility. Did I want to be a cold, bitter woman at her age?

"Let them." I took a deep breath. "There's nothing to report."

Giana tilted her head to the side, considering. "The best way to deal with a scandal is to pretend there isn't one."

"Exactly," Lex said.

"Were you aware of this?" Kellan shoved his hands in his pockets, finally taking a step closer to us. "Did you know it was going on?"

Lex rolled his eyes. "So what if I did? At least Ivy would have had the guts to admit it instead of hiding it for decades. Right, *Dad*?"

I saw the second Kellan's hatred for Lex reached a boiling point. If they were alone, he might have hit him. Lex's memories came back to me, the one where Kellan had admitted to resenting Lex for surviving and lamented that Marcus had been taken instead. I hated him almost as much as I hated my own mother.

"Watch your mouth, Alexei." Kellan's tone voiced a threat he likely wouldn't act upon.

Lex snickered to himself, knowing he'd hit a chord.

"All due respect, Mister President, Madam President, I'd like to speak with the congresswoman alone." Giana crossed her hands in front of her, staring my mother down as Evelyn's jaw clenched and Kellan's face turned beet red.

"Excuse me?" He put his hands on his hips.

"I work for Ivy. Not either of you. If I'm going to spin a story, I need to know the facts. Right now, you're both a distraction." Giana cleared her throat. "Again, respectfully."

No one had talked to my mother like that in a long time. Not my father. Not my mother's employees. Not even Kellan. Evelyn stared at Giana for a moment before glancing at Kellan, who let out a short laugh.

"What do you suggest we do?" Evelyn blinked. "Wait in the sitting room like guests?"

"Or the parlor," Giana suggested, "if you need a drink to settle your nerves."

I physically swallowed down my shock when my mother shook her head and pointed at Giana, narrowing her gaze as she headed toward the hallway. "I knew I liked you."

Kellan didn't say anything as he followed.

"Holy fucking shit." Lex laughed and ran his hands back through his hair, his eyes wild.

"Listen to me," Giana said. "We'll say it's a fake. We'll deny it. But Ivy, there can't be any other surprises." She looked between the two of us. "Are there more skeletons I should know about?"

I pursed my lips and glanced at Lex. Giana had signed an iron-clad NDA. If she besmirched my name or my brand in any way, exposed any of my secrets, I'd own everything she had. But this secret didn't just affect me. Carter would need to consent to it, and I hadn't been able to reach him for hours.

"Giana." Lex shook his head and sighed. "If we told you all the skeletons in our closet, you'd have to marry a Washington so Evelyn could be sure you'd keep your mouth shut."

I pursed my lips and ignored Giana's confused expression. "Someone broke into our house for these shots. They knew they existed. They knew where to look. I have no idea what else they knew how to find."

Giana nodded. "We'll try to prepare for everything."

Every day I thanked God for bringing me such a competent chief of staff, but this was the day I knew that if I helped her, she really would take over the world.

22

LEX

Something about this story, in particular, made it blow up. *The Puck* had written millions of debatably inaccurate things about us over the years—that I'd fucked my way through the entire royal family before settling down with Ivy, that I'd cleaned up my image in an attempt to be with her, that we broke up and fucked around and got back together every other week, that we'd been in love since we were children.

Most of the time, the public barely batted an eye. But the affair between Ivy and Miri caught the world's attention, and it became fucking ravenous for information about where I fit into things.

Did I know? Did I care? Was I a part of it?

I ignored the shame in my mother's eyes when a conservative news network spent forty-five minutes arguing if we participated in a satanic sex cult. Though that wasn't too far-fetched considering how fucked-up the truth actually was. Ivy and I sat through it, fingers intertwined, hands pressed firmly against each other. A united front.

We took the next week to hide out in our house while the media eviscerated us in public. Comedians and late-night talk show hosts poked fun at the situation—me for being the stereotypical douche whose girlfriends went to town while I gawked in the corner like a perv, Ivy and Miri, for being clichéd brainless party girls, willing to do whatever for attention.

From an outside perspective, it must have looked that way. The scrutiny focused solely on Ivy and Miri, but if someone paid enough attention, they would have remembered I hadn't been shy about my sexuality when I was a teenager, and we'd been transparent about being close in college. I didn't care if the public knew I once fucked anything with a pulse. Even if I wasn't openly pansexual, it wouldn't take a genius to figure out that *gawking* had not been what I was doing in the corner.

The injustice infuriated me.

Did they not know the impact of what Ivy had already accomplished? Did they not know we were trying to save the world?

But that's not what got the masses fired up. That's not what sold magazines and clicks on the internet.

No.

All they cared about, all they *ever* cared about, was drama, real or imagined.

Giana delivered the public statement announcing the photos were fake, the work of someone set on damaging our reputations ahead of the upcoming legislation and wedding. Kit had found digital footprint experts to corroborate the story. Princess Miriam and Representative Washington continued to be good friends, and the wedding would proceed as planned. We would answer no questions and provide no further comment on the matter.

Ivy went back to work. So did I. Aside from a few brief stares from colleagues and muffled whispers in coffee rooms, no one mentioned anything to me.

Life went on. But something had been fractured. I sensed it on an instinctual level. Miri hadn't returned any of our calls or texts. We had stopped trying.

"She's scared," Carter told me once I finally got ahold of him. He and Miri had been in touch a few times since then, but even he wasn't safe for her to contact. The royal household monitored her conversations to make sure they were civil and clean. Two old friends and nothing more. "The British press is turning her into a whore, dredging up anyone she's ever slept with. The royal family can't put a lid on it fast enough."

I'd seen the filth they'd been writing, making her out to be a home-wrecker or a seductress. Like me, Miri hadn't been shy about sleeping around when she was younger. It had been easier to conceal in the days before smartphones and social media. Now, everyone was part-time paparazzi.

"Are you going to see her?"

If she wouldn't see Ivy or me, at least Carter could be there.

"I still plan to stop by Danae Enterprises the day she'll be there," Carter said. "She doesn't know, or else she would refuse."

Goddamn stubborn princess.

"Come home."

"Lex." He blew out a desperate breath. "I don't think I can. The media is watching you like a hawk. There's no way I can get in."

"She needs you." I cleared my throat, murmuring the next bit. "I need you."

"I know." The yearning in his voice reached down inside of me, yanking something so hard, I nearly got on a plane to Romania. "Do you know who it was yet?"

"No. We don't even know when the pictures were stolen. We've been combing through security footage from the last four months, but nothing is out of the ordinary."

Carter hummed. "Which means it was someone close."

"Exactly."

How could someone have gotten in and out without being seen? Had they tampered with the cameras? Had they hacked the system? Kit didn't find evidence of that, but that didn't mean shit. Whoever had fucked with us four years ago hadn't left any breadcrumbs, either.

"How's she doing?" Carter took a sip of something, likely whiskey.

I sighed, pinching the bridge of my nose. The separation had not been good for Ivy the first time around. This was way fucking worse. "She's existing."

To say the least. She went to work and put on the good show, her fake politician's mask barely having a crack despite the damage to our brand. I saw through it. Maybe it was because I'd spent so much time in her head, but I understood those forlorn looks and that grim set to her mouth.

She missed our wife, and so did I. For eight years, Miri and I had fought and fucked and made up. She always came around. *Always.* But it had been over two weeks with no word, on top of the sporadic contact the weeks before that. Not a call. Not a text. *Nothing.* She'd never made me wait this long before.

"I'll see her in a few days," he said. "I love you."

"I love you." We ended the call, but the hole in my heart did not heal the way it normally did after a conversation with him. I stood and walked to the end of the hall, poking into Ivy's room. She wasn't there, so I went downstairs to the basement gym, where I found her on the elliptical, sweating and talking on the phone through her earbuds.

"Senator Waters, you know very well why we can't give in to this brazen attempt to distract us from impacting real change." Ivy pushed herself harder, wiping at her brow with the back of her arm. "We need this bill to get through the Senate. It's the right thing for the country."

I raised an eyebrow and circled around to the front of the machine, putting my arms over the display, leaning my head to the side while she talked. I focused on the X across her neck, now brilliant against her pale throat. A bead of sweat trickled down the column of her windpipe, over her sternum, disappearing in between her breasts.

I tracked it, licking my lips, wondering if she'd let me get close enough to taste her. Call me a sick son of a bitch, but I loved a good fuck after a workout. She pushed herself harder, going faster, taking deep, slow breaths so she could keep up with the conversation.

Since Miri had broken things off, Ivy had pushed herself to the breaking point. She'd lost at least fifteen pounds, saying she needed to fit into the wedding dress, but Ivy didn't have the weight to lose to begin with. She'd always been long and lean, and in the past few years, toned from working out every day.

Now she looked tired and wrung out. She barely slept, and when she did, it was for an hour or two at a time. If we were normal humans, I'd say she was depressed. But we weren't normal, and such a finite word didn't begin to describe what was going on with her.

Ivy always hated the anticipation of things to come, but I'd been planning and scheming, biding my time for the prick to show himself. I worked with Poppy to get her ready for the showdown. She needed to be strong. We all did.

"Think about it." Ivy shook her head and grabbed her water bottle, taking a deep sip. "Call me once you've reconsidered." She hung up the phone and pressed stop on the machine, sinking down to the ground. "What?"

I pursed my lips. "You've been down here for over an hour."

"I'm busy." She hopped off the elliptical and bent over to stretch, my eyes catching on the curves of her ass, sloping down into her thighs. *Such a great ass.*

"Carter sends his love."

"Oh?" She raised her eyebrows. "I'll give him a call tonight."

I furrowed my brows. Usually, the mention of her beloved Mister Scott sent Ivy's heart all a pitter patter. No reaction raised my hackles higher. She went to the treadmill and pressed start, pushing the incline up to 5 percent before cranking the speed into a jog. With the *thwack thwack thwack* of her feet hitting the machine and the *swoosh swoosh swoosh* of the belt, she'd barely be able to hear me.

Which had been the fucking point. Ivy didn't want to talk. She didn't want to be around me. Couldn't she see I was heartbroken, too? Couldn't she tell that our love was the only thing keeping me together? She'd once said what we had was real, and I believed her. But at the first sign of trouble, she pulled away.

No.

I didn't like that shit one fucking bit. I'd let her have her space for now, but we had a week until the wedding. Her heart might be breaking, but if the king was planning what I thought he might be, she needed to get her head in the game. I couldn't do this alone.

I turned and walked out of the gym, dialing Miri like some pathetic stalker that couldn't take a restraining order for an answer. I got her voicemail.

Well, at least I hadn't been blocked yet.

"Miri, I know you're scared. I know you think you can't survive this." I looked over my shoulder at my disintegrating fiancée. "But staying away will be worse. Don't make me get on a fucking plane and hunt you down." A long pause where I sucked back on my cigarette, hating the desperation in my voice. "I love you."

I hung up knowing, like I did the thousand times before, she wouldn't return my call.

Whoever said "Any press is good press" never survived a sex scandal. The paparazzi hounded us, more than they ever had before. They waited outside my work, shouting questions as my bodyguards tried to get me to and from the door. I ignored them.

Sixteen-year-old Lex would have given them the finger and shown them exactly where to fuck off. A decade later, I had an image to keep. We told the world there was nothing to see, and lately, there hadn't been. Ivy sublimated, I searched for the truth, and somewhere in the middle, we got ready for the wedding event of the season.

"We've always been friends, but not best man sort of friends." Jon narrowed his gaze as he adjusted his tie in the mirror.

"Well, it's a small wedding party, and I didn't have many options."

Jon turned his ginger head toward me. "Not Carter Scott or the commander of the fairy army?" I snapped my gaze to his, but he smiled and clapped me on the shoulder. "Relax. I'm only fucking with you."

At first, I'd balked about Ivy telling her siblings what happened to us. But now, I was unusually grateful to have someone else to rely on. The three of them were close. As they'd gotten older, Jon had moved to New England, trying to put some separation between himself and his mother. That had only worked for so long. Now graduated from law school, he'd been dragged back to DC, back into the fray, and, fortunately for me, back into my inner circle.

"What about your bachelor party?" Done with his suit, he came to me and grabbed the lapels of my jacket, giving them a good yank so the fabric lay flat over my body.

"No bachelor party."

"What?" Jon's eyes crinkled. "Why not?"

"Because." I shook my head. "Neither of us wanted this. It's not something I'm celebrating."

Jon sighed. "You might not have wanted it at the beginning, but there are some curtains on the fourth floor of the Contemporary Art Museum that say otherwise."

"Fuck off." I shoved his arms away and turned to check myself out in the three mirrors ahead of me. I owned suits at home almost as expensive as this, but when I looked up, I didn't recognize the man staring back.

I had the same eyes, the same cheekbones, the same lips, but Christ. I looked like Marcus. I looked like my Uncle Dmitri when he was young. I was a fucking man. I saw it in the set of my shoulders, the square of my jaw, the haunting expression behind my eyes.

"Look at this fucking asshole," the younger version of myself said from the depths of my subconscious. *"Giving up and giving in, huh? At least you'll look fine as fuck doing it."*

Four years ago, I never thought I'd be standing here. I never thought we'd be seeing this through to the end. My gaze caught on the scars on my hand. *Until the end.* I missed them. I missed Miri. The longer her silence went on, the more I realized this might not be like the last time. This might not blow over.

"Just wait until Evelyn does this to you." I shucked the jacket down my arms and gently laid it on the chair, yanking at the tie to pull it over my head.

"Oh, she'll try." Jon smiled. "And she'll fail."

I pursed my lips, raising a skeptical eyebrow. "You sound confident."

"There's no one left to run for office." Jon shrugged. "Your dad is done. Ivy's a long way out from the White House."

"No one except you."

Jon shook his head and let out a sad laugh. "I'm not interested in politics."

"And yet, here you stand at the heart of it all."

"Well, yeah." He nodded. "My family's here. My siblings need me."

"I fought for months to change my father's mind." I unbuttoned the shirt and whipped it off my arms next. "If Kellan couldn't be swayed, Evelyn definitely won't. I guarantee she already has her eye on someone for you."

"Oh, sure." He nodded. "Probably half of DC. But if she thinks she's good at this game, I assure you, I'm better."

That piqued my interest. "How so?"

"I'm twenty-four." He put his hands in his pockets, giving me a nonchalant shrug. "You were engaged by my age. I've been putting her off this long."

I admired his tenacity even if it was stupid as hell. Evelyn had been playing before any of us had been alive. His arrogance and cockiness may have made me love him even more, if only because it reminded me so damn much of his sister.

"Good luck, brother." I clapped his shoulder.

His grin widened, and it wasn't until he said it back, "Yeah, thanks, brother," that I realized the words I'd used.

In a way, Jon had always been family, the same as Ivy. Where she had always been *mine,* he had been a sibling, a constant presence that didn't grate as much as X's. In fact, of his siblings, Jon might be the most normal. He always had a grounded, even-keeled approach to life.

"I'm worried about Ivy." He cleared his throat and ran a hand over the back of his head. "She's acting like it doesn't matter, but she's a good liar."

She was an *okay* liar, even before I could magically sniff her out. I pursed my lips, considering how to answer.

"She's fucked-up about it." I sighed. "She and Miri were soul mates. Now, Miri won't even talk to her."

Jon's eyes widened. "Why not?"

"The royal family is trying to do damage control. You see what they write about her in the press." Miri had taken the publicity hit over there. They'd dug up old photos of her from her wild teenage years, calling her a disgrace to her lineage. This time, her gran had taken it seriously.

"They write a lot of garbage in the press." Jon scratched the back of his head. He'd also been the subject of *The Puck*'s rumor mill in his youth.

"Yeah, but not everyone believes it. The world's eating this shit up, no matter how hard we try to force feed them Ivy and me."

I still didn't understand why the focus had been on Ivy and Miri; it just didn't make any sense, and the more I spun it, the more pissed off I became. Certainly, the Washingtons had an enemy list a mile long. But who would have access to our house...*without using the door?* Only one person that I could think of, one person who would know we'd taken photographs at Solstice and where I'd hid them.

No. She'd made me a promise. She'd sworn an oath of loyalty, and even if she'd been raised around the fucking fairies, I had to believe she loved Carter and Ivy enough not to fuck us over. Our relationship had gotten stronger in the weeks since I'd been training with her, and I didn't think she'd be capable of something so sinister.

But...what if she had done this *before* we came to terms?

"It'll blow over." Jon patted my shoulder, giving it a fraternal squeeze. "It always does." He took a step back and assessed his jacket one more time. "Remember when my father got caught in the Oval Office with his pants down and an intern on her knees in front of him?"

I snorted and then sighed. "It's not sex if it's not in the vagina." That had been George's excuse, but everyone knew, even Evelyn. They were too big and too rich to divorce, so they suffered through the agony of marital counseling and public evisceration.

"In six months, it'll be some other idiot with his dick shoved somewhere it shouldn't be, and they'll forget about my sister."

Yeah, but it would never go away, not really. Anytime Ivy and Miri were in the same room together, people would speculate. Every time I was with Miri, people would gossip. It would be passed around on hushed whispers in dark corners of any event we attended, the sycophants thriving on draining the life out of us.

We should just tell everyone. That way, they couldn't use it against us.

I sighed, knowing we'd never be able to do that.

Jon nodded. "What about Finn and Siobhan? Any word from them?"

"Sadly, no," I said, my anxiety causing a storm in my chest. We were running out of time, and without them, I had no plan to defeat the king. Poppy had gone mysteriously silent, too. "Just be prepared for anything on the day, all right? Whatever happens, I'm thankful we're in it together."

"Yeah, you got it." Jon smiled and turned back to the mirror to readjust his tux.

23

MIRI

I stared at my cellphone while it buzzed and flashed Lex's name across the top for the fiftieth time, inhaling my cigarette when it went to voicemail. A few seconds later, a notification popped up that he'd left a message, but I ignored that, too. If I answered, Gran would see it. She'd know I was in contact with my former lovers and she'd be...*displeased*.

Perhaps I should have left the glitz and glamour behind, taken Ivy up on her offer to come to the States. Even if I didn't marry Carter, I could live on my own and build a new life. Who was I if not Princess Miriam Stuart? Perhaps I could have found out.

It was the look in Gran's eyes when she reprimanded me that forced me to go along with her despicable plan—marry the prince and dismiss my spouses and pray it all blew over. She saw right through me, down to all the dirty, filthy parts, and she'd gotten tired of them.

When she threatened my title and wealth, a part of me didn't care. My spouses would take care of me the way I'd always taken care of them. But despite it all, selfish me still wanted my birthright. It had been mine since I was born and I owed it to my father to get it.

As it was, I thought about what my parents would want or what they'd do in the same situation. Theirs hadn't been a love match, but they did eventually find partnership while they were together. It was a different time for royalty in the eighties, and the same advantages afforded to my father wouldn't be given to me.

Inhaling deep on the cigarette, I let it out on a sigh and clicked my phone off just as another notification from the local news station came through, this one about my lack of chastity and morals befitting a princess of England. Had they found another former lover to give a tell-all interview? It wouldn't matter either way.

I stared in the mirror, forcing myself to admit I looked like rubbish. I couldn't eat. I couldn't sleep. The distance from my lovers hurt, yes, but my body knew something that my brain hadn't caught up to—or perhaps my brain had permanently shut out.

It was that same gnawing ache that hadn't gone away since my trip to Monaco in January. Every time I thought about stepping foot inside that place again, my muscles tensed and a wave of nausea hit me so hard, I thought I'd fall over.

I'm not safe there.

I knew it down to my bones, but I just didn't know why.

"Miriam, darling," Gran said, walking into my bedroom without knocking. After my *great matter*, she'd taken more liberties than she ever had, telling me I was lucky she still claimed me. I didn't see what luck had to do with it. Her continued public acceptance of me had to do with optics. If she claimed the photos of me with Ivy were fake and then threw me out, no one would believe our royal bullshit. "Time to get dressed. You have a visitor."

Hope sparked in my chest before I could tamper it down. "Who is it?"

"Reginald, of course." She grinned and went to my dressing room, opening the doors while two attendants followed closely behind her.

"Oh." Disappointment dripping into my gut, I went back to staring at my cellphone, wishing I had the courage to do the things I wanted. It was a strange feeling to describe. I knew I needed to keep fighting, I knew I should escape and find my way on the first flight home, to my real home, not this antiquated prison. But something in my gut told me I needed to stay away to keep my spouses safe.

I thought again to the memory of that night in Monaco and the morning after, when I'd woken and hobbled to the bathroom like I'd spent all night at an orgy. But I hadn't. I'd gone to sleep and dreamed of...Well, I wasn't sure of that, either.

Remember, the trees said. *Remember. Remember.*

Remember what, I had no idea. When I asked, they bristled and shivered and refused to say more.

Gran draped a few dresses over her arms before returning to me so she could help me to stand and get me out of my nightgown.

"Oh, do try to cheer up, love." Gran grabbed my chin and held my face up so I had to stare her in the eyes. "He's not all bad."

I forced a smile but didn't truly feel happy about anything.

Once I was presentable, we walked down the hallway to the pink sitting room where the guard waiting outside announced our arrival to our guests before stepping aside so we could enter. Reginald stood, his salt-and-pepper hair even grayer than the last time I'd seen him. He wore an expensive, well-tailored suit, his dark eyes creasing as he stared down his aristocratic nose at me.

"Miriam, it is so lovely to see you again." He bowed, and we exchanged pleasantries. "And on incomparable terms."

"A wedding," Gran piped in. "Such bliss."

Yes, a wedding. I should have been thrilled. In exchange for keeping my dowry and titles after the photo leak, I'd finally agreed to be sold to the prince. We'd be married sometime next year, but it was difficult to feel anything about even that.

I missed Ivy. I missed Lex. The small amounts I talked to Carter weren't enough to sate me, not really. Something had been fundamentally shattered deep down inside, and I just couldn't figure out what it was.

Reginald and Gran talked about politics and the upcoming Grand

Prix, but I focused on the swirling haze forming in my mind's eye. The last time I'd seen Reginald at his palace in Monaco, he'd kissed me on the cheek and offered me a good night. But that shimmer around the memory had me forcing my energy harder at it, knowing whatever was wrong with me had to do with what happened after that.

"Miriam," Reginald whispered, turning to face me with a small grin. "I admit, it took me far too long to reach out."

I gave him a small smile, unwilling to meet his gaze. The thought of touching him, of being near him, rankled my nerves. What happened between us? What was it I was missing?

"I left so early in the morning, but I wanted to check in on you... regarding your *nightmares*." He said the word like it was a euphemism for something haughty.

I furrowed my brows and forced a grin, not understanding what he meant. "Nightmares?"

"Yes, the staff said they heard you making noises in your sleep, tossing and turning, bumping the bed about, moaning about Carter Scott. The next morning, there were...fluids on the sheets." He smiled, but it didn't quite reach his eyes. "I'll let you know that once we're married, I won't tolerate a public affair, no matter how far back your affiliation goes."

Carter?

I racked my memory about that night and the morning after. Undoubtedly, I had woken up feeling sore between the legs, but I'd gotten my period, so I attributed it to that. Had I been dreaming about Carter that night? Had the king found me and done something more?

Reginald cleared his throat and wiped at his mouth. "Especially after all that's happened."

I should have reacted to the dig about my recent indiscretion, but the glimmering distracted me, as if the entire night had been put in a vintage filter, making it seem warmer and more surreal than it should have been.

There could be only one explanation.

The king.

A deep, sinister laugh rose up from the depths of my subconscious, villainous and outrageous, freezing the disgust at the center of my sternum. A piece of the memory had broken free, a piece designed to taunt me into compliance.

"Oh, Little Thistle. Are we having fun yet?" It was his voice, his raspy, sinister snarl.

I jolted out of my seat, the chair flinging onto its back behind me.

"Miriam?" Reginald said, rising to put a hand on my shoulder to steady me. "Are you—"

I didn't let him finish. I turned on my heel, tears burning my eyes, and marched out of that bloody charade before I lost my mind.

"Bring me the child," the king demanded. *"Bring me my wife. Then I'll give you what you seek."*

"I don't have your bloody family," I snarled, shoving into my apartments before slamming the doors shut. The staff must have thought I'd had a mental breakdown, and they wouldn't be too far from the truth.

I didn't know who to trust. I didn't know what was real. I couldn't even rely on my own memories. Panic seized my chest, overwhelming me as I melted against the plaster walls and slid down to the ground, allowing myself these few private moments to fall apart.

What did you do to me? What did I do to myself?

I couldn't remember. But truth be told, whatever happened that night paled in comparison to how the king had violated me *again*. He had entered my mind and distorted whatever he wanted *again*.

How had he done it? How had he convinced me I was dreaming, that none of it was real? Or perhaps, I was still dreaming. Perhaps I had never woken up that day my parents died.

Bleeding Christ, I don't know. I don't know.

Why was I so vulnerable?

Go to them, a part of me said. *We're stronger together.*

I quickly shut that down. I couldn't even protect myself. If the king could manipulate my memories so easily, what else was he capable of doing to me?

No, it was even more important for me to stay away from my spouses now. To protect them. To protect us all. I didn't know what was real and what wasn't, but most importantly, I was a liability, tarnished to the very core.

My phone buzzed again, this time flashing Carter across the top of the screen. My thumb hovered over the answer button, but I didn't have the strength to push it down.

Maybe one day I would.

Maybe. One day.

24

IVY

TWO DAYS BEFORE THE WEDDING

The days went by with no sign of Siobhan, Finn, or Donnelly.

I didn't hear from Miri. She was an adult; she could make her own choices.

And she hadn't chosen me.

My heart throbbed, and I glanced down at the scars on my hand, the remnants of vows we made when we were younger and more naive.

Enough now.

I wanted to move past it. I wanted it to not hurt anymore. Hell, even I had started to pity myself. But...it just wasn't right without her here. A few nights ago, I had gotten the courage to call her, knowing it would only bring me more heartache.

The phone had rang and rang while my skin crawled. It must have been 7 or 8 a.m. in London, certainly she was awake. A click had brought me back to the present.

"Hello?" My knees had crumpled under me, and I'd slumped to a couch. "Miri? Is that you?"

Nothing had come from the other end.

"Miri, please. I miss you. Say something." Tears had burned my eyes and sobs had threatened to spill out of my throat. I'd shoved them back down into my chest. "Yeah, I get it. You'll be okay...okay? Just hang in there."

Still, no words had come from the other side, just the soft whisper of someone breathing. Was it her? Had it been some royal creep listening in?

"Miri, I love you. I haven't forgotten my promise." My murmurs had turned to whispers and, finally, to pleas. Hot tears had slid down my cheeks as I gave in to the angst building in my chest. "Please let me back in. We all miss you. We can't do this without you, Miri, my darling. My love. Please."

Then the line had gone dead.

I'd gasped and stared at my phone. That had to have been her. She must have heard me; her desperate breathing gave her away. I'd tried to call the number again, but it had gone straight to voicemail, as if the phone had been turned off or gone dead.

For any other person, this would have softened their resolve and maybe they would have gotten a clue by now. But it only poked the wild beast stirring inside me.

Once upon a time, I'd made a promise to her I wouldn't let her get away from me again. Something so fucking trivial, like the paparazzi making up rumors about us, shouldn't have been enough to tear us apart. We were stronger than this. We'd made vows. We'd been through worse.

Whatever this was, it wasn't Miri, and I was willing to bet everything on that. It was that secret I sensed the last time I'd seen her, the one that had been hidden from even her. It was whatever lived inside of her that she didn't know about. Carter called every night from his tour, and when he met with Miri tomorrow, we'd have our answers.

In the weeks since the scandal broke, I'd reached out to Miri's grandmother, thinking if I could talk some sense into that woman, maybe she'd let my wife off the hook. Now, at my rehearsal dinner, I finally had an answer. I looked down at my phone and pulled up the formal response from the royal family.

"Her Royal Majesty, Queen Elizabeth of England, regrets to formally decline your request for an audience. The queen's intensive schedule does not allow for diplomatic affairs outside of what has been previously arranged with the United States embassy. The queen has supplied this comment: 'If my granddaughter has ended your friendship, best leave it be. All my love to my dear friends, your mother and future father-in-law. Best wishes on your upcoming nuptials.' The queen has donated a generous sum to the charity listed on your registry as a gesture of solidarity and goodwill."

I closed my phone and took a sip of wine, feeling more helpless than an abandoned kitten. I didn't know how I would pull this off. I mean, how in the hell could I defeat a king of fairies when I couldn't even keep my own family together?

Looking around at this menagerie of collected power figures made me even more disheartened. Dmitri and most of Lex's family had flown in for the festivities. Since this was the biggest occasion since the last royal wedding, everyone who was anyone in the world's aristocracy was here. Mount Vernon overflowed with old money, and every room at my family's ancestral mansion had been filled by relatives. Most of them, I'd never met before, or if I had, it had been a long time since I'd seen them—cousins, aunts, uncles, people with the Washington last name or ties to it but had the good fortune of not being *the* Washington family, the firstborn of the first-born going all the way back.

I stood in the parlor, watching my mother flit from guest to guest —politician smile wide, arms out in greeting. Like this was the most joyous thing to ever happen: her eldest daughter, finally sold off to the neighbor. I finished my pinot in one gulp.

"Slow down," Lex murmured, coming to stand next to me. My attention caught on Kit talking to a Kennedy in the corner. I wasn't sure which one—Hugh, Lexington, another John. It didn't matter. She'd be next on the chopping block, no matter what I tried to do to stop it. I grabbed a glass off the tray of a passing server, handing him my empty one in exchange.

"Only two days before the end, Lucifer." I smirked. "You can still run."

He chuckled. "I'd never run from you, X."

I stared at him, echoes of our game in his gaze. What would this crowd of rich old farts think if they knew that only a few days ago, he and our husband had held me down and spit roasted me like a kabob? I snorted at the image.

They thought what I did with Miri was bad? *Good fucking Lord.*

"Ma'am." Reagan cut across the room and headed right toward me, standing close so they could whisper in my ear. "We've been given the heads-up that your bill is unlikely to pass through the Senate."

I sighed, my lungs turning to lead as they sank into my stomach. Just another goddamned thing. When it rains, it's a hurricane.

"I forwarded the email to you. But...it's not good news."

"Okay." I pulled back to nod. "Thank you, Reagan."

Their brown eyes met mine with sympathy as they squeezed my hand.

"You'll get through this," they said. "Just focus on the wedding for now. Giana's got everything else covered."

I had no doubt she did. Reagan kissed me on the cheek and turned to walk away. I'd failed in every way. I couldn't figure out a way to destroy the fairy king or find the fairy queen. I hadn't heard from Siobhan since she left, and we were supposed to capture the king in two days. I couldn't stop this marriage from happening or get my wife back. I couldn't even do my one fucking job in Congress.

My evening gown tightened, suddenly suffocating me. I couldn't breathe. "I'll be right back, Lucifer."

"You okay, X?"

I nodded, pursed my lips, and casually walked to the balcony, looking out over the gardens and the Potomac River in the distance. I'd stood in this exact spot thousands of times, contemplating my life and what to do with it. I couldn't decide which failure hurt worse, for there had been plenty since then.

"Hey," came the deep voice from behind me. My father walked closer, one hand in his pocket, a glass of whiskey in his other, the typical accessory for him these days.

I straightened and turned to face him, plastering on a fake smile as I tried to bottle up my emotions. "Hello."

"How are you doing?"

I shrugged. "Living the dream."

He laughed and held up his glass for me to cheers.

"My bill failed in the Senate. So, there's that."

Father sighed, staring out at the river with an expression so like my own. Hell, it was like looking in a mirror sometimes. "Ah."

"Ah?" I shook my head. Not that he'd ever been a beacon of fatherly wisdom, nor had we ever been very close, but that noise sounded loaded.

He gave me an encouraging nod. "You're young. You've got a lot of time to try again."

"What if I don't want to?" The words flew out before I could stop them. Hell, I didn't even know I felt that way until I said it.

He narrowed his eyes as he considered me, taking a drink of his liquor. "That's the great game, Ivy." He shook his head. "You put yourself out there. You do the best you can. They chew you up and spit you back out. The ones who keep going, they're the ones left standing at the end."

Far be it from me to take advice from a man who had forced me into this situation, a man who had once chided me for protesting it at all.

"You're either in this family or you're not. Exitus acta probat."

In the days since, time had beaten him down. How long had it been defeating him before that? How many times had this town chewed him up and spit him back out? How many times would it do it to me? Was I so like him that I wouldn't stop, no matter what? The next time I got caught, the next time someone broke into my house, my cell phone, my laptop, and leaked my secrets to the media? Would I keep going once they knew about Poppy and Carter, once they destroyed my image and my brand and everything to do with my personal life?

I drifted my focus across the crowd to where my mother laughed at something Senator Jacobs said, clutching both him and his wife. I wondered how much of my current situation she was responsible for. She might have forced the breakup with Carter and Miri four years ago and leaked the pictures to the public so I wouldn't be tempted to call this off in favor of Miri. Had she manipulated my whole life?

More importantly...if I did become her, if I took up the mantle of the Washington matriarch, what would I do to my children? Would I be capable of doing what was done to me for the sake of national policy?

"Are you happy, Father?"

It had been a long time since I'd addressed him as anything other than "Sir," and he turned to face me with his eyebrows furrowed. "Why would you ask me that?"

I shrugged and gazed up at him, hoping for the cold, honest truth. "Just wondering if you'd do anything differently, if you could do it again."

"Oh, well." He sighed and looked down to the ground, swirling his whiskey in his glass. "Of course. Everyone feels that way."

"Would you marry Mother again?"

He snapped his gaze to meet mine, his features dropping. "Of course, Ivy. It wasn't just an arrangement. She used to make me laugh." One side of his mouth pulled into a smile as memories flipped behind his eyes. I'd give anything to put my hands on him and see what he was seeing. But no, those were just for him. Just for *them*. "She's tired." He shook his head and took another sip. "She thinks the weight of the world is on her shoulders, like she has to fix everything. She doesn't, and she can't."

Anything else he could have said wouldn't have impacted me

nearly as much. I'd been compared to Evelyn my entire life, as she had been compared to her mother and so on before that. Washington women were the backbone of this family, and without us, not even the first George would have done what he did.

It nearly broke my heart. If I didn't want to be like her, I didn't have to be. That started with taking a stand—for myself, for my siblings, for my father. And most importantly, for her.

If I was going to sabotage this wedding anyway by inviting a dark fairy king to crash it, then why not go all in?

25

LEX

"*Malysh! Malysh!*" Aunt Vera wrapped her arms around me and pulled me into a hug, kissing the side of my face before licking her thumb and wiping off the lipstick she left behind. It didn't matter how old I got; I'd always be a little boy around her. "You're getting married! Such a beautiful thing!"

Vera had always been most comfortable in Russian, so we kept the conversation in her native tongue. I greeted her and turned to Uncle Dmitri, who'd arrived with four or five bodyguards currently roaming the outskirts of the Washington estate.

"*Dyadya,* good to see you." I shook his hand, and he pulled me into a big hug.

"Good to see you, too." He laughed and clapped my shoulder, inhaling his cigar. In the two years since I'd dropped Poppy at his doorstep, he hadn't aged at all. He was still the big, burly man with the gold chain and the expensive suit.

"Look at you, huh?" He grabbed my chin and gave it a rough shake. "A full grown man now!" Dmitri kissed either side of my face before turning to the crowd. "Where's my beautiful sister?"

My mother, Anna, appeared with my father, throwing out her arms so she could embrace her sibling. I didn't know the last time they'd seen each other, but it had certainly been longer than it had for me.

"There she is!" Dmitri kissed my mother and hugged her tight.

"So happy you two could make it." Mother and Vera talked about their trip in, and Dmitri asked my father about a foreign policy the emperor wanted to push through. I sensed my presence was superfluous, so I tried to take a step back, figuring we would catch up about my previous request later. My uncle put his hand on my shoulder to stop me.

"Alexei, I wondered if you might give me a tour of the grounds. I have something I wish to discuss with you."

Oh?

I looked from my uncle to my father. He straightened, an eyebrow going up his forehead.

"Romanov to Romanov." Dmitri smiled, giving Father a knowing look that demanded he not ask for an invite.

"Of course," I said. "Excuse us."

My father didn't like being told to fuck off at his own party, but I'd admit, a little smirk came to my face as we walked past him. I led Dmitri onto the balcony and down the steps to the backyard, my thoughts going to the funeral we'd held for my brother all those years ago. I'd first kissed Ivy by that bench over there, and then she'd slugged the shit out of me. I smiled at the memory, putting my hands in my pockets as we walked.

"How is the engagement going?" Dmitri puffed on his cigar. "Are you happy with your new wife?"

I shrugged, and maybe I was feeling nostalgic because I muttered, "There are worse people I could marry." It was the same flimsy excuse I'd given Ivy when our parents first announced this farce.

He laughed. "She's very beautiful. She'll make you a man."

She already did.

"What's on your mind, *dyadya?* Is this about my phone call a few weeks ago?"

He frowned and tilted his head to the side. "Yes...and no."

"Oh?" I lit a cigarette while we fell into a stroll. "What does that mean?"

He chuckled. "That depends on what you tell me."

I narrowed my eyes and took a long drag on my cigarette.

"Sometimes, when your Poppy goes to sleep, I check on her in the middle of the night and she's not there." Dmitri shrugged. "You say you've come to get her, but no vehicles have been by my house."

I cleared my throat.

"When I look into her eyes, I can see there is something else going on." Dmitri watched me, gauging my reaction.

I swallowed down my non-surprise that she hadn't been good about hiding what she could do.

"As a child, my nanny used to tell me stories about the *vila*, beautiful women that lived in the woods. They changed their form at will, teleported long distances." Dmitri shook his head. "I'm not saying I believe in such things. But..." He stopped and turned to face me, staring down at me like he, too, could detect the truth in other people. "If I did, would you say you believed in them?"

I raked my gaze over my uncle, focusing on his stern expression. I'd never known him to be a liar, or someone to fuck with me just for the sake of fucking with me, and I did thrust this child on him with very little explanation or concern for what she'd be capable of doing to him as a result. I never said I made all the right choices. I only did what I thought was best.

"I would say I did, yes."

"And if I asked you...is this child a *vila*? What would you say to that?" His eyebrow shot up his forehead as he considered me.

I took another long drag on my smoke and nodded. "She's not a *vila*. But she's not...from around here."

He pursed his lips. "And you gave this child to me without telling me this?"

I let out a sardonic laugh. "I told her not to give herself away."

"She's not good at keeping secrets." He tsked, continuing to walk down the riverbank. I knew that, too, as I still suspected she'd been keeping the location of the queen from us. "Oh, Alexei, I could have you killed for this."

I chuckled. "But you won't."

"I won't. It would not be fair to Ivy to deliver a corpse as a groom on her wedding day." He shook his head. "My mother did not raise me to have such ill manners."

"I apologize. I didn't think she'd be living with you this long."

He held up his hand. "Alexei, I would do anything for you. My sister's son, you are very dear to my heart." Dmitri shook his head and gave me a genuine smile, clapping me on the side of the cheek. "I have a gift for you."

"A gift?" Anticipation rose in my chest.

"Come with me." He led me farther away from the house where a black Range Rover with tinted windows was parked. Power emanated from inside the vehicle, a strange magic I recognized from Faerie. This wasn't dark and twisted like the king. This was light and airy, and it made me want to fall to my knees with idolatry.

When two of his guards circled around us, going to the back door, I almost told them to stop. One guard opened it, and the other reached inside to yank out a tall blond woman in soiled white robes.

The queen.

"Holy shit. You did it." I took a step forward, and her wild eyes darted between me and the other men.

"Of course I did it. Who do you think I am?" Dmitri smirked.

She'd been gagged with a piece of cloth and her wrists were zip-tied together in front of her body. Her skin had turned a pale, ghostly white, and that once radiant look in her eye was now faded to a haunted imitation of what it used to be. Slicing cold terror replaced that excitement inside me, and my stomach dropped. Even on this side of the realm, she still radiated with the eternal, vibrant energy that terrified and exhilarated me.

"How did you find her? Where did you find her?"

"My guards caught her sneaking around Poppy's rooms. You were right." Dmitri waved his hand to his guards. "Poppy has been hiding her this whole time."

I fucking knew it.

If the queen remembered me, she didn't act like it. She struggled against the bodyguards, trying to use her weight to attempt to escape, and the more she struggled, the tighter they held her. Bruises lined her wrists and biceps. It must have been a long journey to get to this point.

"Wait, stop!" I took a step closer and held up my hand. "Be gentle."

She was the queen of the fairies, for fuck's sake.

"Your Highness." I came closer, and she eyed me up and down, still suspicious but cautiously interested. "Do you remember me from Samhain a few years ago?"

Her panicked gaze flicked between us like she didn't understand and waited for someone else to translate. When no one did, she struggled and tried to hit one of them in the face. He ducked out of the way and grabbed her wrists, tossing her in the back seat before slamming the door shut.

"She's a wild animal," the guard said.

"She bit me." The other guard held up a red bruise on his forearm.

"She's scared." I turned to Dmitri. "I'll be back with help. We'll take her from here."

His eyes narrowed. "What are you caught up in, *malysh*?"

I shook my head. "You wouldn't believe me if I told you."

"I've believed a lot."

I nodded and put my hand on his shoulder. "One day, Uncle. You'll get me drunk, and I'll explain the whole thing."

"One day." He eyed me skeptically. "Before I leave this trip. Yes?"

"Yes."

"Uh-huh." He turned to head back toward the house, and I

followed him. "As for Poppy." He shrugged. "She didn't want to come to the wedding. I cannot force her."

"She's still in Russia?" It was my attempt at making sure she was still going through with the plan...at least until she realized her queen had been taken. She had to appear as normal as possible, as hidden as possible, until the time was right.

He nodded. "She was when I left. As for where she is right now?" Dmitri shrugged.

"That's okay." I pulled out my phone and sent a message to Ivy to meet me out here. We had to figure out how to hide a fairy queen until the wedding was over. With Siobhan not answering and two days to figure out a new plan, we were fucking screwed no matter what.

"Do you need anything else from me, Alexei? Manpower? Protection?"

"No, Uncle. Protect yourself. I'll be okay."

He narrowed his eyes and shook his head. "I do not like this. Take three of my most trusted guards. They will stay until after the wedding, until you can sort this out."

"I can't ask you to do that." Moreover, I didn't trust guys I didn't know.

"You didn't ask," he said. "I insist. You can't tell your mother. This is what uncles are for, huh?"

I laughed. "Thank you. I'm not worthy."

"You're Romanov. That is enough." He smiled and kissed my cheek again. "For now."

"Holy shit." Ivy stared into the back of the van with her mouth open. "Dmitri just found her wandering around his house?"

I nodded. "She's been looking for Poppy. That explains why she came to the cabin over Solstice; Poppy was there."

"Your Highness," Ivy said to the queen. "Please, let me first say—"

I shook my head. "She doesn't understand. Donnelly was right. She's been bewitched."

The queen's eyes darted from me to Ivy and back again, eyebrows furrowed as we talked. She'd settled down now that I'd cut the bindings on her hands and taken the gag out. She still didn't seem to remember me or Ivy, but I believed she could tell we meant her no harm.

I inhaled my cigarette and glanced back at the house where our relatives mingled, drinking alcohol like the world wasn't ending. No one could see us out here, no one could know about her. "I tried to make her tell the truth, but that went as well this time as it did last."

Right on cue, the queen babbled something in a language that didn't sound real. Ivy took a deep breath and took a step forward, holding her hands up in solidarity. The queen backed away at first, but she must have found something in Ivy that seemed peaceful because she slowly leaned forward.

She put a hand on Diana's wrist, a gentle, simple touch, nothing to suggest anything untoward. Their eyes closed, and I held my breath, waiting to see if Ivy's gift would work where mine hadn't. But she shook her head and dropped her hand to her side.

"I can't get through, either. It's like...she has a force field around her mind. It's powerful."

"Well, shit." I stabbed my cigarette out and threw the butt in a nearby garbage. "Any ideas what to do with her?"

Ivy shook her head. "Christ, we can't keep her in the Range Rover all night."

"What about the servants' quarters?" Mount Vernon had been ripped apart and renovated five different times since the original Washingtons owned it, and sometime during the Victorian era, an entire servants' corridor had been added in the basement, replacing the old wine cellars and kitchen.

"It would take one outburst for everyone to hear her."

I rubbed at the crease between my eyebrows, a headache brewing on the horizon. "We could take her home, maybe keep her there until this is all over."

"I mean, Siobhan told us to find her, right? That she was the only thing that could protect us from Alberich?"

I mulled that over. "Yeah, but what good is she in this condition?"

Ivy crossed her arms and looked back at the house. "Taking her home is probably the safest. The house is warded. The king won't be able to enter without a welcome."

"Dmitri gave me a few guys to watch her. I'll ask them to keep her entertained." I gestured to the big dudes standing next to another black SUV a few yards away. "They'll stay with her for the wedding."

Ivy shook her head and pursed her lips. "I don't like this."

"Do you have a better idea?"

She pulled her lip between her teeth. "Lex...maybe we should stop this? We haven't heard from Siobhan or Poppy or any of the others. We were supposed to regroup three days ago."

I should have told her Poppy had been hiding Diana all this time, but that too would have to wait. "Whatever shit they had to do to rally the troops, it didn't sound like it would be easy."

"What if they're dead?" Ivy's eyes radiated all the anxiety in her body. "What if we're on our own?"

"We don't know that, and until the day of the wedding, we have no idea what's going to happen. Take a deep breath and be patient."

"What if Siobhan and Ashley don't come?" Ivy folded her hands together and pressed them to her mouth. "Lex, we should cancel this and tell all these people to go home, to run as far away from us as they can."

"We have two things he wants. Poppy and the queen. He's on our playing field. He has to come *to us.*" I wrapped an arm around her body and tried to pull her into a hug. She let me up until I said, "That gives us an advantage."

Ivy groaned and shoved me away, rubbing her hands over her face. "You sound so arrogant."

"Okay, what's your big plan?" Anger surged in my chest, the thrill of fighting with Ivy rising up in me. "March in there with all our family and friends and tell them we need to postpone the biggest media event of the fucking year because a fairy king might be our guest of honor?"

She put her hands on her hips and stared at the queen, currently running her fingertips over the fabric-covered ceiling of the SUV. "What if he kills everyone?"

I shook my head, betting it all on the fact that he wouldn't do that. It wouldn't be what I would do. "That's not a smart move."

No, the better move would be to pick us off one by one, wait until we were the most vulnerable to hit us with the kill strike. If he came tomorrow, it would be to make a scene. He'd want to establish his power, which was fine because it meant we could establish ours.

We weren't weak fucking no ones. We were also powerful, and this was our realm, goddamn it.

"So you're suggesting we go through with this when we suspect it'll turn into a bloodbath? That's what you want?"

I winced. "A bloodbath is unlikely."

"Lex," she groaned my name, sounding exasperated and stressed out.

"Look, this was my plan from the start, lure him out to where we have the advantage." I ran my hands over her upper arms, hoping to soothe her and ease her mind. "Your family has lived on this property for two hundred years. This is *your* home. If anyone can protect it, it's you."

I sounded like Carter.

I'd like to thank the Academy.

The truth was that I, too, thought this would turn out to be a nightmare, but I didn't see how we had any other choice. There was no stopping this avalanche. We had to let it smother us and hope we could dig out in the cold light of day.

She took a deep breath and sighed. "I guess you're right. There's no way we can get out of this." Ivy stepped closer to me and wrapped her arms around my neck, pushing up on her toes to give me a kiss of solidarity.

I chuckled, remembering the last time we'd kissed out here and half expecting her to haul off and smack me again. She didn't, just pulled away and looked at the fairy in the back of the SUV. The queen squealed in delight, clapping at our kiss while saying something in a jovial, encouraging tone.

"How are we going to sneak home and back without anyone noticing?" Ivy asked with a grimace.

I ran my hands over the back of my hair and sighed. "Ahh, fuck."

Ivy texted Kit and Abigail to cover us, and I could only imagine the stories those two came up with to explain our absence. When we pulled into the garage of our townhouse, the three bodyguards helped the queen out of the vehicle and flanked either side of her as we walked up the stairs and across the back porch.

When we got to the entryway, the queen stopped and peered inside while I unlocked the door. My breath fogged around me on this chilly spring night, but the queen seemed completely undisturbed by the weather. I stepped inside and turned to face Diana, trying not to smile at the silly grin she gave me. She looked so eager and excited to be involved, such a contrast to my fiancée at her side, who nervously glanced around to ensure none of the neighbors could see us.

"Queen of Faerie, we invite you inside our home." The queen's smile widened as she walked through the door, her hands behind her, scoping the place out. The guards came in next, managing to keep their cool while she looked up at the giant chandelier over our dining room table and spun around in a circle to admire it.

"Ahh," she said, pointing at it. "Spritzen!"

"Right." Ivy grabbed her hand and put it down, wrapping an arm over the queen's shoulders to usher her through the living room and over to the stairs. We intended to put her in the guest room for now, but she needed a shower and some clean clothes immediately.

The queen nodded, folded her hands in front of her, and tiptoed around with a look of astonishment.

"This way." Ivy led the group down the hallway to our guest room, the one Miri normally slept in. She hadn't been here in so long, it had become an abandoned space, lifeless and cold. We didn't go in here anymore, but it would have to do. I opened the door and gestured them inside. The queen's mouth dropped when she spotted the bed, and she ran up to it, grabbing her legs before springing cannonball style into the center.

"Jesus Christ." I pinched the bridge of my nose. "That's not the same woman we met at Samhain." This person was a far cry from the powerful forest nymph who'd put me in my place when I tried to use my gift on her. Did she even remember who *she* was?

Ivy snorted and shrugged. "Even queens like jumping on the bed."

The air had once tasted magnetic in her presence, her magic coating my skin and my tongue in awareness of *her*. In this realm, her light had dimmed to nothing. Would it be the same with the king? Or had he stolen something essential from her in order to get what he wanted?

Ivy fiddled with her phone, pressing a button and bringing it to her ear. When it went to the automated voicemail, she shook her head and said, "Fuck, I still can't reach Siobhan."

"The three of them made a pact with us. They're coming back."

"What if they don't? What if the entire *Fianna* is dead?"

"Stop ruminating," I said. "We don't have time for that." I looked at the three guards and said in Russian, *"She stays here. Don't let her leave, and don't harm her again, you understand?"*

Each of the bodyguards nodded.

I turned to the queen, hoping something I said would break through her barrier. "You'll keep out of trouble, yes?"

She narrowed her eyebrows for a moment, but nodded again, smiling with her bottom lip tucked between her teeth. I went to the bathroom and clicked on the light. "You can shower in here."

"I'll bring you some of my clothes," Ivy said.

The queen clapped and nodded, jumping off the bed to throw her arms around my neck and kiss me on the cheek before doing the same to my fiancée.

What the fuck had the king done to her?

I met Ivy's gaze, who seemed as confused and concerned as me.

I put my hands on the queen's shoulders and pushed her back, trying to put as much sincerity in my eyes as I could. "You're safe here, okay?"

I didn't think she understood my words, but she nodded and that was enough for me. She gave me another hug and went to the shower, turning on the heat before stripping her robe over her head, careless of the five other people in the room. The guards turned away to give her some privacy.

Okay. She seems content enough.

I turned and shut the bathroom door behind me. Ivy rubbed at the spot on her neck where her X appeared and came closer so the guards couldn't hear.

"Do you think she can still do magic?"

"If she could, she would have used it by now." She ran her hands over her face. "This is such a bad idea."

"Hey." I snatched her chin and forced her to look up at me, my hands on either side of her cheeks. "Don't fucking do that. We're in the homestretch, and I need you, X."

She nodded and steeled her gaze, swallowing down whatever anxiety she'd let bubble to the surface.

A few moments later, the bathroom door opened and Diana emerged wearing a towel. Ivy brought her an old pair of my gray sweatpants and a TWU hoodie. She put them on, caring little for propriety as she shucked the towel down to the ground before slipping the clothes over her body. Even dressed, she lacked that certain something that had made her the queen.

"Feeling better?" Ivy asked.

Diana smiled, pointing at Ivy and saying something that sounded jovial and uplifting. I imagined she liked my fiancée.

"We have to go back to Mount Vernon."

The queen turned to face me.

"I wish we could do this any other way. I know you don't like this, but..." I stood and went to her, holding her wrists between us. *"Tell me the truth. Are you still in there?"* I glanced between her eyes, and she blinked, grimacing for barely a second before ultimately nodding.

Did it work?

I tried again. "How do we break this curse? How do we fix you? *Tell me the truth."*

She winced this time and pulled her arms away, moaning and rubbing at the places I touched her. She made incoherent and rambling sounds, occasionally scoffing and rolling her eyes. I had no idea what she was saying, but I understood all the same.

Don't fucking touch me.

Despite the rejection, the response gave me fucking hope. That was the first sign of the real queen I'd seen since Dmitri gave her to me.

"You stay here. Understand?"

I had no idea if she really did, of course. But we couldn't risk her getting out or the king finding her, so with one more stern word to the guards, we left them there and headed back to our party.

26

MIRI

THE DAY BEFORE THE WEDDING

"As you can tell, Miriam," the CEO of Danae Enterprises said, pointing to the screen in front of me, "profits are up. Even if the joint US structure falls through, you've made a substantial impact to our cause."

The room applauded, and I did my best to stay humble. "I couldn't have done it without all of you. Truly." I graciously smiled and pushed to my feet, keeping the grin on my face despite the wooziness behind my eyes. This had been a planned media excursion, one of the few Gran would let me have these days, and she'd been sure to assess me before I left.

I'd shrunk three sizes in the weeks since I broke things off with my spouses, and even the press had commented about the hollow look in my eyes.

"Miriam is heartbroken," one of the newscasters had said. *"I'd believe the leaked pictures are real based on that alone. Has anyone seen Ivy Washington these days? She's a complete wreck."*

I had to swallow down the insult and carry on with my life like they weren't bordering too close to the truth. Shame writhed in my gut like a snake, spewing its venom into my veins anytime I thought about my lost loves.

This is better, I reminded myself. *Safer.*

That was what kept me stock-still and frozen in Kensington, hiding in my ivory tower to wait for the villain to come to me.

All the news coverage had been about Lex and Ivy's big day tomorrow, and the place where my heart used to be clenched again.

I have to protect them. I have to keep them safe.

I still didn't remember what I'd done the night Reginald's staff had supposedly overheard my "nightmare." But perhaps ignorance was bliss. Perhaps it was better I not know. This did not change the fact I had become a liability in either case.

Perhaps you'd be safer with them, the logical part of my brain said, *the way Ivy is.*

It's safer to stay away, the dark side repeated. *Safer to be alone.*

I felt so fragmented that I'd been paralyzed into inaction. I couldn't go home to my loves, but staying still and quiet would get us all killed. Shoving all of that into a compartment somewhere in the agony of my heartbreak, I refocused on the present.

"Brilliant. I'm quite overjoyed to hear this," I said. "And I do look forward to seeing what you come up with next." I eyed my assistant at the corner of the room, and she pointed to her watch as if to indicate it was time to move on to my next appointment. I'd glanced at the itinerary this morning, but I hadn't paid much attention because Yana kept me on task no matter what, the brilliant woman. I made my goodbyes and told everyone I'd see them at lunch before following her down the hallway to another meeting space. This one had no window on the door, and when she opened it for me, she stayed outside and nodded for me to go ahead of her.

No bodyguards first? No scoping out the space? Confused, I took a hesitant step inside and glanced around at the boxes of printer paper and the copy machines up ahead. "Is this a supplies cabinet?"

Yana shut the door in my face.

"Yana?"

"Good to see you, Juliet."

The voice coated my spine like a warm campfire. Deep and melodic, it could have belonged to only one person. I turned on my heels and came face-to-face with Carter Scott leaning up against the plaster wall, looking like a walking wet dream with that panty-dropper grin on his stupid handsome face.

My Romeo.

My star-crossed lover.

My best friend until the end.

Emotions overwhelmed me, and I jumped into his embrace before I could stop myself, my arms going around his neck. God, he smelled exactly the same, like sunshine and soap and *male.* I missed him terribly, as much as I missed the others. My eyes burned and, silly me, I couldn't hold back my emotions. Tears spilled over my cheeks and down my chin.

He laughed when he put me down, wiping at my face with his thumbs.

"Are you really here?" I whimpered.

"I'm here, Juliet."

"How did you get me alone?"

He laughed and kissed me. Not the way Ivy or Lex would have kissed me, but deep and passionate all the same. We were bound together, he and I. We had something no one else would ever under-stand, even if it was different from what we had with the other two.

"I bribed your assistant." He grinned. "She's a big fan, and she found out you and I have matching tattoos." He held up his palm and pretended to be shocked. "What? Carter Scott and Miriam Stuart are besties? Is that what all that time out in California was about?"

I laughed and shoved his shoulders, playfully squaring my jaw. In that brilliant moment of reconnection, I forgot the reason why I'd stayed away. I forgot I had a filthy secret I struggled to hide as well as I used to. I had to stay away from them, from *all* of them. This could turn bad so quickly, and I'd be powerless to stop it.

Carter ran his eyes over me, the weight of his gaze nearly

drowning my lungs. I looked terrible; I knew I did. My eyes had sunk into my head and my cheeks had curved in. Every bone stuck out along my ribs, and no doubt he could feel that when he touched me. He didn't say anything but didn't have to. The thin set to his lips and the concern radiating out of his eyes said it all.

I cleared my throat and wrapped my arms around my torso, a self-conscious burn echoing over my skin. "It's not what you think."

"Jesus, Miri." He ran his hands over my upper arms and shoulders to my neck, cupping my face. "You look horrible."

"Shh." I put my fingers over his lips. "Keep your voice down."

"What's going on? Are you okay?" His indigo eyes turned serious, and he put his hands on my shoulders, holding me still so he could get a good read on me. "Juliet?"

I licked my lips and sighed, tensing my muscles to keep them from trembling. "I don't know."

He blinked. "What? What do you mean you don't know?" His expression dropped. "Have you seen a doctor?"

"Yes," I hissed. "There's nothing physically wrong with me. It's just...stress." I couldn't tell him the truth, not now. Maybe not ever. I knew very well what was wrong with me, and he couldn't do anything to fix it. None of them could.

"Stress." Carter blew out a disbelieving breath and shook his head. "You should see Ivy."

I snapped my gaze to his. I'd seen photos of her online and a few press junkets in the days leading up to the wedding. She had lost some weight, but she looked otherwise okay. "What are you saying?"

"You can't be away from each other, and you know it." His gaze pierced me, echoing the hurt and betrayal he must have felt inside. "It's time to come home."

"No." I took a step back, breaking the connection between us as scalding tears slid down my cheeks. "This is for the best, Carter. I can't—" I cleared my throat when it broke and tried again. "I'm tired of coming in third."

That physically hurt him. Agony replaced the confusion in his expression, his brows furrowing, his lips pouting before thinning in response. He'd always been so beautiful, and I hated what I had to do to make him go. The lies I had to tell nearly gutted me, but I had to say them all the same. This would keep everyone safe, make sure I couldn't hurt them.

"Third?" He shook his head. "Is that what you think?"

More tears slid down my cheeks, but these weren't from the joy of seeing an old friend. This was the shame of knowing that all of this was my fault. I couldn't keep the thistles going, and the king had likely gotten out because of it. All of this started because of me, because of what I'd done to him on Samhain, and now he could take my memories away from me and enter my mind whenever he wanted. I couldn't trust myself. As long as I stayed away, they would be safe. I was too vulnerable where the king was concerned.

Besides, I didn't have a right to call them my own, not anymore, no matter what the scars on our hands said. I'd agreed to marry someone else, and there was no going back now.

"Ivy and Lex, Ivy and you," I continued, justifying my nonsense, "I can't compete with that, and I'm done trying."

Carter balked, his jaw falling open like I'd slugged him in the bollocks. "Ivy and..." He trailed off like he didn't know what to say.

"It's obvious that no matter what happens, Ivy is going to end up with one of you. And what do I get, huh?" It wasn't true, and I only said it to hurt him. If Carter knew how vulnerable I was, if he knew that I'd agreed to the engagement with the prince, that I couldn't trust my own mind...

No one will want you anymore, the darkness whispered. *Oh, Little Thistle. Are we having fun yet?*

It was all my fault. I was dirty, soiled, pathetic. I swallowed back the terrible memory and shook my head, sobbing as more tears spilled over my face. None of that mattered anymore. The same reasons that held us back before were still there today. In fact, the *biggest* reason was happening tomorrow on international television, much to my complete and utter agony.

"What do you get?" His voice smacked with the pain and desperation that had been building in the weeks since we'd seen each other. "What the fuck is that supposed to mean?"

"Nothing." I scrubbed my hands over my face, trying to regain the composure I had walking in here. Our joyful reunion had to end. I couldn't be caught alone in a closet with him. The Prince of Monaco would *definitely* not like that. "Forget I said it. Carter, you have to go."

"What is going on with you?" He closed the distance between us, wrapping his arms around me again. I tensed and broke away, needing more space, ignoring the hurt look in his eyes. "What happened to all we have is us?"

"I don't have a choice." My heart shattered as I said it, all of the torture from the weeks apart seeping out of me.

He squared his jaw, the belligerent knight in shining armor coming to the forefront of his personality. "Come to America. Marry me, Juliet. Marry Lex. Can't you see we need you?" His words rang through me, the truest thing I'd ever felt in my life. "And you need us. I mean, fuck. Look at you."

My knees gave out, and I sank to the floor, unable to hold my own weight while I cried. Carter followed me, squatting down so he could wrap his arms around me and hold me. "You're not safe with me, not anymore, not anymore." I could barely get the words out, but I needed him to hear them.

"I love you," he murmured, kissing the side of my head. "You're not third anything. It's all of us, Miri, all the time. Weeds is a fucking mess without you."

"Ivy is strong."

"Lex is a stone-hearted monster."

The thought of my beloved prince of darkness made me chuckle, and Carter cupped my jaw so he could look me in the eyes again.

"Things are getting bad." He shook his head. "I was sent to get you. My tour is almost over, and once it's up, I'm heading back to DC."

None of that had been a surprise. I'd felt it the minute the king had gotten out, but it didn't matter anymore. The princess would save everyone in this fairy tale, and that started with staying away from them to protect them.

The king's voice echoed in the back of my mind.

"Little Thistle, you'll come to owe me quite a bit before we're through."

I shivered and couldn't hide it, making Carter hold me tighter.

"You're not safe here by yourself. Please come with me."

"What, right now?" I balked and met his gaze.

"Yes, right now. Roxy's down in the car. We could get you out. You could start a new life in the States with us. We need your help. Please."

I'd be lying if I said I didn't want to do it. Bleeding Christ, a huge part of me wanted to squeal for joy and jump in his arms, eagerly accepting his proposition. I yearned for my spouses the same way they yearned for me.

But I couldn't. It was safer for everyone if I stayed away. The king could manipulate me in ways he couldn't with the others, and the closer he got to me, the more vulnerable I made the people around me. If he could manipulate my mind anytime he wanted, I didn't know what else I was capable of, what sins he'd make me commit and hide from everyone else.

"I can't," I said. "I love you, but I can't."

He looked crestfallen, my words shooting him right through the gut.

"You have to go," I told him, suddenly afraid that someone would see him and report it back to Gran. She couldn't know he was here, that I'd been in touch with any of them. Hell, she'd nearly killed me when I'd listened to Ivy on the phone a few weeks ago. If she knew I'd seen one of them in person? "Carter, please. Don't make it harder for me."

"None of us wanted this, but we're all a part of it. That includes you, like it or not." He kept his voice as low and as level as he could, but I knew I was killing him. "You can break it off with them, but you can't get away from me." His voice broke and he cleared his throat, blinking back tears. "Not me, Miri. Not me."

"Okay," I relented, my chest heaving. "Okay, Carter. I'll figure it out. I'll call you."

As if coming to some resolution within himself, he nodded and said, "Okay." He gave me one last kiss before standing and going for the door. "He's coming, Miri. You need to be ready to tear this all down when he does." I didn't say anything as he opened it and left me standing there, shaking and terrified for what I'd just agreed to.

ACT V

The iron tongue of midnight hath told twelve.
Lovers, to bed! 'Tis almost fairy time.
-Theseus, Act V, Scene I

27

IVY

WEDDING EVE

Lex and I had spent the better part of the night trying to get through the queen's defenses before we gave up and went back to Mount Vernon. When I still hadn't heard from Siobhan the next morning, I asked Kit to put out an APB and find her the way she had last time.

"It doesn't work like that," she'd told me. "There's a lot of ground to cover."

By the rehearsal the next day, I had come to the resounding conclusion this was going to be a disaster. The closer we got to the actual wedding, the more I dreaded it. Despite what Lex thought, by going through with this, we were dangling a shrimp in front of a giant blue whale and daring him not to eat us with the bait.

We don't know he'll come. We don't know what will happen, I tried to tell myself. There was no sense in panicking before I had all the facts.

Speak of the devil...

My sister eyed me from inside the dining room, giving a smile to a few of Lex's relatives as she walked out onto the balcony next to me. Bodies moved on the lawn below, all of the people hard at work setting up for a wedding that had been twenty-six years in the making.

"I'm still working on it," Kit said. "When I ran the diagnostic, I found something interesting."

"Oh?"

She rattled off a bunch of computer jargon that only partially made sense, something about a firewall and leaving a back door open. She could only figure that out because we were in the place where it happened. It had to do with who had screwed with us after Carter and Miri moved to California and who had leaked the photos to the media.

There could have only been one outcome from an affair between us going public, and that was exactly what happened. Miri left me. I hadn't seen her since. My mother had as much motivation as anyone. But why not out Carter, too? Why only Miri and me?

Hopefully, Kit could find something...*anything*...to point me in the right direction.

With the queen showing up and the attack from the king, I had forgotten all about the leaked photos. That all seemed insignificant compared to what I worried we might truly be up against. Still, if it turned out to be my mother, my own flesh and blood, I wasn't sure I'd be able to stop myself from exposing her. This might be enough to finally push me over the edge, to go public with the way she treated me. Hell, I might as well go public with all of her skeletons.

"Jury's still out on Siobhan. But I'll keep trying."

"Thank you, Kit." I grabbed her hand and squeezed it. "I owe you."

"You bet your sweet ass you do." She winked. "You fucking loser."

"You insufferable twat."

She laughed and pulled me into a side hug.

"I saw you talking to a Kennedy yesterday." I raised an eyebrow.

She shook her head. "Oh, fuckface? Yeah, good conversation. He rattled on about his daddy's big plans for his political future." She stirred her tiny straw in her cocktail. "As if I gave a shit."

I teased, "You'll never win a husband like that."

"Hmm, just what I need on top of fairy royalty trying to destroy the world." She shrugged. "The Kennedy is a distraction. If Mother thinks I'm interested, she won't meddle, and I can keep minding my business."

I nodded, but internally I winced. Evelyn wouldn't care if we knew or what we thought about it. If she did, she wouldn't have done it. This was all politics to her—our lives, our careers, all part of the Washington brand. That left no room to be an individual, and the pressure had suffocated me all my life. Now, it stifled my siblings.

All of this would be solved if I used my gifts to my advantage, but I couldn't hide when I was inside someone's mind, and my mother would be a tough nut to crack. Trying to expose her would expose me, and I still hadn't figured out how to explain all of this to her.

"Places everyone," the wedding day coordinator said. I internally groaned and forced a smile, plastering that politician mask on the way I always had.

Off we went, down the stairs to the back lawn, over two thousand chairs lined the grass on either side of the aisle, positioned facing the altar made out of ivy and roses. The Potomac would provide the backdrop to our nuptials as it had for hundreds of Washingtons before me.

The wedding coordinator, Marcia, went over the particulars, where the men should stand, how they should stand, when the ladies should walk down the aisle, how long to wait in between each person.

Kit, Abigail, and I took our places inside the door leading to the basement, waiting for Lex, Henry, and Jon to stand at the altar.

"Has anyone seen the groom's party?" Marcia put her hands on her hips and trotted off around the corner to find my fiancé. My father stood next to me, and from this angle, hiding behind the stone wall, we couldn't see the head of the altar or the chairs leading up to it. No one could see us, either.

"Getting through the vows is the worst part," Father said, patting my hand when I grabbed his elbow. "No one prepares you for standing up there for so long."

Why would he say that?

The few moments right before we went on were the worst, and even if this was just rehearsal, there were still going to be people standing around watching us with their judgmental eyes. Even if I'd gotten over the stage fright, the anxious anticipation was so deeply ingrained that it showed up by habit.

The music started, and Abigail took her place at the head of the bridal party, waiting for Marcia's cue before starting her walk. A few moments went by before Kit went.

Fuck. Fuck. Fuck.

My stomach churned and saliva pooled at the back of my mouth, and maybe it was all the stress leading up to this, but I was definitely going to puke. I didn't care that it was just a rehearsal; there were too many people looking at me. The music changed to a string version of the bridal chorus. I waited until Marcia gave me the go-ahead before I took a deep breath and prayed for the best. I couldn't stop now.

The show must go on.

"Ivy," my father said, gesturing to the front.

I looked up to where my fiancé stood next to the minister. Never in my life had I been so relieved to see Alexei Fairfax, to make eye contact with him and know he had my back. We were doing this together. A weight lifted off my chest and I sighed, keeping his stare as I walked forward. The knowing look in his gaze sent a shiver down my spine. For twenty-six years, we'd lived our lives together, all of it leading up to this.

Sure, this was pretend for tomorrow, but I imagined him standing in his tux with his hair done and that snarky twist to his lips. A flush went through me, headed straight down my body.

For years, I'd bucked against this marriage. I'd fought it and reviled it and begged to be released from it. But after all we'd been through together, after the last few weeks in particular, I found myself grateful to be meeting *him* at the end of this aisle.

It wasn't the life I would have chosen for myself. It wasn't the most ideal circumstance. But if I couldn't have what I wanted, then… well, to quote Lex, there were worse people I could marry.

Of course, now that I'd come to accept it, we were preparing to tear the whole thing apart.

"Hello, X." Lex smiled when I finally reached him.

"Hello, Lucifer."

"Who presents this woman for marriage?" the minister said.

"I do, on behalf of her family." My father placed my hand in Lex's before turning to take his seat next to my mother. The minister carried on with the practice run, but my eyes locked with Lex's hazel counterparts, and for the first time in months, I let him inside my mind.

He sighed out a small laugh and shook his head, glancing down to the ground. *"Careful. You almost look like you want to marry me."*

"Don't get it twisted," I said, raising an eyebrow. *"I couldn't stand the thought of being up here in front of all these people by myself. You know I do better with a co-star."*

He pulled his lips into the devil's grin I once hated. Now, it wasn't so bad.

"How's the queen?"

He took a deep breath. *"Still asleep. The guards said she didn't wake up this morning, but she's breathing. Any word from Carter?"*

"I tried to call him. No answer."

Lex sighed.

"And now a reading from the Book of Corinthians," the minister said, gesturing to my younger brother, Henry.

He stood and cleared his throat, brushing the dark hair off his eyes. "Love is patient. Love is kind."

"How about Poppy?" I asked Lex.

"No luck. She's avoiding us."

"Do you think she knows we have the queen?"

He shrugged. If she did, she could be plotting her own method of destroying us. Either that, or she'd already been taken by the king. If that was the case, I'd go for her. I'd throw myself at the mercy of Alberich to guarantee her safety.

"Do you have the rings?" The minister gave us both a smile before turning to Jon with his hand out.

Jon reached into his pocket to pull out the wedding rings my mother had chosen for us. Mine contained stones that once belonged to a great-grandmother Washington, and Lex's had been inherited by his mother through the men on her side.

"Ivette Washington, do you take Alexei Fairfax to be your wedded husband, to have and to hold, through sickness and health, for the rest of your lives?"

Echoes of the first time we'd gotten married went through my mind, drunk on fairy wine in the enchanted woods, lying in those ruins after having fucked in the creek.

"I would marry all of you," Carter had said.

"I would, too," Lex agreed.

"Really, Lucifer? Even me?" I'd been teasing. I hadn't actually expected him to say yes.

"Especially you, X."

We'd been betrothed for real at the time, barely twenty-two and wide-eyed in the world. As the memories played out in my head, they echoed in Lex's, too.

"I do," I said. *"Until the end."*

"And do you, Alexei Fairfax—" The minister repeated the same words to him, but Lex's eyes never left mine.

"I do," Lex said. *"Until the end."*

I smiled as he stepped closer and kissed me.

The flood of emotion that came through that small contact nearly toppled me. This wasn't the real ceremony, but I couldn't stop my heart from exploding with overwhelming raw adoration for him.

My story with Lex had been fucked up from the start—in puppy love with his brother, sworn to hate him for my entire life, betrothed to him before I graduated from college. Through that, I'd gained a confidant, an ally, someone who understood me better than anyone.

I would not have made it this far without him. I would not have made it the last few weeks without him. When I was lost, he found me. When I couldn't stand on my own, Lex held me up.

"I love you, X."

"I love you, Lucifer."

And this time, I meant it. This time, it was real. Really and incomprehensibly real.

The revelation rocketed through me, making me shiver, and I could no longer deny the effect he had on me. True, Lex Fairfax and I were complicated. But I perhaps loved that the most.

"Ugh, get a fucking room already," Kit sneered from behind me, which made Abigail snicker.

WE FINISHED the rehearsal and went inside for dinner. My mother made an obnoxious speech about the sanctity of our union and how it would bring blessings to both our families. Kellan said some words about the great honor of being Lex's father and how he looked forward to the long line of Fairfax-Washingtons after us.

To which my mother corrected, "Washington-Fairfaxes."

Lex thanked everyone for coming and brought the crowd back to life with hilarious tales of us as children. Four years ago, I envisioned myself sitting here, frustrated I'd had to marry my worst nightmare. Watching him thrill the crowd with our former antics reminded me of what'd he told me. I'd belonged to him from the time he'd been born and he'd belonged to me. Nothing could stop that. Ever.

I was supposed to stay in my childhood room that night. It was bad luck for the groom to see the bride before the wedding, but I didn't care. My body craved his in a way it never had before. It wasn't the lust, but something close to it. If I didn't know any better, I'd say I'd fallen in love with him and *actually* wanted to fuck him because I liked it.

Hell, we might die tomorrow. The fairy king could show up and kill everyone and this could be my last night alive. I wanted to spend it with someone who loved me, and despite it all, Lex and I had loved each other since the moment we met.

I knew that now. Perhaps I'd always known it.

I waited until the house quieted, well past midnight, so I could be sure no one would see me. Then I tiptoed out of my room, down the hallway, and into the southern corridor, not bothering to knock before I slipped inside.

I walked to his bed and stood at the edge of it, staring down at Lex as he relaxed on his mattress. His head was propped up against the headboard, the faint glow of the cigarette between his lips illuminating his chiseled features. He raked his hazel eyes over my body, all the way down before coming back up again, saying so much without saying anything.

He wanted me naked. I yanked at the string holding my nightie together at my breasts, causing the fabric to flit over my arms and puddle at my feet. I raised an eyebrow and matched his expression with one of my own.

Yes.

He cleared his throat, sat up straighter, and stabbed out the cigarette in the crystal by the bed. Lex swallowed and tilted his head to the side, eyes narrowing.

In the twenty-six years we'd been together, I never *once* came to him like this, willing and vulnerable and desperate for him specifically. His expression demanded to know *why now?*

I didn't answer, just crawled onto the bed and straddled his body, cupping his face, tilting his chin up so he faced me.

"No matter what happens tomorrow, I'm happy it's you." I kissed him gently, much more gently than I'd ever kissed him, cradling his face like it was made of porcelain. With those marble cheekbones and his hard, cold heart, I couldn't be sure he wasn't.

He furrowed his brows and stared up at me. *"What's going on with you?"*

"Shh." I pushed him back, dragging the blankets down so I could slip my hand over his half-erect cock. I scooted down his body until I wrapped my lips around it, sucking it the way he liked. I looked up his body at him before I continued. *"If you want me to stop, tell me to stop."*

Lex groaned and fisted the back of my hair, hissing in a breath when I swirled my tongue around the head. *God,* I loved driving him wild like this, loved it even more when he got so hard, so quick.

He tightened his grip, letting me into his mind, forcing his way into mine. *"X, what's wrong? Is it the lust?"*

"No, Lucifer." I let his cock go with a loud *pop.* "Can't a girl fuck her husband before their second wedding?"

He laughed. "I'll take your pity fuck, but I need to know it's real."

"It's not a pity fuck." I gave his cock another lick, all the way from the balls up to the tip and back down again. "It's real, Lucifer, and I get it now."

His eyes lit up, mischief and hope glittering behind them. "Get what?"

"What I have to do."

He looked like he was going to ask more questions, but he didn't get a chance. I climbed up his body, positioned him at my entrance, and sheathed him inside me, all the way down. It took me a minute to adjust, but I didn't mind the pain, especially when he inhaled a sharp gasp.

There was nothing like that first shove inside—the warmth in my lower belly, the jolt of pleasure erupting all over my skin, the intimate connection to another human. All of it overpowered me, forcing away thoughts of the king and Miri and what might happen come morning.

He sat up and bit my breast, knowing I normally liked it rough between us. But not tonight. No. Tonight, I wanted to love him, to revel in this one thing we'd get to have between us. No one else was being forced to get married tomorrow. No one else was completely surrounded by their horrible, maniacal family. No one else was being tracked and stalked by an evil fairy bent on killing the entire human race.

This night, tomorrow, they were about us, me and him. I grabbed his hands and intertwined our fingers, leaning down so I could pin them above his head.

Lex didn't normally take the submissive role when we had sex. He liked to win, and I let him. But I wanted to remind him we were equals, that as much as I liked to give in to him, he also liked to give in to me.

He caved with very little effort. He let me hold him down with one hand while I rode him the way I wanted. He let me finger my clit, and he watched, his mouth hanging open, his head thrown back in euphoria, deep sighs on his lips. I angled myself so he hit the spot inside me that had both of us moaning and gasping. My climax rose, bubbling up my spine and down my legs.

"Ride the wave with me, Lucifer." I opened the floodgates between us, so his pleasure was mine and mine was his and every single nerve ending in our bodies became one. We were one soul. One mind. One body. Our molecules warped and changed and molded together.

When I ran my thumb over his bottom lip, I felt it on my own. I pushed inside his mouth, and he sucked it back, rolling his tongue around the tip, sending a shock of lust to my clit.

He groaned.

"Do you feel me?" I didn't mean physically. I meant subconsciously. Spiritually. I felt him everywhere, all at once, like a million icy pinpricks on my scalding-hot inferno.

"I feel you, X. I feel you."

When my orgasm finally crested, it shot out of me, right into him, and his peak hit me between the eyes. Our bodies vibrated with hormones and magic and the tether that had bound us together. Call it fate, karma, whatever, it had led us to this euphoric point in time.

Just me and Lex, like always.

The universe split wide open. Lex and I surfed a higher consciousness. We were together in a way no two humans had ever been connected before. We stayed like that for hundreds of years. Thousands. Millions. Time did not mean anything to beings like us anymore. My soul expanded to an effervescent all-knowing thing, and so had his because we were the same.

We hovered there, on the brink of this profound, ethereal weightlessness. Then it collapsed down, and we sank into our bodies, Lex and Ivy once more in a guest room at Mount Vernon.

Time passed like centuries in the moments after. I lay next to him, breathing down the high, and he rolled on his side to face me. Lex grabbed my hands, our thumbs hooking around each other, and he pressed his lips to my knuckles. We didn't say anything. Nothing needed to be said.

We were in the presence of each other's company, finding comfort in both the familiarity and the contact. My thoughts went to younger versions of us, holding each other wordlessly after learning that Marcus had died. How different those children seemed compared to the people we'd become.

Yet, in so many ways, nothing had changed at all. As much as I loved him, it wasn't complete. *We* weren't complete. While we were made for each other, we were never meant to be a two. Others had been made for us as well.

My heart swelled to think of Carter, beautiful, magnetic Carter, and I longed for him, even as I lay next to our husband. Then my heart drifted to Miri, and I sighed. It had been weeks since I'd seen her, the most we'd gone since before Samhain. Her absence ached like a glass splinter in my brain. I could tell it was there, but I didn't know where to push to pry it out.

"We'll get her back, X." Lex pressed another kiss to my knuckles, his hazel eyes searching mine for sincerity. *"I promise. We will."*

I bit back a sob and met his gaze, the rising tide of panic nearly crushing my chest. Going through with this was a stupid idea. If I were the king, if I knew where my enemy's entire family would be, I would go in guns blazing. I'd take them all out, or threaten to until I got what I wanted.

"We should call off the wedding."

He shook his head and sighed. "We can't. You know that."

Did I?

I couldn't imagine having that conversation with my mother, but that didn't mean it couldn't happen. Especially if I found out she had something to do with the photo leak.

"What if we ran away?" I turned to face him.

"Disappear into the woods?" He raised an eyebrow. *"Like you suggested that day by the creek?"*

I smiled at the memory. *"Yeah."*

"There's a pretty thought."

I swallowed down the uneasiness. Something didn't sit right inside, a growing sense of dread nearly boiling my blood. I grabbed Lex's hand tighter, letting the sensation flow through me into him. *"You feel that?"*

He nodded. *"Is it Siobhan?"*

I shook my head, glancing around as my mind struggled to catch up. "This may end up being the stupidest thing we've ever done, Lucifer."

He pursed his lips, but he didn't argue. For once in his life, he agreed with me, and it didn't make me feel any better.

28

IVY
THE WEDDING

It was a sham wedding.

I might as well be honest about that.

I *hated* Alexei Fairfax. I always had. I always would. Yet, as I traced over the scars on my palm, a permanent reminder of what we'd done together all those years ago, there could be no doubt I loved him more deeply than I ought to. More deeply than this marriage would require.

Our lives were so entangled and chained together that we would never be free of one another. I had stopped trying long ago.

"Ivy?" Kit gave me a hesitant smile and took a few steps inside, her dark hair twisted up on the back of her head. "Wow, you look stunning. Absolutely stunning."

"You look beautiful, too," I told her, and she grabbed my hand, staring out over the beginnings of the party below. The Potomac glistened in the afternoon light, and boats littered the channel with paparazzi hoping to get a photo of the Washington-Fairfax wedding.

The event of the season. Of the year.

"Did he bolt?" I asked.

She laughed. "Not a chance. You know he won't back down from you. He never has."

"Tell him I'm planning to murder him in our marital bed."

Kit hummed an amused noise. "I think he already suspects that."

I cleared my throat and looked down at the scars on my palm, right along my lifeline, tracing over a particular grouping as the aching chasm in my heart deepened. We still hadn't heard from anyone. It was as if Siobhan and the others dropped off the face of the planet. Had they been captured? Had they been killed? If the fairy king came, who would protect us? Could we protect ourselves?

Miri wasn't here. Carter wasn't here. That hurt the worst. Not that I expected them to come, not after everything that had happened. It was too fucked, and given the danger I suspected headed straight for us, I didn't blame them. If I could, I would have left me years ago.

Just me and Lex again. Like always.

"Ivette," my mother said, waltzing into the room with that same judgmental arrogance she'd had all week. She stopped when she saw the look on my face. "Why so glum? It's your wedding day. At least pretend like you're excited."

Ah, yes. *Pretend* this was my idea, that the relationship between Lex and me had been real from the start, that I wanted any part of this.

I should. Lex was a handsome, powerful man. We had all the money in the world. Our marriage would be broadcast to over twenty-seven countries. But the hollow, sinking feeling in my gut only worsened.

It seemed so trivial now. The last thing I should be doing was getting married. All of this, all of *them,* so insignificant.

"Look at me, child," Evelyn said. I forced my chin up and tried to smile, hoping she couldn't see the fractures through the duct tape. "You're making the right decision. You both are." She straightened her spine. "I know this isn't what you wanted, but we all have to make choices we don't like for the good of the country." She touched my cheek, the way she used to do when I was a little girl, and gave me a pitying smile. "I've been where you're standing. And I wouldn't change my decision."

It was the wrong time to compare her and my father to me and Lex.

Especially since Kit and I had spent part of this week trying to find out how far her manipulation went.

My mother gave me a fake peck on the cheek and announced I had fifteen minutes to get downstairs if we wanted to start this thing fashionably late. As soon as the door shut behind her, I made up my mind.

"Ivy." Kit turned to me, taking my hands. "I debated telling you this after the wedding, but you should know something." She took my hands. "And you're not going to like it."

I raised an eyebrow.

"It's about that thing you asked me to look into, that weird thing I found on Mother's firewall."

The look on her face told me everything I needed to know.

"Is it what I think?" I said. "Was it her?"

Kit's features dropped, and she pursed her lips, giving me a solemn nod. "I think so. Whoever hacked you and your spouses, they did one sloppy thing. Just one. But—" She sighed. "I'm pretty sure Mother is the reason you broke up the first time. And the photo leak?" Kit pursed her lips. "I found the cache myself."

Words could not describe the fury that shot through my blood. Rage at my mother, at the media, at all of *them* for doing this to me. To us. Sadness that we had missed out on so much because of it, because of the roles we all had to play.

Well, I was done playing it.

I couldn't do anymore.

After everything that's happened, they didn't deserve it. Lex's voice played in the back of my head. *"Bunch of sycophants, all of them."* He was right. Lex had always been right about everything. Screw the polling numbers. Screw the rumors. I didn't care. They'd taken everything from me.

I should let this wedding go on, let it all fall to pieces. If the fairy king was coming for us, then tear us apart, you bastard.

Evelyn Washington deserved my wrath, and god-fucking-damn it, I'd hit my breaking point.

No one had heard from Poppy, Siobhan, or the other fairies in weeks. The queen had been asleep for two days in our guest room. Miri had gone MIA. I couldn't get a hold of Carter. The media had not stopped skewering me, despite being invited and attending my wedding. My big bill had fallen flat on its face. To top it off, my mother had violated a personal part of my life and manipulated me into years of pain.

Enough.

Time to tear it down. I turned on my heels and met my sister's sympathetic gaze.

"What?" She narrowed her skeptical gray eyes. "You look like you're about to do something stupid."

"Maybe I am."

"What?" More serious now, she gasped and tried to reach for my hand, but I was already out the door, picking up my dress so I could run down the hallway on the balls of my feet.

"Mother!"

I caught up with her halfway there. She stopped and turned to face me. "Yes?"

All the terrible things that had happened up to this point rushed through my mind, and most of them were her fault. In fact, if she hadn't arranged this marriage between Lex and me, Siobhan wouldn't have noticed me. We would have gone on with our lives, happily oblivious to this warped, twisted reality.

Maybe I was looking for someone to blame, or maybe I had realized that none of this mattered. I knew the consequences of what I was about to do. Hell, my career would likely be over. But I didn't want it anymore if it came with her strings attached. Making that decision freed me. I raised an eyebrow and took a menacing step toward her.

"What are you doing?" She planted her feet and held firm.

"Whatever *I* want for a change."

She balked, her brows furrowing. "Ivette, what has gotten—"

"No," I cut her off, grabbing her elbow so I could back her up against the plaster wall. "No, the time for you to speak is done."

I twisted her bony arm in my fist, and I stared her in the eyes, allowing my gift to take over, giving myself this moment, this millisecond, to unleash my anger on her.

"I know what you did, Mother," I told her, picking through her memories, crawling through her mind like a spider in the deep, dark webs of her subconscious. *"Why? Tell me why."*

"Ivette, what is happening?" Her voice came out fast and high-pitched, sounding terrified and transfixed. Perhaps it was impulsive to do this now when so many other things were happening, but nothing could have stopped me.

"Tell me," I bellowed. *"Did you cause the breakup with Carter? Did you leak the photos to the press? Did you do this to me?"* I squeezed my hand tighter, almost to the point of pinching. Her agony ricocheted up her arm, around her spine, slipping into her brain so I felt it with my own.

She stayed silent for a moment, then muttered a simple, "Yes."

The memories came next. She'd hired the best people in the business to monitor our computers, our smartphones, all of our tech. She'd made sure, even months after Carter and Miri had left, that we didn't see each other. When she found out we were back together, when she found out we'd gone to the cabin for Christmas instead of coming home and playing house, that had been the last straw. She had the same people hack our security system, go inside our house, and find the pictures, find anything that could be used against us.

Yeah, she could have leaked the whole thing, and if this were about more than forcing me to do what she wanted for the good of the family, she might have. What point was there to that? The same result could be achieved with minimum collateral damage. If it was just me, if it was just my reputation to repair, I'd been so drama free my whole life, I could take the hit.

My hatred for her boiled in my veins, sending a spike through our connection, into her brain.

"What are you doing to me?" she pleaded again. *"What are you? A monster?"*

"Ivy," Lex's voice cut through all of it, pulling me from my outrage and bringing me back to the present. *"X, stop it."*

I let go and stepped back, gasping for air to fill my lungs. My fingers and toes vibrated, my legs wobbly, barely able to hold my weight. My mother wilted before catching herself and pushing herself upright.

"You're a demon," she whimpered. "What did you do to me?"

Lex twisted my body around to face him, cupping my cheeks. "X, look at me. Take a breath." Kit stood just to the right, staring at our mother with her hands over her mouth.

I focused on my fiancé.

"Deep breath in," he told me, *"and a deep breath out."*

I repeated the mantra as he calmed my nerves and all of the rage directed at the one person who'd made my life hell. A practical part of me was already freaking out and worrying about what she'd do to me as a result, but this new vengeful side didn't care anymore. Even if she did, who would believe her?

Then it hit me, a crushing wave of power so strong it nearly dropped me to my knees. The hair on the back of my neck stood on end. The overwhelming strength of Alberich's foreign magic twisted its way down my spine and into my thighs, turning my body to Jello. Lex's hands clawed into my forearms.

"Ivy?" Lex said.

I nodded, my heart sinking into my gut. "He's here."

The king.

29

LEX

It was a sham marriage.

Everyone knew it.

I knew it. Ivy knew it.

Four years of faking it, and here we were, staring down a day that would most definitely live in infamy, but for all the wrong reasons. The public wanted the glitz and the glam. They wanted the star-studded event with the free booze and the photo ops. That wasn't us anymore. That hadn't been us for a long time. Not since Ireland. Not since Samhain and Poppy and the clusterfuck in the woods.

We'd be lucky to make it out alive. We'd be lucky if this event didn't end in bloodshed.

The sun had faded behind dark, smoky tendrils, the once brilliant Saturday morning now turned to shades of gray.

We were so fucked.

"Lex." Ivy's eyes implored me to listen. "We can't wait any longer. Siobhan isn't coming. We need to get everyone out of here."

I took a deep breath, reminding myself of the great plan. This had to happen. He had to come here, and we had to face him.

Except, that was when I thought we had Poppy on our side. I'd been texting her for hours with no response. I'd tried calling her after she didn't make her scheduled check-in, and when it told me the number had been disconnected, I suspected we might be screwed.

The sky grew darker, and the guests below stood, grabbing onto their dresses and sweaters as they rushed inside. The winds blew harder, and my heart beat faster as I racked my fucking imagination for a game plan. The black tendrils swirled outside the window, and we backed away, Ivy gripping my hand tighter as it seeped in through the cracks like smoke.

"Fuck!" Kit startled and jumped away. "Guys, make up your mind."

I had planned for this. I had suspected Siobhan and her lovers wouldn't make it back in time, and now that we were dealing with that reality, I had to fall back on plan C—the one where we ran and he chased.

"We're getting out of here." I grabbed Ivy's hand to lead her back over to the door.

"We're leaving?" Ivy's eyes bulged. "What about all these people?"

"If we leave, he'll come after us." I ushered everyone over to the door.

"To where?" Jon ran a hand over the back of his head. "Where are we supposed to hide?"

"The closest place that's warded is our house. That was the plan when Siobhan and Finn were here."

"That's where the queen is," Ivy said. "We'll lead him right to her."

"Then we go to Kit's or Jon's," I said. "Anywhere. We just need to go."

Ivy took a deep breath. "Yeah. Okay."

"What?" Jon's eyes narrowed. "He'll catch us in a second and crush us in two."

"We don't have another choice." Ivy gave her brother a reas-suring nod.

I decided not to read too much into her quick agreement.

"C'mon," she said, tugging me over to the door. "I can sense him getting closer."

"Where's Henry and Abigail?" Kit asked.

"I don't know!" Ivy shook her head. We walked out into the hallway just as they appeared at the top of the stairs.

"There you are!" Abigail said.

"The minister thinks the weather is about to take a turn." Henry looked between us. "We should get started soon."

"Yeah, it's not the weather." Ivy gave Abigail a knowing look, and she grabbed Henry, hauling him along with us as we headed toward the back stairs.

"What's happening?" Henry narrowed his ice-blue eyes on our panicked state.

"There's no time to explain," Abigail said. "You have to trust us and do what I say."

"Isn't that my whole life?" Henry rolled his eyes but trotted dutifully along. We ducked behind the door and took the steps two at a time. Ivy struggled in her enormous, obnoxious dress, her arms one giant poof of sparkling fabric as she walked. I held up the back of it, and goddamn it, if this was just the train, what did the rest of the thing weigh?

The king used his black mist to peck at the top of the floor-to-ceiling windows like a million tiny birds. It surged upward, a dark blanket consuming everything it touched. *Chirp. Chirp. Peck. Chirp. Peck.* The sounds unnerved me, tickling my molars like nails on a chalkboard.

Once we were on the lowest level, Ivy pulled her phone out of her purse to call Carter one last time. On the second ring, he finally answered. She put it on speaker.

"Carter, he's here," Ivy said, cutting him off.

"Fuck." He sounded restless and exhausted. "Where are you?"

"We're still in Mount Vernon," Ivy said.

I took the spot in front of her, grabbing her hand while I led her through the hallways we'd used to run through as children. "We're leading him away. We have one of his primary targets."

Fury burned through me as we ran, at fucking Evelyn for being such a goddamn pain in the ass, at the king for being such a show-off, and at Siobhan for not coming through for us. I thought fairies were supposed to be honor bound by their oaths or some shit. Where was that now?

Fuck her, fuck Donnelly, and fuck Finn. All that planning, all that scheming, all for nothing.

"Is he still in London?" I asked, my hand on her waist to halt her from turning around the corner. I peeked first, checking both directions before guiding her and her siblings into the basement hallway. The world grew blacker and that dreadful sinking feeling in my stomach intensified, putting even more pressure on my lungs as we walked. The atmosphere reeked of magic, seeping in through the cracks in the cinderblock walls like mist. Unlike the queen's energy, which radiated with vibrance and life, this echoed the pain of hollowness. This scratched at my insides like the worst depression in the world, like absolute torture that would never end.

"Yeah," Carter said. "But I can be in DC soon. I'll call Miri."

I held back a growl as the thought of Miri broke my heart. "Have you talked to her?"

"Yeah," he said. "It's not good."

Not good? What could be so complicated she couldn't share it with us? Whatever. Not the time to discuss it. We needed to get to safety first.

"Be careful," Ivy told him.

"Of course, Weeds," Carter said. "I love you."

"I love you."

The muffled conversation on the other end of the phone made me pause. It sounded like Carter said, *"Lizzie?"*

Lizzie? What the hell was his sister doing at his hotel?

"Poppy? What are you doing?"

"Poppy?" That got my attention. "Did he say Poppy?"

Ivy froze, and her siblings looked at each other while Poppy and Carter argued. *"Is the king making you do this?"*

"No, it's not the king," Poppy said. *"I just thought you should say goodbye."*

The fear and trepidation rose in me, and I understood what was happening. Poppy had Lizzie. Was this what the king had asked of her? Why hadn't she contacted me? Or did she realize we had the queen and retaliated?

"Carter!" I shouted, trying to get his attention, trying to tell him to get Lizzie and get out of there.

But it was no use because Carter shouted, *"Poppy, no. Wait. Poppy. Stop!"*

And then the line went silent.

"Carter!" Ivy tried to call him again, but it went to voicemail. "Shit!"

Her red-rimmed eyes met mine, and I ran my hands through my hair. I had told Poppy not to make any drastic decisions without cluing me in. Something was wrong. Was she stealing family members? Was this part of his plan?

"C'mon. We have to go." Ivy's voice sounded as rough and devastated as I felt.

"This way." Jon opened the door that led to the side of the house, and we crossed the lawn to the litany of vehicles near the garage. My heart pounded as I looked at the sky. Smoke spiraled around us, frightening and beautiful, making it infinitely more difficult to see.

Ivy lagged behind me, her dress weighing her down even after Kit and Jon grabbed a piece of the monstrosity so we could go faster. One of our wedding guests stood a hundred yards in the distance, slack-jawed and staring at the sky. From this distance, it was difficult to make out, but I could swear his eyes were pitch black. I stopped, taking a moment to look. Other people stood around in the same position, wearing similar expressions of dumbstruck wonder.

That was the least of my worries.

"C'mon, X!" I stood by the back door of the nearest Range Rover while Ivy ran faster. Kit climbed in first, followed by Abigail, Jon, and Henry. Ivy tried to get in the passenger seat, but the train of her dress was too big for her to squeeze through the door.

"Get it off me," Ivy said, scrambling for the zipper on her back, but she was tied in this thing tighter than anything I'd ever roped her up with.

"We don't have time for this," Kit said.

I grabbed the delicate lace holding her in with both hands and gave it a sharp tug, ripping the seams down the middle and peeling it from the front of her body. Wearing only her petticoats and her bra, she hopped into the seat and slammed the door closed behind her. I circled the hood, watching as the king's madness descended on us.

Fuck. No matter if Siobhan had shown up with the *Fianna,* we still would have been greatly outmatched. I gazed at the spectacle. What a fucking drama queen to show up like this. To hypnotize my entire family. To chase us down like dogs. It indicated a level of narcissism and righteousness I knew all too well. Perhaps Siobhan had been right. Perhaps there had been a reason the four of us were chosen.

I got in the driver's seat, started the engine, and put it into drive, leaving our family and Ivy's pretentious three-million-dollar dress behind. I turned right at the end of the driveway, and the clouds followed us, swirling through the atmosphere on either side of the SUV. It reminded me of the night we'd gone to see Siobhan.

Except this time, when the vehicle pulled to a stop, it wasn't henchmen that stood in our way.

No.

It was *him.*

30
IVY

All of the mist sank back in on itself, churning together like water in a drain. It formed a man with a black cloak draped over his shoulders, hanging down to his shins. His dark hair had gotten longer since we last saw him, now shoulder length and slicked back away from his face. His beard remained the same, pitch against his mouth, matching the shadows in his eyes.

"Jesus Christ, that's him?" Kit asked.

Lex and I leaned forward, putting ourselves between our family and this monster, this fairy-tale villain come to life.

"What is that?" Henry screeched.

"Shut up," I said. "Everyone, shut the fuck up."

For two years, we'd tried to prepare for this moment. Now that it was here, anything we could have done would have fallen woefully short. What idiots we were to think we could ever take him on by ourselves. We were so fucked.

There was no stopping the king. Whatever he'd done to Poppy had squashed any hope we thought we had. Siobhan, Finn, Donnelly? They'd likely run for the hills, or worse. Smythe had tried to warn us. The king was all-powerful and all-consuming, and I had no fucking clue how we'd defeat him or get him back to his own realm.

For as terrifying as he was, he was equally mesmerizing in the same preternatural way the queen had once been. If I had to guess, I'd say he'd stolen whatever the queen had to amplify his own magnificence. The last time I'd seen him, it hadn't felt this crushing or overwhelming.

Maybe it was this newfound link to him brewing inside of me, but when he coalesced into a physical being, everything in my body wanted to be near him. I wrapped my hand around the oh-shit handle to make sure I didn't jump out of the car and launch myself in his direction. I didn't know where that impulse came from or why, but it terrified me.

"Alexei." I heard the words, but the king's mouth didn't move. His dark eyes met mine through the windshield before shifting to Lex at my side. His gaze slithered over both of us like cold molasses, sticky and encompassing, holding me in place. "Ivette. Please get out of the vehicle." He crossed his hands in front of him and took a step forward. "We are long overdue for a chat."

"About what?" I said, my chin tilting up in defiance. "We don't have anything to say to you."

"You have something I want." Another slow step brought him around to the passenger side, his incredible eyes leering into the window at my side. "And I have something you need."

I swallowed.

"We don't need anything from you." I shook my head, remaining strong, but being this close to him made me tremble with recognition. I'd seen him somewhere before, and not just in my nightmares. No, this was a long time ago, some ancient place that I could hardly remember. Nostalgia settled in my gut, warming me to him, making me want to give in to his demands.

That is his magic. Stay focused.

"No? Nothing?" He arched both eyebrows and paused, glancing from the front of the SUV to the back. "You want this...*gift*...removed, do you not?" He said the word like it held more weight than we knew. "I want my wife. This is an easy deal to make."

Of all the scenarios that had played out in my head, I did not see this one coming.

"Why would you help us?" Despite my rattling nerves, my voice stayed calm and steady. "I thought you despised humans."

He chuckled softly, shaking his head as he tried the door handle. *Locked.* Something about this silly human movement struck me at the time, but I put that in a compartment to analyze later.

"That does not mean I am unreasonable."

Lex grabbed my hand and whispered, *"Careful,"* through our bond. Fairies offered gold-encrusted dreams on silver platters with a thousand invisible strings attached.

"We were told no one could undo the gift." I straightened and held his gaze with a firm one of my own. "Not even the one who gave it to us."

He let out a soft, sardonic laugh. "I am the king of fairies. I can do whatever I want."

That pissed me off even more because it was that bullshit that got us into this in the first place. No, he couldn't do whatever he wanted. No one could, especially not in my fucking realm.

"No deal," I said. "Go back to Faerie and terrorize your own kind."

The king's sparkling eyes widened as his gaze shifted again between Lex and me, his lips twisting into an amused smile. I'd expected anger, but he seemed delighted in the way a rotten kid revels in burning insects with a microscope.

"Very well." His attention went to Jon and Kit behind me as the darkness fogged out of him again, deep, dark wisps of smoke that crept in through the windows and the doors, through every crack in the vehicle, filling the interior like gas. "Since you have taken two lives that belong to me, I shall do the same."

The black clouds surrounded me, blocking out the light, blocking out everything. Lex thrashed against it, flailing his arms to get it off him, but I embraced it. I closed my eyes and let it wrap around my throat to choke me.

The memories assaulted me again.

Poppy asking for his help and refuge from her human captors, her big eyes welling with tears.

A relentless search for the queen that had yielded nothing.

A visit with Miri that—

"Ahh, Ivette." Alberich's voice slithered down my spine like battery acid, poisoning me from the inside out. "I see you poking around in there."

The tendrils squeezed my windpipe harder, but I knew he wouldn't kill me. He didn't have his queen, and this would have been far too easy a victory for him if he could. By the way he'd showboated this afternoon, I'd bet he wanted to pick us apart slowly, bit by bit.

I ignored him and went deeper in his mind, sifting and searching for the heart of him. I'd experienced that last night with Lex. I'd seen the bright ball of our existence when we climaxed together, and I'd held his love for me inside my soul.

If the king had once loved the queen, that same kind of affection must still exist somewhere inside him.

I can find it. I can find what makes him tick.

I focused on the queen, flipping through memories, forcing him to relive the best of their multiple lifetimes together, and just when I'd gotten to one he kept deeply buried inside his twisted soul, he realized what I was doing.

Pressure rebelled in my mind, and he shoved me out of his head, out of his fog. But oh no. I wouldn't go down that easily. He wanted to put on a show, the big scary king and his big cloud of smoke.

Well, guess what? I'm Ivy fucking Washington, and this is my realm.

You wanted me? Now you got me.

I pushed against his mental barriers harder, gritting my teeth, clenching my eyes shut, using every bit of energy I had to bang my telepathic battering ram at his immense force of will. Lex's hand was still in mine, so when he realized what was going on, he joined me.

Our link strengthened us. Siobhan had given us this gift, connected Lex and me like this for a reason.

"Get out of my city!" My battle cry hit the king like a blinding white sledgehammer, and the pressure in my mind snapped. A weight lifted off my chest and throat. When I opened my eyes, the king had disappeared, the tendrils had evaporated, and the sky had cleared.

Alberich was gone.

No...

I'd forced Alberich to leave. *We'd* forced him to retreat.

And when I threw my arms around Lex to celebrate, Abigail's scream from the back seat stole my attention. Henry and my youngest sister still sat in the third row.

But Jon and Kit were gone.

WANT MORE?

Thank you for reading *Solstice,* and if you enjoyed it, please leave a review on Goodreads, Amazon, and/or anywhere else you get your books. Not only do they help other readers, but the algorithm uses reviews to promote and categorize the book.

The next book in the series, *Beltane,* releases on February 25, 2025.

If you want more while you wait, I have a novella featuring Siobhan, Finn, and Donnelly. It's a 13k short that takes place before *Midsummer*. If you liked these characters and wanted to know more about them, be sure to check it out!

If you're interested, please follow this link: https://books.jenadoyle.com/WeWildThings

Thanks again. Keep reading for a sneak peek at *Beltane*.

BELTANE

YOU HAVE BUT SLUMBERED HERE
WHILE THESE VISIONS DID APPEAR

JENA DOYLE

BELTANE BLURB

<u>Miri</u>

I know what happens if I stay away from my spouses, but I need to keep them safe. I can't be near them, not if the king of fairies can manipulate my memories so easily.

When the Washington-Fairfax wedding doesn't go to plan, I have no choice but to face the loves of my life and deal with the consequences of my actions.

The end is drawing near, the queen of fairies doesn't remember who she is, and even those closest to us can't be trusted. Fairy-tales aren't supposed to end in heartache, but I can't see how we get out of this one unscathed.

<u>Carter</u>

I thought watching the girl of my dreams marry my best friend would gut me alive, but that day messed me up for very different reasons. Betrayal aches like salt in a wound, especially when I didn't see it coming.

Planning to take down a fairy king wasn't how I wanted to spend time with my spouses, but I've always been sentimental. I'd do whatever it takes to save them, even if it means sacrificing myself.

Endings have always been hard, and this one is going to hurt like a son of a bitch.

BELTANE

PROLOGUE

MIRI

AFTER THE END

It was not a sham marriage.

We were in love, all of us, together. We were always meant to be a four.

The world looked at our relationship and judged us for it, but I no longer cared what they thought. I couldn't, not when my wife brought out my inner fire, not when one of my husbands lived in the darkness with me and the other was as blinding as endless sunshine.

"Are you sure about this?" Ivy asked, wrapping her fingers in mine as we walked through the woods. The pads of my bare feet sank into the wet undergrowth, but I barely felt it.

Once, long ago, the trees would have whispered to me of their secret schemes. They would have told me if this was a good idea or if I should turn back, but I hadn't heard them in years...not since the end. Not since that night in Killwater when we'd lost so much and gained much more in return.

"I'm sure," I said, more confident than I'd ever been about anything. I'd been dreaming about this for months. The woods had been calling me, reaching out however they could. So many times, I had ventured out here and shoved my fingers into the dirt, hoping and praying I'd vibrate with that same vitality the plants had once used to communicate. I'd close my eyes and unfurl my senses to dead air.

Ivy was no longer able to get inside our minds. Lex tried to get the truth out of his clients, but the words held no magic. Carter's luck had finally run out.

A part of me, perhaps the part that had always had a special connection to the trees, lamented what we'd lost...what we'd given up so we could win. But in my darkest moments, I'd admit I'd do it all again if it brought the same results. I'd go through the tears, the heartache, the threat of a terrible, irreversible loss only to know unimaginable joy.

Until the end, we once promised. *Until the end* had been branded on our hands for four years.

The end had come and gone and we'd survived. All of us. All four of us. Here to bring in the new day.

"If I thought we could get it back," Lex said, catching up to me on the side opposite Ivy. "I would have suggested this after we rescued you from—"

"I'm certain," I cut him off, refusing to even think about the memory he mentioned. Those were dark days, indeed, and now that we were on the other side, I refused to relive them. I had made mistakes. I had loved them dearly, only to disappoint them when it mattered most.

I was unworthy of their forgiveness, and yet, they had offered it anyway.

"Yes, but how?" Lex said as he brushed his dark hair out of his mesmerizing eyes, no less beautiful for the years between now and when I'd first met him.

"I just know," I said.

"Are you hearing the trees again, Juliet?" Carter asked, grabbing my shoulders with a loving squeeze.

"No," I said, "but this is the right thing to do, regardless."

"It *is* Midsummer," Ivy said. "We made the original vow on Midsummer."

"Yeah, on the grounds of a sacred ruin in Faerie," Lex added with a scoff and a roll of his eyes. "Don't tell me you've found another veil for us to slip through."

"Goodness, no," I said. "But this land is sacred."

Lex looked unconvinced but Carter wrapped his arms around my prince's shoulders and tucked his head into the crease of his neck. "C'mon, DC. Give her a chance."

"I don't take chances," Lex said. "Not anymore."

"Regardless of whether we get our gifts back, we need to renew our vow," Ivy said, bringing my hand to her mouth to kiss my knuckles.

"Hmm." Lex curled his lips into a devilish grin. "Didn't I just make you do that last night when I had my cock in your a—"

"Our *actual* vow, Lucifer." Ivy laughed, and it pleased me to be a witness to their interactions these days. They still bickered like they hated each other, but now I understood that was their dynamic. They loved as much as they fought, and in that turmoil, they sated a side of their personalities that could only be soothed by the other person. I loved their love, just as they adored the affection I had for Carter. There could only ever be one Ivy for Lex, and only one Romeo for my Juliet, and around and around the earth spun.

"Here," I said, stopping inside the clearing I'd found two weeks ago on one of my walks. The meadow formed a perfect circle with the trees, naturally made considering this was too far away from the cabin for anyone to have done it purposely. It thrummed with an otherworldly energy, something I sensed even without my fairy gift.

"Oh," Carter said, breaking away from us to walk ahead and glance around. The trees had grown tall on all sides, and despite the natural cover, wildflowers bloomed in the center. It was beautiful, idyllic, reminding me of the meadow outside the ruins in Killwater. "This is perfect, Juliet."

I smiled and walked toward him to grab his neck and pull him down for a kiss. "I don't care if we never get our gifts back. I want you to know I still love you...that I still want to be married to you."

"Well, you do crawl into our bed every night," Lex said, grinning as he snaked an arm around my waist to tug me away from our husband.

"I can't explain how I know it will work," I said. "I just know that it will."

"What if the lust hits us again?" Ivy said. "What if we get stuck out here for the next few days?"

"We're not expected anywhere," I said. "It'll be okay."

Ivy took a deep breath and nodded, sinking to her knees in the grass before opening the bag we'd brought with us. We'd been discussing this for a while, researching different ways to renew what we'd once had no choice in creating. Ivy grabbed the candles and put them on the ground as I sat down next to her to light them. I used scissors to cut off a piece of my long white dress before handing them to Carter to do the same to his white T-shirt. Lex cut off a strip of his matching shirt and handed it to me as Ivy sliced through her dress for a scrap of the same.

Once I had the four pieces of linen, I tied them together into a tight knot and held my hand out in the middle, overtop of the open flame. I grabbed the ceremonial knife that had been cleaned and sanitized before coming out here and made a tiny incision in the palm of my hand, right where the words had once shined bright against my alabaster skin. Crimson blood bubbled over the cut, and I watched as my spouses did the same to their hands before placing them over mine. Ivy gripped my palm and Carter laid his on top of hers. Lex went under me, holding us up with his indomitable strength, truly the king of our world, the gravity around which we spun.

I wrapped the fabric around our combined embrace, over and under and over again until Ivy helped me knot it on top.

Blood dripped from Carter and Ivy over my hand and down onto Lex's, combining each of us, mixing our life force together. Ivy's fire soothed Lex's ice and emboldened Carter's autumn chill. Each of them complemented the sunny frost of my springtime spirit. We were always meant to be a four, and after everything that had happened, I thanked God that had not changed.

"Okay," I said, glancing at each one of them before returning my attention to our embrace. "Here goes nothing."

Acknowledgments

Dear Reader,

I knoooowwwwwww. Another cliffhanger? How very dare I? Alas, I am but a merciful sadistic author. If you're reading this as I'm publishing it, *Beltane* is right around the corner. If you happen to pick this up in the future, go on over to that bookstore and get the next one because you're going to need to know how this ends.

Our lovers are staring down the end of a very long shotgun, just waiting for it to go off. The king is up to no good, the queen has (quite literally) lost her mind, and Poppy seems to be just as maniacal as the king claimed her to be. Siobhan, Finn, and Donnelly are scattered to the wind. How in the world are our heroes going to pull this off?

Stick with me, dear reader. I promise there's a happily ever after in store. I cry every time I read it.

If you want to hear more about my process for *Midsummer, Samhain, Solstice,* and *Beltane,* hop on over to Spotify and check out "Shh, We're Reading Dirty Books." I sat down with Saylet and Calina to talk about how I came up with this idea and how I went about putting the characters together (inspiration, dream cast, dynamic relationships, etc.) I had such a good time talking to them!

To my beta readers — Leslie Grace, Maggie Sims, and Shannon L. Thank you from the depths of my heart. You literally read the worst versions of everything I write, and none of my stories would be the same without you and your valuable input.

To my ARC readers — thank you for sticking by me through my

writing journey. Some of you have been there since the very beginning, and I promise I won't ever forget it.

To my partner — I love you, and thank you for walking this road with me. You are the jelly to my peanut butter.

To my editors — Misha and Kimberly, who have been so gracious and kind with their wisdom. I appreciate having both of you on my team. I bow to your guidance.

Nae, Willow, Amethyst, Becca, and my other shadow work friends — It is with your support and gracious motivation that I continue to keep my head up. Together, we are stronger. I love you all.

To you, dear reader — Thank you for picking up this story. Thank you for giving me a shot. And thank you for pushing through the angst. We're in the home stretch now.

To Odin — I said you'd get a book. Here it is. I owe this one to you. Thank you, Alfather.

And finally, to the people who made up Shakespeare. To the queers that history forgot.

To anyone who ever dared to write what they wanted, despite the critics. To anyone who ever got up on a stage and performed their little heart out. I see you, I love you, and I'll never forget you. Thank you.

Cheers!

-Jena

Also by Jena Doyle

MIDSUMMER

We Wild Things (Prequel Novella)

Midsummer

Samhain

Solstice

Beltane

STEEL ROSES MC

They Called Him Saint (Prequel Novella)

Crimson Chaos

Savage Saint

Oleander Oaths

Mischief Mayhem

Ruthless Reign

ROYAL BASTARDS MC: HELENA, MT

Blood and Whiskey